KINGS & CONSORTS

# TWISTED DEVOTION

# TWISTED DEVOTION

KINGS & CONSORTS

POPPY ST. JOHN

# AUTHOR'S NOTE

This book contains content that may be triggering to some readers. For a full list of TWs, please visit the author's website before proceeding.

If you're still with me, sit the fuck down and turn that page like a good girl.

♥

# PROLOGUE

Discreet. Exclusive. Indulgent. Worth every penny.

Masks were club policy at Delirium, but I wasn't fooling anyone with mine. I could cover my face, but I couldn't cover the tattoos. Not with each finger on my left hand inked down to the first knuckle and bold black lines carving up my neck to touch my throat. Even in the suit I wore, they were impossible to hide.

Anonymity was paramount for the survival of the club but each and every person here knew my name. Knew that I answered to none of them.

Only upon the word of a current member and a direct invitation from me could they be allowed the honor of entry to my kingdom.

The constraints of our members' real lives didn't matter anymore the instant they stepped foot on the property. They paid handsomely for that illusion. To become faceless, nameless avatars that lived for pleasure. Our waitlist rivaled Ivy League colleges, and annual membership cost as much as tuition.

The top brass of society were the main clientele. Trophy wives, fuck boys, and mistresses weren't enough for them. They sought *more*. Something darker. Dirtier. They wanted taboo. And I gave it to them in fucking spades.

When the owner of the city's biggest telecom company liked to spend his weekends getting whipped on a St. Andrew's cross, he needed somewhere safe and private to do that. When the revered city priest needed a place to come to be drilled in the ass by a massive cock, I welcomed him.

I pulled my mask down, tying the ribbon strands behind my head. The filigreed gold covered half my face, leaving only my jaw visible. I slipped my tie off my neck, popping the button at my throat, revealing more ink-blackened skin.

Taking the central staircase down two floors to the ground level, I strode across the high-ceilinged foyer. Nobody walking into the estate would suspect that half of the gothic mansion was a sex club patronized by the most powerful people in this city.

Not until they opened the doors.

The original eighteenth-century locks were just for show. Popping the lid off of the hidden security panel, I scanned my retina, opening the private entrance.

If you entered the club through the other side, the first thing you went through was the security check and cloakroom. No phones or any recording devices allowed, no exceptions.

Footage of what went on here could sink political aspirations and ruin careers. Not to mention end a few marriages.

Resonant, bass-heavy music and haunting vocals played just loud enough to conceal conversations, but not so that others in attendance couldn't hear the animalistic sounds of passion and pain.

The air hung heavy with the sinful, thick energy of bodies and unbridled desire. The sultry interior provided the backdrop for another world. One brimming with desire, fetish, and kink.

Masked patrons in various states of undress looked over, watching me enter, before returning to their partners. Talking, fucking, indulging in everything they were too cowardly to *take* anywhere else.

Ninety percent of our clients were men. Politicians, businessmen, the occasional artist or actor, and of course all the old money degenerates who had memberships at places like this wherever they happened to own property.

Their dates were pre-approved before they were allowed into the club. Models mostly. Escorts. Mistresses. Rarely wives. All of them having signed non-disclosure agreements. And then of course there were my women. The ones well trained in every sexual artform, willing to give and take in equal measure.

Many walls from floor to ceiling were painted flat black, others coated in the richest damask wallpaper in darkest shimmering red. Dampened lighting set off the color, making it glow as if painted with fresh blood. Candles on brass holders and gothic carvings garlanded the entire space.

I nodded to one of my girls as she passed me in the narrow corridor between private rooms that led to a great hall. Her naked tits bounced with each step and she lowered her head in respect as I passed.

The main hall opened to semi-private rooms through carved archways. Clients drank, gambled, and fucked on velvet coated tables to voyeuristic audiences. In the main hall, couples and groups lounged on luxurious sofas. A large fire roared all night in the grand, carved fireplace.

Two staircases, one on each far corner of the hall led to the mezzanine style second-floor, where the private VIP rooms were located.

Besides beds obviously, the rooms were stocked with anything guests could imagine. High-quality leather whips, restraints, wooden paddles, candles, gags, vibrators, dildos, the list was endless. Anything we didn't have, which was rare, we special ordered in.

This bounty could be enjoyed for the small annual membership fee of $80,000.

To be fair, that was the cost of the highest membership level. That came with free use of my provided pussy.

There were cheaper memberships as well, going down to $40,000 for the less discerning of our patrons. Out of all the rackets I ran, Delirium was the most lucrative.

And not just financially.

Knowing scandalous personal details about some of the most powerful men on the east coast, in the entire country, came with its own priceless reward.

These men wrote the rules but I was above all of them. The masked king. A secret whispered in the night. The boogeyman in a closet that they wanted to keep shut.

My chest swelled with pride looking over my kingdom. The hall heaved with activity tonight.

People spilled in and out of the semi-private rooms. Couples and groups scattered on sofas and seats throughout the open ballroom. In the middle, a raised platform nicknamed *the altar* would inevitably become the center of attention.

Late enough every night, one enterprising couple would start fucking on it, often turning the hall into an orgy of heaving, sweaty masked bodies.

Moans and screams pierced the ambient din of music and conversation and I stepped to the side as a naked man in a minotaur mask crawled collared on his hands and knees, led by a woman in lingerie so skimpy, she might as well have been naked.

Peering into one of the rooms, I was greeted by the sight of a rope-bound woman being shared by three men. Her guttural moans were music to my ears.

I stayed semi-cocked whenever I came in here but I didn't touch. Delirium was their space, not mine.

My tastes were beyond the scope of the clientele here. Better enjoyed in private.

I moved to head up the stairs to watch from the mezzanine when I felt a gaze on me. Close to the fire, an older man swirled a glass of scotch. His companion, a woman in black lingerie, couldn't have been more than three years out of college.

The woman, draped over the man's lap, sank to her knees before him with a grace not often seen within these walls. She folded herself almost as though in prayer, bowing to the altar of his cock as she clasped it between her palms and fed it deep into her throat, drawing a groan from the man's lips.

The man stared at me through his veiled masquerade

mask, a slight upturning of his lips as she continued to do God's good work on her knees.

I wandered closer, wanting to get a better vantage point as the girl choked on his cock, gagging loudly, but never ceasing, barely coming up for air

The semi in my pants raged closer to a full hard on, and I clenched my teeth as it pressed into my pants, constricted when it should've been free.

"You like her?" the man asked, drawing my attention back to him.

I raised an eyebrow. The girl sucked the tip of his cock before popping her lips free to glance over at me. She was long and thin, with a firm ass and minuscule waist I bet I could join my hands around. Not one of mine. An approved escort I'd never seen here before.

"Take her," the man offered. "My treat."

The girl's lips parted in a silent gasp, but looking between her date and me, it was clear who she would rather be servicing.

"She seems busy," I purred and the little vixen went back to her work, languidly stroking the man's base as she swirled her tongue around his tip, bringing him back to fullness.

"She's yours if I can watch," he said.

I scoffed, shaking my head.

"I don't play."

Public sex wasn't one of my kinks. I watched, but I didn't care for an audience.

The man's mask covered most of his expression but his lips pursed. He was probably hoping to get cucked tonight. He still could be, it just wouldn't be with me.

"What do you like to do?" he asked.

"I've never met anyone who could talk so much with their cock in a beautiful woman's mouth."

He chuckled, nodding his head.

I inclined my head, leaving the man to his desires.

Going up the stairs to stand in the center of the mezzanine platform, I watched the scene below.

Heels clicked against the floor behind me and I knew without turning who I'd find.

The young woman from downstairs leaned over the railing next to me, her tits pushed together, her lower lip between her teeth.

"Hi," she said coyly and I smirked.

"Can I help you?"

"I think maybe you could."

"Does your date know you're here?"

"Yes. He encouraged me to come," she insisted.

"What's he paying you?"

"Two thousand."

Escort, as I'd already assumed.

"This your usual work?"

Her cheeks turned pink. "First time."

*Fuck.*

Under the hazy light, the smooth planes of her body made her look like a statue. Something that might break if you dropped it.

...and how I longed to watch her fall. Shatter.

"How's he going to feel about me fucking you on his time?"

"It can be your time if you want."

*I did.*

My desire reared up, surprising me. It'd been a few

weeks since I'd taken a woman. I didn't fuck anyone twice, which made finding new conquests a challenge.

I crooked a finger at her to come closer. She did, taking the invitation to put her arms around my neck and try to kiss me. I stopped her with a finger against her swollen lips.

"You have to do everything I ask you to."

"Anything you want," she promised, eager.

I leaned in.

"I said *everything*," I repeated, allowing her to see the meaning in my eyes, the darkness that roiled within, mere inches from the surface at all times.

She flinched and her black-rimmed eyes fluttered, but she maintained eye contact. I ghosted my fingers over her nipples and they hardened under my fingertips.

"No safe words, no limits. You do not tell me no," I said, speaking every word as clearly as possible, so there was no way she might misunderstand me.

Her breathing hitched as I twisted a nipple between my fingers, testing her pain tolerance.

"Do you understand?"

"I understand," she said, her voice reduced to a timid squeak.

"The masks stay on. When we're finished you will never return to Delirium."

That got the cogs turning. Her blue irises shifted back and forth as she considered how much she wanted me to fuck her; whether it was worth losing out on long-term income.

"Fifty thousand," I added. "That's my offer."

Her eyes widened. "For fifty thousand, you can do whatever you want to me."

I grinned wickedly and released her, motioning for her

to follow me toward the entrance, out to the security and cloakroom area. My men disregarded her, looking to me. Waiting for orders.

"Have her sign my personal NDA. Make sure she pays special attention to *the list*. Then have her brought to the courtyard. Blindfolded," I instructed.

The girl paled. "Why do I need to sign something? I already signed the NDA to enter with Mr. Haggerty."

"This is a different kind of contract, love," I told her. "Protects us both."

Her brows furrowed. "In case of what?"

"Lots of things."

...accidental death among them.

My men nodded, taking her by the arms to lead her to the little office where she'd sign away her soul to the devil for one night.

# 1

## EMILY

*Face down on the bed, her limbs were secured to its four posts. His open palm came down on her, cracking against heated, tender skin. She wailed, writhing uselessly against her restraints.*

*"Please," she begged, face pressed to the mattress. She clenched as he circled the bed.*

*"What did I say would happen if you let that man touch you," he snapped. Fear and humiliation burned like a furnace inside her. She deserved her punishment, every agonizing second of it.*

*His hand cracked sharply against her skin a second time.*

*"What did I say?" he demanded.*

My nose wrinkled. *What the fuck?*

Tessa's wide-eyed face looked at me expectantly. Gingerly, I closed the book I was holding, placing it carefully on the table between us.

"Yeah, I don't know about this one, Tess. Not really my thing, you know?"

"You can't say that after reading *one* page. More like *half* a page," she complained.

Half was enough.

I eyed the book like it was going to jump up and bite me.

"I'm sure the writer did a great job," I said, smiling weakly, reaching for my cup.

It was filled to the brim with bottom-shelf cabernet Tessa brought over. I tried not to grimace as the overly sweetened red wine coated my tongue. At least it was getting the job done, helping me slough off the monotony of my day to day in favor of something that felt a little more like living.

A pleasant lightness in my head had me sighing, the wine's warmth heating me up from the inside. Tessa was drinking too, which meant she was sleeping over. As a semi-regular visitor to Snow Funeral Services, she was one of the rare guests that walked in on her own two feet.

"Just try it. I know you'll like it. The last one I gave you might have been a little too spicy. This one is more tame," Tessa reported.

"*Tame?*" I scoffed, reaching for the book. Cracking it open to a random page in the middle, I read the first line I saw.

"*He touched the cool blade to her skin. She flinched from its cold hardness. Flattened to the tender flesh of her abdomen, one flick of his wrist and he could cut her.*" I cocked my head, staring at her. "You call that *tame?*"

She shrugged, compressing her lips into an unapologetic smile.

"Yeah, you didn't even get to the part where he—"

I held my hands up for her to stop.

## Chapter 1

"*Okay*, okay. I'll read it. Probably. One day." I closed the book.

It was joining the last couple of books Tessa gave me. They were forming a small tower on my nightstand, spines smooth and unbroken because I didn't read them yet. They were a little too out there for me but she got them for free from her job and I couldn't say no.

"It's good, I swear," she pushed.

My head nodded dutifully, taking a long draw of my wine.

"If you say so."

She snorted, emptying the wine bottle between us into her cup.

"*If you say so*," she said, mimicking me. I cut my eyes at her.

"Sorry, I think reading about a man flaying someone like a yellowtail a little off-putting. Sue me," I said.

"He doesn't *kill* her," she said.

"Well, does either one of them die?" I asked and she smirked, thinking my ask meant I was interested, when in reality I just refused to read anything where one of the main characters kicked the bucket. I dealt with corpses all day. I didn't want to read about them. And I *definitely* didn't want to experience their loss, even if it was only fictional.

"I don't know. Read it and find out."

"I give up." I rolled my eyes, leaning back in my chair.

I could still see the sharp yellow light from the illuminated bulb above us through my closed eyelids. Out on the patio overlooking the woods behind my cabin, we were mostly sheltered from the wind, but it was getting cold out.

The forest here looked impenetrably dark at night. In the daylight, though, it could look almost idyllic. Deer sometimes milled around the border of the property. A tiny creek babbled quietly down the footpath. And hundreds of birds woke me every morning with their songs.

Given the fact that our main revenue came from cremating corpses in the main building, this place had no business looking so damn story-book in the light of day.

The cabin was a glorified shed when I was a kid, used for storage and little else until my dad renovated it after mom died, turning it into the tiny home it was today.

Down on the far side of the property, this part of the land sloped down towards the woods and a creek. As if at any moment it could roll away into the trees, taking me with it into the all-consuming dark.

On the other side of the property near the road was my dad's house: my childhood home. He renovated that too when mom died. Nothing like a little grief to kickstart new hobbies and interests. Nobody was more productive than a person who wanted to stay distracted.

My distraction of choice had been mom's books. I obsessively read her collection of anatomy, funerary, and science books. Her notes in the margins made me feel close to her in a way that looking at old photos couldn't.

It helped that at twelve-years-old I'd gained an encyclo-pedic knowledge on the science of decomposition. She had studied mortuary and funeral science after meeting my dad during med school. He left his medical career to support her opening Snow Funeral Services when I was barely out of diapers.

My dad had run it since she died ten years ago, bringing me in as soon as I was tall enough to reach the top cooling lockers myself.

"You should be thanking me. That book doesn't even

come out until next week. That's why I'm heading out to Chicago next weekend," she said.

"Thanks for taking time out of your jet-set lifestyle to see me," I teased.

"I could probably score you a ticket to come," she said, waggling her eyebrows suggestively. She filled them in red to match the mass of coppery waves on her head.

I'd kill for some of that body. My straight black hair couldn't hold a curl to save its life. As a mostly virtual personal assistant, it didn't matter whether she was here at Snow Funeral Services or her own home when she worked.

Her employers were the authors who wrote the books that she kept giving me. At least once every month or two, she had to fly out to help at book signings, tours or festivals.

Our lives couldn't have been more opposite.

I *lived* at work. In the daytime if I squinted hard enough, I could see the mortuary and crematorium through the trees outside my bedroom window.

"I don't think I can get the time off on such short notice. Dad would have to work doubles the whole time I'm gone."

She sighed dramatically.

"Yay for another exciting weekend of contouring a dead grandma's face," she snarked.

"Someone has to do it."

"Yeah, *you*. Every day for the rest of your life until it's your turn to lie on the table."

The wine soured in my mouth.

I looked everywhere but at her, not wanting her to see how much what she said affected me. I loved my work, but dying before ever properly living was probably my greatest fear.

The forest in front of us, a blackened mass under the

dim crescent moon seemed to heave forward, threatening to engulf me.

I blinked hard, dispelling the illusion with another long swallow of saccharine wine.

It wasn't like I could leave. Dad couldn't run the mortuary alone. If I left, he'd have to hire help that we couldn't afford. He'd go even more into debt. The doors to Snow's would be forced to close and he couldn't do that. It was her legacy.

It was also mine, whether I liked it or not.

This place; the woods, the creek, the mortuary, prepping dead bodies with my dad. Day after day. That was my fate. I forced some more wine down my throat.

"Tessa?"

"Yeah?"

"What does that guy use the knife for?" I asked, changing the subject. Tessa turned slowly to face me, a devilish smile on her lips.

"What do you think he uses it for?"

Her devious smile scared me a little. Hopefully he used it to prepare a lovely charcuterie board for them to share. There was only so much you could do with a knife. I mean... unless *that* was what they were doing. I frowned, not wanting to take it there because there was no way...

*Was there?*

My eyes bulged and Tessa erupted in manic cackles.

"You know what? I'm sorry I asked." An involuntary shiver shook through me. "Why do you like that stuff?"

"Honestly, just read it and you'll be into it too. I swear."

I was certain she was wrong, but I didn't argue. A few moments of silence passed before she spoke again.

"Hey," she said, turning to look at me, her index finger

drawing a nervous ring around the rim of her wine glass. "What does a dead body look like?"

The wine I was sipping took a detour down the wrong tube. I sputtered and coughed, eyes watering, trying not to spill my wine. Tessa's laugh echoed into the night. I gasped, coming back up for air.

"Thanks a lot," I sniffed, Putting my cup down. Tessa chuckled.

"No, really. I've never wondered before, not really, but I... I kind of want to see one. I mean, if you work with them all day it can't be that bad right."

Wrong. Dead wrong. Depending on how they died. And I was used to it. Tessa? Tessa would be fucking scarred for life.

I shook my head. "Girl, you're drunk. You do not want to see a corpse."

"*I do*," she argued, sitting up straighter. "Just take me inside and let me have a peek at one."

I shook my head some more. "Nope. Not happening. Fresh out of corpses."

"This is literally a morgue, Em. You have dead bodies in the basement or in the fridge or whatever. You literally told me earlier that one was brought in this morning and—"

"That's it. You're cut off."

"Come on, Em," she insisted, her voice pitching high in an exaggerated whine.

I stopped, staring at her. She may have been keeping it light, but her clear green eyes were focused. She was serious.

My brow furrowed.

"I just want to see what one looks like and then we can come right back."

For real? What they looked like depended wholly on how they died.

Road accidents? Grizzly. Sometimes torn limb from limb or decapitated.

Same with suicides, depending on the method.

If you were lucky enough to die in your sleep you got the pleasure of being an attractive corpse, for all that was worth. Then, you literally just looked asleep. Pale, deathly pale. Your extremities turned purple, your body got lumpy and cold, but generally, asleep.

Snow Funeral Services was family run, small, so we saw only about forty bodies a month. By now though, I'd seen it all. The most tragic part about dead bodies was that on some level, everybody was just *meat*.

"Well, after dying, bodies swell. They can get so big that they look double their usual size. That's when they start to stink and the insects show up. Then everything that isn't hair, bone or cartilage liquefies," I said fluttering my lashes. "Do they put that stuff in those books you like?"

Tessa shivered, swallowing hard. "N-no, usually they leave that part out," she said. Good call. I would too. I picked up the empty wine bottle and got up, done entertaining her morbid curiosity.

"I'll be right back."

I slipped into the silent warmth of my cabin. The fire in my pellet stove still glowed, making the mild night on the patio feel colder than it was.

Soon, it would be warm enough that I wouldn't need the stove at night. I walked through my living room, and through to the kitchen to retrieve the second wine bottle. The remnants of our dinner, cooked on my little two-plate burner stove, filled the sink, the number of dishes seeming to explode exponentially whenever I had company.

Tessa always slept over to make the trip over here worth it. We were twenty-five minutes out of the city and her being the more mobile one, we tended to spend girl's nights here. Much to her dismay a lot of the time.

With her bright hair and even brighter personality, she was out of place at the mortuary where most people were dead or close to it. We'd been friends since fourth grade so the spook factor of the property was gone for her.

It had been a lot harder to convince my ex, Cody to come over but usually, the promise of sex was enough for him to get over the fact that *there were bodies over there*.

I came back to the patio with the wine, unscrewing the cap and pouring her glass first.

"Will your dad say yes if I ask him?" she asked. I opened my mouth to ask what she wanted to ask him, then sighed, remembering where the conversation left off before I went inside. She wasn't letting this go.

"No, probably not," I answered honestly. "Why do you even want to see one?"

"I don't know." Tess shrugged, swishing her wine around in her glass. "Just curious, I guess. I've been to funerals but never open-casket. And you're my best friend and you work with them all day. I guess I kind of want to see what you do. Plus." She paused, motioning to the book on the table. "That definitely helped."

I frowned. It wasn't adding up. What the hell was in that book? What was she reading about? Fucking psychos who tied girls up and held knives to their stomachs? Oh and don't forget dead bodies, too?

"You scare me," I joked with a raised brow and she chuckled in response.

"Don't yuck my yum," she teased. "And if anyone should be afraid, it should definitely be me. You've touched more dead men than living men."

"Ouch." I winced, reflecting on my nonexistent love life that Dad might as well have thrown in the incinerator with the last Jane Doe.

"Just because I like a little something *extra* with my romance doesn't make me any weirder than you."

Tess narrowed her eyes at me. "Besides prepping dead bodies, what else do you even do around here?"

"You know what I do. Assist with autopsies. Embalming. I prep the bodies for viewing. I have to talk to—"

"No, I know *that*, but you're acting like there's way too much in your schedule to read one measly three-hundred-page book. You barely make it out to the city to see me and you're not dating anyone right now..."

The sound of a particularly loud cricket filled the silence.

She didn't have to call me out like that but as one of the living residents of Snow Funeral Services, I probably got out as much as one of the corpses.

"I said I'd read the freaking book," I said, picking it up and examining the moody, red, and black cover with a sigh.

"Maybe read it outside, like, in the sun."

I whacked her with the book. "Are you saying I'm pale now, too?"

"No offense but you look like Morticia Adams circa 1960," she said and I bit the inside of my cheek, trying to think of a comeback, and coming up dry.

I couldn't argue with that. Everyone who ever said I

looked like the actress who played Morticia Addams, then said 'yeah, makes sense' when I told them what I did for a living would agree with her.

Carolyn Jones was gorgeous and I appreciated the compliment but the only way I looked like her was if you squinted real hard. I tossed the book down then glanced at the time on my phone.

12:38.

Dad said never to enter the mortuary after midnight but...

*Fuck it.*

I narrowed my eyes on Tess, the wine mixing with the blood in my veins whispering *why the hell not.* "You sure you want to see a dead body?" I asked. "Because you can't unsee one."

Tessa's eyes widened over the rim of her glass. "Seriously?"

"Yep. You win."

I stood, leaving her floundering to catch up as I ditched my wine and kicked on my boots, making for the path to the mortuary.

"Hurry up, before I change my mind."

Tessa scrambled to get up and followed me down the patio steps. The mortuary was up a gentle incline from my cabin.

"I need you to be quiet, okay?" I said over my shoulder.

"Why?" Tessa chuckled. "Are they gonna wake up if I'm too loud?"

No, unfortunately. That would have offered some much-needed excitement around here but I'd have to hold out for the zombie apocalypse.

"No, but Dad might."

For as long as I could remember he'd warned me about entering the mortuary after midnight. It was nothing but idiotic superstition, but I didn't rebel. I spent enough time there during the day to not want to spend my evenings with the dead, too.

I could bend the rules, just this once.

We tiptoed along the hedges behind the family home where I grew up, staying low as we darted across the gravel drive toward the main building.

Tess giggled, high on the rush and I hushed her sharply even though the wine was making it low key difficult not to want to laugh with her. We weren't actually trespassing though. Not *really* breaking any laws. You couldn't B and E a building you owned.

"*Shhh*?" I urged her, unable to keep from grinning.

"Sorry!"

We came up behind the mortuary. My keys were still in my pocket from closing up at six and I reached for them, then saw the sliver of light leaking from the edges of the solid metal door. It was open.

A prickle of unease ratcheted up my spine, making me shiver.

Did dad leave it like that? He wouldn't ever forget to lock the mortuary. Was he still inside? Maybe there was a last minute drop off.

"What are you waiting for?" Tess whispered loudly and I swallowed, trying to remember if I *did* lock the door when I left but I couldn't remember.

"Em?"

Pushing the door open, I led the way in, figuring it had to be me who left it unlocked and thanking my lucky stars that Tess had the idiotic idea to come see a dead body before Dad noticed my screw up. It wouldn't have been the first time.

Crossing the short distance to the stairs that went down to the basement cooling room, I heard banging. I froze, about to ask Tessa whether she heard it too but her hand gripping my arm like a vice told me she had. I shooed her back outside.

"What the fuck was that?" she shout-whispered when we were outside. I fought the urge to say it was a ghost.

"Things like that happen sometimes. Let me go and look."

She grabbed my arm, tugging. "What do you mean things like that happen?" I peeled her surprisingly strong grip from my arm, looking into her wide eyes.

"Just wait here," I insisted. "It's probably nothing. Remember, everyone in there is dead anyway."

Her shifty expression hadn't calmed but she wasn't squeezing the life out of my arm anymore.

Shit. If another raccoon got in, Dad was going to kill me. If I could just get to the supply closet at the bottom of the stairs I could grab a broom and shooed it back outside.

"Em, don't leave me out here alone," Tess hissed as I stepped back inside.

"I'll be back in like two seconds, relax."

Steeling myself in case of a trash panda attack, I slunk silently down the steps. Hazy light filtered around the edges of the open cooling room door. Raccoons definitely couldn't open doors, right?

A late night drop off then. It had to be. Those weren't super uncommon. The dead didn't always respect business hours and we were the first choice when there was hospital overflow.

"Who was this guy?" my dad asked, his voice distant, muffled through the door.

"Why don't you ask him and find out," a deep voice snapped sarcastically.

My body stiffened, foot hovering over the next step.

That was *not* my father. The shock gave way to immediate curiosity and I couldn't help easing my way down the rest of the steps, close enough to see into the room.

Sweat broke out over my temples when he came into view. Not my father.

*Him.*

The owner of the other voice.

The imposing, tall dark-haired man pushed the trolley from the room. Crafted of shadows and sharp lines, his chin and jaw were stubbled, his hair mostly pushed back from his face with a curl of deep brown falling over his smooth forehead.

He twisted his head to one side and my mouth went dry at the sight of deep black ink clawing up one side of his neck. The stranger wore a fitted button down shirt with the sleeves rolled up to the creases of his elbows, revealing even more heavily inked skin, down to the knuckles on each of his fingers.

His voice may have stopped me in my tracks, but his face ripped all the air from my lungs. Hard, masculine lines shaped his cheekbones, nose, and brow. I couldn't tell his eye color from here but they were severe, piercing under straight, dark eyebrows. His jaw gave his face an almost regal bearing.

I silently closed my gaping mouth, working my jaw as my neck and cheeks flushed.

His searing energy seemed to twist and bend everything

around it; scrambling thoughts and warping metal. I wanted to back away from him but I couldn't seem to move.

He looked thirty, maybe? Not as old as my dad, but older than me for sure. Questions about him interrupted my thoughts so loudly that I didn't realize there was a body on the trolley he was pushing.

Was he being embalmed? And if he was, why was *this guy* pushing the cart? Why was he even down here?

The body on the trolley was still dressed and not yet cleaned. I couldn't even see a toe tag.

Heat rose through my body, setting my teeth on edge. Something was wrong.

I slipped my phone out of my pocket, ready to call the cops. But, no, I couldn't do that, my dad was in there.

A bolt of unease ricocheted up my spine, triggering a cold sweat over my chest as I shakily slid my phone back into my pocket and swallowed hard.

"That was what we discussed," said the man with the deep voice and I realized he was answering a question from Dad that I'd been too deaf with nerves to hear, the ringing in my ears slowly dissipating now.

"Can't we renegotiate? That's what business partners do, isn't it?"

"Is that we are? Partners?" he asked.

I shivered at his words, at the implication, but the rough sound of his voice made me squirm. The hard edge as attractive as it was dangerous. Who was this guy?

"But we—"

"Did you think I came here tonight to talk about the disposal fee with you, undertaker?"

The disposal...

*What?*

Bodies were *interred, cremated, laid to rest*; all kinds of things.

Typically, they weren't *disposed of* unless they needed to be hidden. I jumped to my feet and ran up the stairs, his words chasing me as I ran.

I burst out the door, panting. Tessa stood up from her position crouched against the back of the building.

"There you are, I thought you had—"

"You need to go back to the cabin," I gasped.

"What? Why?" Her face fell.

*Because there was a body being* disposed of *in my dad's mortuary.*

"Th-there was... it's a body. Last minute drop-off from the hospital," I stammered, the lie fighting me on its way out.

"Are you kidding me?"

"They need it tomorrow."

Tessa frowned. I hated lying to her but I didn't even know what I stumbled on downstairs. She couldn't see it. She couldn't be a part of whatever it was.

"Don't hospitals have morgues? People die there all the time."

I glanced quickly over my shoulder, so frazzled I swore I heard something back there.

"They get overflow sometimes and we're close," I said, only halfway lying now. "I need to help my dad. I'll be back as soon as I can."

"You work too much," she grumbled, gathering the lapels of her leather jacket with a little shiver against the chill in the air as she turned.

"I'm going to finish the bottle without you if you don't hurry your ass up," she called back and I waited until she was out of sight, nearly back to the cabin, before going back inside.

My heart bleated out a discordant rhythm as I passed the threshold, inhaling deeply to settle the flutter of anxiety in my stomach.

A man stood where the stairs should have been.

I staggered back with a muted gasp, my muscles knotting, fear gripping my throat so tight I almost choked.

His hands, bloody now, hung at his sides. His shoulders, wide enough to nearly fill the passage to the stairs, made him even more imposing up close.

A magnetism radiated off him, pushing me away and pulling me close simultaneously. Drawing me like a moth to a flame. Making me want to run like prey from a predator.

His stare settled on me, eerily placid save for the lifting of a single brow.

"And who are you, little lamb," he purred. That voice curled around me, making me clench. I steadied my stance, standing straighter to look him in the eye as I lifted my chin. I was scared as hell, but I'd be damned if I let him know that.

"Emily Snow," I stated, my voice coming out stronger than it had any right to sound with my pulse throbbing in my ears. "Who the hell are you?"

He'd been handsome from a distance. Five feet away from me, he was startlingly beautiful. Hard and unyielding but perfectly formed, like lace carved from stone. His eyes under the fluorescent bulbs were so light, they looked clear.

"I fucking live here," I lobbied back.

His brow rose slightly and his lip twitched. Was he making fun of me? Was he amused?

"I gave you my name, who are *you*?"

A small smile spread across his lips, and a muscle in my jaw twitched.

"A ghost."

He turned and walked back down the stairs.

With his gaze finally off me, my whole body uncoiled.

A fucking *ghost*?

I stared down the steps after him. He walked into the basement like he owned the place. My dad would lose his shit if I followed him down and my fingernails dug deeply into my palms with the effort of keeping myself from charging after the man. Whoever he was, he had more mortuary privileges than me.

I listened for a moment, just long enough to hear Dad's voice as he spoke to the man. To confirm the blood on his hands belonged to the man on the trolley and not my father.

A shiver ran over my skin as I spun on my heel and left the building. I wrapped my arms around myself, teeth chattering as I tried to warm the ice water in my veins.

## 2

---

### RUARC

B lood.

     The shit got everywhere.

I inspected the dried stain near my left elbow. I'd rolled my sleeves up first but still, another Brioni shirt ruined. I had no doubt the suit and shirt casualties totaled in the tens of thousands by now. I should've sent this fucker the bill before killing him. Or invested in Brioni stock.

"Call the undertaker," I ordered Nixon.

"I'm surprised it's not past his bedtime, yet," he quipped.

Irate and still edgy from the kill, I stared deadpan at Nixon who shook his eyes at my lack of humor.

The slight, white-haired man who ran Snow's didn't live up to his title in the least. He didn't look like the guy in the morgue who dealt a person's final rites; he looked more like one of the mice that lived under the building's floorboards.

"We're getting rid of him now?" he asked, crouching down next to the bloodied pulp of pimp filth.

I sunk a blade under his ribs after Nixon and I took our time torturing any useful information from his thin lips. I'd have let Nix and the others handle it, but this was personal. No one encroached on my territory without meeting the business end of one of my blades personally.

A dark, almost black pool of blood shone on the ground around the corpse. The next time we came in here, it would be gone. My housekeepers had grown accustomed to cleaning blood as if it were spilled milk.

Nixon straightened to his full six foot height. I checked the time. 11:30. By the time we arrived at the undertaker's doorstep it'd be after midnight as was part of the agreement.

"Yes, now," I said, the contempt still bitter in my mouth. I was fast-tracking his trip to hell tonight. The fucker had been harassing our escorts, trying to get them to break contract with me and join under him. I might've let him off with a warning if he hadn't touched one of them.

Nobody touched what belonged to me. Not unless they paid the fee and bent the knee.

My fists clenched, thirsty for more of his blood.

Our girls didn't go near the streets.

White collar hotels only. Trusted clients were approved for trips and outcalls. Otherwise, they were on call only so we controlled security and screening. When I took my cut, it was because I earned it. We offered something they wouldn't find with the likes of this scum.

I met a lot of his kind in my time. My mother went through about five just like him. On her knees in parking lots giving head to jackasses who went home to beat their wives and were only willing to pay $50 for her time.

My girls didn't even meet a client until he was vetted and paid upfront.

The pile of worthless flesh and bones on the ground thought our girls would settle for that demeaning existence after working with me. It was fucking laughable.

"Help me move him."

Nixon took his legs and I took his head. He left a trail of blood on the ground as we walked him out to the car. We were on the property, at the stables. They hadn't been used to store horses for about eighty years. My dad used to use them for the same thing I did. You couldn't even hear a gunshot out here from the house. About a quarter mile from the main estate, nestled in a grove of trees, nothing could be seen, either.

We hauled him into the back of the car and closed the trunk.

"I'll take him," Nixon offered, but I shook my head.

"No. I want to watch the bastard burn."

Nixon paused. I saw him about to challenge my directive, but change his mind, standing down instead. He was the only person I would take that kind of insubordination from. My second in command, my shadow, my brother even if not by blood.

Everything I had would be his if I kicked it, but if the devil hadn't taken me yet I doubted he ever would. My soul too rotten even for his taste.

I was born alone, my mom's only child. The only pregnancy she carried to term. Her sperm donor wasn't in the picture. After she abandoned me, luck, or god, *something* got me in the way of Thane Monroe, the king before me. He left the house and the syndicate to me when he died. Gave me his name along with the kingdom.

When he died, I almost felt something. Something more than rage or disdain.

If I bit a bullet, I knew Nix would fucking eviscerate the man responsible.

We had enough shit on each other to sink the other irreparably, which made it easier to let him get away with shit I didn't allow for the others. I had no one I'd call 'friend' besides him.

He knew everything about me worth knowing.

A screeching bat flew out from under the eaves of the stables, flapping wildly into the black night. Slamming the trunk closed, Nixon made his way back to the house.

"Say hi to the old bastard for me, would you?" he called back to me as he departed.

Nix was the one who usually handled pass offs to the undertaker, but it was good to let the people under my thumb see my face every now and again. Remind them who ran the show.

The mansion loomed like a goliath over the rest of the property. Even in the dark, its strong, stark black façade demanded attention. The towering turrets seemed to pierce the sky. It was an imposing gothic mansion that had been in the Monroe family since it was built in the mid-19th century. Over 12,000 square feet on thirty acres.

Fit for a King. Fit for a Monroe.

The early years of my takeover weren't without some pushback. Cut brake-lines, drive-bys, even a particularly sneaky fucker who tried to bury a landmine outside my front door and blew himself up instead.

I had to claw my way to my throne, earning my place and my reputation, but after expanding the syndicate's reach, influence and profits, no one questioned my authority.

Gravel crunched beneath the tires as I drove around the stable to the rear of the house, taking the private driveway our members used to access the club. Security let me out and I started up the road to the mortuary.

The undertaker's name was Snow.

Before we struck our bargain, he ran it with his wife, but she was gone now. We'd been working together since the start of last winter. Years ago when Thane still lived, he'd proposed the same arrangement to Snow. The man had said no at the time, but since losing his wife, his tune changed.

I'd say money problems if I had to guess, but in truth I didn't give a fuck what the reason was. It was a good arrangement, especially considering the short distance between his mortuary and my estate. The fact that he only had one employee besides himself on site, and they were a blood relative to my knowledge made it even more appealing.

The location was perfect. Out of town, isolated, and barely ten minutes from the house. The undertaker was clean, not even a speeding ticket to his name. I drove off the road up the driveway to the stark, white mortuary building. The lights were off inside, but the door opened and the undertaker appeared like a ghostly apparition in the doorway. My nose wrinkled at the sight of him. Despite the otherwise choice arrangement, there was something about the old man that didn't sit right with me.

His face was just a little too gaunt. Eyes just a little too beady. Tall, but slender and lanky, with arms too long and shoulders too narrow.

Pulling a cash-filled envelope out of the glove compartment and wedging it in my waistband, I pushed out of the car.

"He's in the back," I said, offering no other information.

The undertaker nodded, coming around the back with me. Wordlessly, he lifted the pimp's legs, and I took the head. Between us, we moved the body easily into the building, heading to the stairs that led to the cold basement where he kept other corpses on ice.

We placed the guy on a metal slab, ready to roll him through to the incinerator.

"Who was this guy?" the undertaker asked.

"Why don't you ask him and find out."

I pulled the envelope out of my waistband, holding it out to him. I spotted him eyeing my bloody hand before taking it. He looked inside, his lips pursed. Was he counting it? My eye twitched. Usually, he had the smarts to wait to do that after I left.

"Is there a problem?"

He closed the envelope, folding it gingerly.

"It's four thousand," he said.

Fucking perfect. My teeth ground in annoyance. The last thing I wanted to do tonight was discuss a pay hike with this rat of a man in his goddamn corpse refrigerator.

"That's what we discussed."

He swallowed. "I'd like to renegotiate."

Why? It was already twice what he charged normal customers for direct cremations.

I stared at him, deadpan.

He recoiled, fiddling with the envelope as he found his balls and continued. "That's what business partners do, isn't it?"

"Is that what you think we are? *Partners*?"

I saw him shrink, retreat into himself like a turtle into its shell.

"I need a service and I pay you for said service."

I pointed to myself. "Employer."

Pointed to him. "Employ*ee*."

"But we—"

"But nothing," I snapped, my patience waning. "Did you think I came here tonight to talk about the disposal fee with you? If you have a fucking problem, why didn't you—"

My head snapped towards the still open door. It was faint but I heard it. Rustling. The shift of clothing over skin, of soft soled shoes over tile floor.

Unless his dead tenants liked to take late-night walks, someone was out there.

"Is something wrong?" the undertaker asked.

I glared at him. Did he really not hear it?

"Stay here," I hissed, leaving both bags of bones behind as I walked up the stairs, slowly, making sure I didn't make a sound on the steps.

Voices. More than one. My fists tightened involuntarily. I'd have Snow's head on a fucking spike if he'd hired more help without clearing it with me, first. Part of our deal was that his was the only living face we'd encounter while disposing of our enemies. He swore up and down no one else resided on the property.

At the top of the steps, what looked like a back door was hanging ajar. The voices filtered through. I frowned, straining to hear.

It sounded like... women?

His wife died years ago and there was no way that old fucker was getting any tail out here.

Anger smoldered within.

"Are you kidding me?" one voice said.

"They need it tomorrow," the other replied.

"Don't hospitals have morgues? People die there all the time."

"'They get overflow sometimes and we're close. I need to help my dad. I'll be back as soon as I can."

Her *dad?* Convenient of the man to neglect to tell me he had a daughter.

The door creaked open, flooding dull white light into the passage as she tiptoed inside.

Pale under the weak light, she froze stiff when she saw me. Full, pink lips parted, but she said nothing. She stared; shock, more than fear in her green eyes.

"And who are you, little lamb," I asked.

Her feet shifted. I thought she'd bolt, but she firmed up her stance instead, standing her ground.

On the taller side of average you'd expect her to be flatter in the areas where curvy girls excelled, but even in the oversized sweatshirt she wore I could see the unmistakable hourglass figure she hid beneath her clothes.

Her hair, black as the night with an almost imperceptible sheen of indigo, hung in messy waves around her heart shaped face.

"Emily Snow. Who the hell are you?"

A searing flare of want burned through me.

My fingers tingled with heat, aching to touch her. To punish her for daring to speak to me that way.

She might have been perfect.

Her wicked almond eyes shone with indignance. Contempt.

I had to have her.

The conclusion sat so comfortably, it was like slotting the last piece into a puzzle.

"You shouldn't have come here," I rasped against the physical effort of holding myself back.

"I fucking live here," she bit back.

The best ones always did. A smile pulled at my lips.

"I gave you my name, who are you?" she demanded, trying and failing to conceal a tremble running up her arms from her clenched fists.

Who was I?

Her worst nightmare and her deepest desire.

From this day forward, she'd never forget my face.

"A ghost."

Turning away from her took Herculean effort. My body burned with the need to possess her, right there on the grass outside her father's mortuary. But downstairs, I had a body to burn. And drawing out the anticipation would only make it that much sweeter once I had her.

I flexed my fingers, tipping my head to one side to crack my neck as the thrill of the hunt tried to overtake everything else.

It was her I heard when I was downstairs. Had she heard us? What did she know?

The image of her flashed behind my eyes as I made my way back to the man that I highly doubted shared any real blood with the goddess upstairs.

Her sturdy stance, erect posture, direct, almost insolent gaze; she wasn't afraid, not like she should've been. She was challenging me.

Those types didn't like to lose.

They pushed back when you pushed them.

I allowed myself the mental image of her stripped

down, bound, begging. Her fair skin reddened, her knees bent, giving herself wholly to me. Bowing to her king. My cock thickened in my pants, throbbing until I needed to clench my jaw against its awakening.

She'd be my greatest conquest.

The undertaker just gave me a reason to come back.

## 3

### EMILY

The sharp-angled eaves of the mortuary seemed to cut the gloomy morning sky. It'd never looked more like what it was than it did today: a building that housed the dead. Daunting. A place to be feared.

I rubbed my sweating palms on the front of my jeans, swallowing past the lump in my throat as I approached from the rear entrance like I always did. A soup of dread bubbled in my gut like acid.

Pausing at the door, I inhaled deeply and closed my eyes. The air filled my lungs, crisp with the smell of morning dew. The gentle sounds of the birds, and the creek rushing around the back of the property gave me a measure of peace, no matter how false it felt.

If my father asked whether I was near the mortuary last night, all I had to do was lie.

What I heard and witnessed last night played over in my head.

If he had secrets, so could I.

I let myself in, padding down the steps into the colder air below.

I strained my ears to hear any sign of life as if I was going to hear him in conversation like I had the night before. The tattooed man, the ghost with the bloody hands, flashed behind my closed eyelids and I pushed him back, blinking him away. Unnerved by the shock of heat rushing through my core, making my skin flush.

*And who are you, little lamb?*

I shook my head, hearing nothing but the soft shuffle of my Dad's loafers on the tile as I entered the basement.

He slid open one of the lockers, looking over and at me with a thin smile on his lips.

"Early morning today?" he asked.

Was it?

I looked up at the large face clock on the wall. I was fifteen minutes early. I left Tessa asleep in the cabin, she'd let herself out whenever she woke up. I'd stayed home as long as I could, wide awake and jumpy as a new foal, before giving in and making my way up the hill.

"Couldn't sleep," I said, trying to sound and look less anxious than I was.

"Oh? Tessa keep you up?"

Not exactly. The ghost's voice droned in my head for hours. Every creak and groan I heard through the night made me think he'd come to get me.

"Yeah," I lied. "What about you?"

I watched him warily as I shrugged my coat on. Clearly the man who'd been here with him hadn't mentioned seeing me and I wasn't sure if that was a relief or something quite the fucking opposite.

Gerard Snow, only my mother ever called him Jerry, was

hardly intimidating. His green eyes, the only thing he gave me were kind but often distracted and for the first time I wondered what the real reason behind that was. What sort of secrets he was hiding from me. Whether he hid them from mom too when she was still alive.

"No complaints here. We have a busy day today. Three this afternoon. One embalming, and two autopsies. The embalming is for an open casket funeral so you know what you need to do."

I rarely had an opportunity to wear makeup in my own life, but when it came to beautifying the dead for their final public appearances, I was the one many grieving families asked for by name.

The cosmetic side of funeral preparations here naturally fell on me as it did my mom before me. Dad always covered the autopsies, having done the proper schooling, whereas everything I knew I'd learned from Mom's books or on the job, apprenticing beneath him.

"Great, anything else?" I said, shoving my hands in my pockets so I wouldn't fidget, eager to put some distance between us before he got suspicious.

Dad pursed his lips, thinking for a second, then shook his head. "That should be it. Are you still working on the one you started yesterday?"

I told him I was. Cancer patients were tricky. Chemo sped up decomp so embalming took longer. He opened a locker to a gust of frosty air, revealing the covered body inside, ready to start his workday. I blinked, still bracing myself for the worst, but nothing came.

Was that it?

I watched Dad, heart in my throat as he wheeled a trolley over to the slab. My heart pulsed in my ears waiting for him to say he knew everything and that I was in trouble. He finally looked up; his green eyes expectant.

"Don't just stand there. Come help," he said.

"*Oh*," I jumped, hurrying over to help him transfer the body to the trolley, then again to the preparation table.

I was off the hook, if I was ever on it to begin with.

"'Kay Dad, I'm going to get started. Back in a bit."

"Mmm," he muttered, already setting about getting his tools ready.

Besides today's main work, I had to do inventory and prepare a suicide for transportation, receiving the family as they came to escort the hearse to the wake.

Storage was on the second floor, but I lingered in the foyer instead of continuing up the stairs. One of the doors on that level led to a smaller, lesser used refrigeration room where we stored the cleaned and prepped dead in their coffins before pickup. Next to that was my father's office.

Rule number two; no entering his office.

Unlike the rule of never entering the mortuary after midnight, this rule had been in place since I was a little girl.

I had been inside exactly two times, both to fetch something for him. Something he gave explicit instructions to grab along with the item's exact location. No dallying. No snooping. And I never had.

What else was he hiding?

If I were him, that was where I would keep my secrets. The one place on this property no one went but him.

I hurried to the door before I changed my mind and tried the knob. It opened with a gentle push and my lips parted on a shuddering breath.

Glancing over my shoulder, I clamped my mouth shut and scurried inside. Dad's office was large and unassuming.

A large desk with a computer sitting on top of it held the middle of the space. His bookshelf held all my mom's old books to my right.

I realized I had no idea what I was looking for or even where to start.

His desk. It made the most sense, right?

I pulled the top drawer open first.

Nothing.

It was scattered with office supplies; paper clips, spare pens, old receipts, and pencils. I tried the next one. Envelopes of old mail, some bills, nothing interesting nor alarming. I tried the last one and stumbled back as the item inside knocked loudly against the wood. Terror gripped my chest.

I recoiled from the small black pistol as if it could sprout legs and arms and shoot me all by itself.

Dad hated guns. *Hated* them. Or so he said.

Mouth dry, I blinked furiously, as if I could make it disappear through sheer force of will.

I reached out to touch it, but withdrew just shy of my clammy fingers brushing the metal barrel.

Why did he have it? Why would he need it?

We were almost completely isolated out here. No one came onto the property unless it was for business purposes. And I couldn't think of anyone who would want to break into a fucking mortuary.

My brows drew, noticing what the weapon was lying on. A thick, bulging envelope filled the drawer beneath it. Curiosity overcame my fear and I carefully plucked the envelope from under the gun.

Peeking inside, I saw an almost two-inch thick stack of bills.

My dread was so thick it clogged my throat, making me choke on it.

It had to be at least four thousand dollars. That would cover direct cremation for two bodies without any extra for an urn or storage or any of the other fees normally charged to our clientele. And who the hell paid in cash?

These days, fucking *no one*.

I set the cash filled envelope down on the desk and reached deeper into the drawer, my fingers finding two more envelopes. No, not envelopes. File folders. My hand shook as I pulled them out.

Opening the first one, I saw the familiar font and template of an autopsy report. I scanned the page. *Male, 32, suicide. Gunshot wound to the chest.*

My mouth dried out and I triple checked the date on the report. We didn't have any corpses of this description brought in on that date.

Adrenaline opened the next envelope for me. It was another report.

*Male, 32, gunshot wound to the chest.*

Ice crept up my fingers holding the sheet.

*Suspected murder. Awaiting autopsy report.*

I stuffed the reports, legitimate and doctored, back into the drawer along with the cash and fled the room. I ran straight out of the front door.

The empty driveway and road were peacefully quiet next to the riot that raged inside me. I wrapped my arms around myself, shaking. My stomach soured and I gagged, struggling to catch my breath. Each exhale fighting its way out of my mouth, burning my lungs.

*No.*

There was no fucking way. *No.*

My vision doubled.

I leaned against the wall next to the door, sinking down to the floor.

This was not happening.

I closed my eyes.

The money, the gun, the reports.

What the hell did I see last night? I forced myself to relive it.

The tattooed man, the *ghost* flashed in my memory. A stark reality against the dark night. A monster carved of stone with blood on his hands.

My stomach twisted and I shut my eyes, leaning my forehead against the cool exterior of the building, paralyzed until I heard the car coming up the road. Someone was here.

My Pavlovian response took over. Working here, I'd learned how to calmly talk to grieving loved ones with a straight yet empathetic face from a young age.

*Remember,* Dad would tell me, *no matter how bad of a day you might be having, they are having one which is much worse.*

I tucked away my anxiety, swallowing it back until it compacted in my stomach like heavy brick to be dealt with later.

Forcing myself to my feet, I straightened my hair and waited as the car parked. A withdrawn man exited, explaining his need for services.

I went through the motions, explaining our services and determining what he wanted as I filled us each a glass of lemonade. The day wore on, the worst of my shock passed, but I couldn't look my dad in the face.

"Do you want to come over for dinner?" he asked as we finished up.

"No," I blurted out before he even finished. He looked up, lips parted, speechless. He looked hurt. I scrambled.

"No. *Sorry*, no. I'm just not hungry. Think I'm going to head to bed early, I'm beat," I rambled, trying to deflect from my mistake. His lips closed, but his eyes were still guarded.

"All right," he said, something too close to suspicion in his eyes for my liking. Did he know how to use that gun? It was like he was a stranger in my Dad's clothes, and I hated it. Wished I was strong enough to confront him.

"Bright and early tomorrow," Dad called to me as I left, reminding me we had double the workload of today tomorrow to get ready for all the funerals next weekend.

Outside, only a small sliver of daylight still peaked up from the horizon. I walked back to my cabin in the twilight, stopping just short of opening the front door.

The cool wind slicing around the cabin howled, bringing with it a sense of unease. My hand tightened on the doorknob, turning to look over my shoulder when the hairs on the back of my neck rose.

The silhouette of the trees swayed sedately in the wind. The distant trickle of the creek continued its song, unbothered. There was nothing outside of the norm and yet I couldn't help the nagging feeling that as I looked out into the woods, something out there was looking back at me.

I shook off the unease and pushed inside, the warm silence of my cabin wrapping me up in its reassuring embrace.

I took comfort in the never changing sameness of my existence. The low couch in the small living room with the hand-me-down TV on the hand-me-down tv stand.

The kitchenette, with the old tool chest I repurposed as

a kitchen island still littered with remnants of last night's snacks and wine.

Normally, I'd feel nothing but an all-consuming, mind-numbing, boredom on my return home, but right now, the predictability was the comfort I needed.

I cranked the shower on in the bathroom, giving the water time to heat before rushing back through the cabin to the front door, deciding to lock it.

Swallowing through the tightness in my throat, I peered outside one last time, trying to shove away morbid imaginings of monsters coming out of the dark to take me. There was nothing there. No one. Just me and the bugs.

*Chill out, Em*, I chastised myself. *Just because Dad may or may not be doing shady business with shady people doesn't mean anyone's coming for you.*

I pulled my t-shirt off, stripping down on the way to the bathroom, needing the hot water to wash away all my sins, soothe my overtightened muscles.

I dumped my dirty laundry into the hamper and stepped under the hot stream of the shower. Through the fogged-over glass of the shower cubicle, I could see the familiar shapes of the toilet, mirror, and door, but just barely. If someone was in here with me, I would see them too.

*Stop being paranoid, Em.*

Running my soapy, slippery hands over my naked body, *he* burst back into my thoughts. His face like a Renaissance statue. And those eyes. I shivered despite the scalding water. He was dangerous.

I wondered if he would be back.

The energy around me was turbulent and full of static. My ears and eyes told me I was alone, but that knowing sensation haunted me all the way out of the shower and into bed.

I flicked through my phone, shooting off another apology text to Tess, but wound up jumping from app to app, my mind too unsettled to focus on anything. Dropping it on my nightstand, I hesitated before lifting the top book on a stack gifted to me by Tessa. I smoothed my thumb over the cover, a close up of a man with piercing gray eyes and tattoos over his collar, arching over his brow.

I bit my lip, cracked the first page, and settled into my pillow.

An hour was gone before I knew it. Then two. My promise of just one more chapter turned into five as I devoured page after page of a romance story so dark it had me questioning my own morals.

I read until my eyes couldn't stay open another second, drifting off to sleep with images of tattooed hands around pretty throats crowding my foggy mind.

# 4

## RUARC

The application email on the screen was one of many I received every week for entry to Delirium. The sender was asking for a private meeting with me to discuss membership in the club. Like the others, this lawyer had gotten a word-of-mouth recommendation from a member and they wanted in.

As if it were that simple.

Delirium was at capacity. There would be no draw if the club wasn't as exclusive as it was. Sometimes they tried to sweeten the deal, buy their way in, adding a little gratuity on top of the membership fee.

It didn't work.

The best I could offer to the impatient ones was the one-time event package that went for a cool $250,000. That booked the space, the women, catering, and use of any and all equipment including any special requests.

Someone knocked at the door, then pushed it open. Not even the housekeepers had that kind of freedom. I didn't need to look away from the screen to know it was Nixon.

"What is it?"

"You're not going to like this."

"Then spit it out."

"It's the undertaker," he started. "Don't know what's gotten into him, but he's asking for more money."

My hand reached absently for the heavy, brass paperweight shaped like a lion's head on my large, oak desk.

"Is he offering new services?" I snapped, an annoyed edge making its way into my voice.

"Nah, he's just greedy."

Having Snow's services at my beck and call was too convenient to want to give up, but that didn't mean the man couldn't be replaced.

"How much does he want?"

"A twenty percent increase," Nixon reported. I squeezed the brass paperweight in my fist, its jagged edges pressing into my skin.

Money was no object, respect, however...

Snow was even more the fool than I thought he was.

"No," I decided.

"I'll tell him."

"No. I'll do it."

I dropped the paperweight, feeling dull points of pain where its edges dug into my skin. Nixon frowned, confusion furrowing his brow. "You sure? I'm happy to do it, boss."

Some messages were better communicated in person. Punctuated by pain.

"He needs a reminder of who's in charge."

"I'll come with."

I shook my head, coming around at the desk.

The undertaker was no threat, even when he was making demands. He was discreet and efficient, but he wasn't intimidating. Not a fighter. He felt big enough to ask for more money because he wasn't asking in person. He wasn't asking me to my face.

"No need."

"At least take your piece," Nix urged, indicating my glock still in its holster atop my desk. I was *not* going to need it and bringing it would only increase my chances of injuring him badly enough to prevent him from doing the job I needed him to do.

The fucker wasn't asking for more money because he thought he could get it or even because of some misguided belief that he deserved it. He was testing his boundaries like a child. Seeing how far he could push, what he could get away with.

I sighed, taking the gun if only because I knew flashing a piece would help get my point across even if I didn't intend to use it.

There was still a sliver of sun in the sky as I pulled into the gravel drive, parking up directly in front of the building, below the long darkened windows set high above the ground.

"Bright and early tomorrow," the undertaker's voice echoed from the back of the building as I stepped out of the car.

My teeth clenched and I let the door close silently behind me, listening to light footsteps retreat down a footpath behind the mortuary.

I cut into the woods along the edge of the property, dried leaves and twigs crunched under my boots. They sunk into the damp soil on the banks of the creek that snaked around the back of their property and I stopped dead in my tracks, sinking in the soft ground as I watched her walking alone down a path deeper into the trees.

Her long jet-black hair was back in a ponytail. Wearing loose jeans and a long-sleeved t-shirt, she walked alone, and I followed her like a shadow in her wake.

A small cabin crouched in a copse of trees at the edge of the property, just before the trees thickened into a forest too dense to traverse.

You'd never know it was there unless you'd come back here yourself.

The old man was hiding more than a few secrets from me and for good reason.

I cut deeper into the woods as she went inside, peering over her shoulder first as if she'd heard me.

The windows lit like beacons against the encroaching night as she filled the sleepy cabin with life. I watched, sinking low in the brush.

My vision tunneled for any sight of her and when her face appeared in the window my breaths shallowed. Desire surged through my muscles, feral in its intensity. I wet my lips, watching every tiny shift in her expression, finding worry in the crease between her brows. A tightness around her smooth jaw.

Sharply, she whipped her head to the left, looking right at me, but not seeing me. The skin around her eyes crinkled as she squinted to see into the shadows, her shoulders heaving with a sigh.

The gulf between us might as well have been ten miles wide. My fingers itched to touch her. To trace the strong line from the base of her delicate ear to her chin, lower to the ridge of her collarbone, lower still.

Everything inside me seized, stiffening in anticipation of something I wouldn't allow myself. Not yet.

I moved to the front of the cabin, crouching next to an oak tree to get a better vantage point. With every curtain and blind open to the night, I watched unimpeded as Emily Snow pulled the gray shirt she was wearing over her head and turned, offering me only a glimpse of her perky breasts from the side before she vanished.

I slammed my palm into the rough bark of the tree, sucking air through my teeth.

Little lamb wasn't so innocent.

She *knew*.

She knew I was out here.

If not me, then she knew *something* was. The trepidation in her expression at the window was unmistakable. I pawed myself through my pants, clenching against the start of an aching hard on.

She knew she was being watched but still she took her top off in the window? She *wanted* me to see.

I rose to my full height and stalked around the porch to the steps, climbing up, keeping close to the wall as I found a better view, one that allowed me to see deeper into the little cabin.

A savage want coursed through my veins, tightening my muscles. I reached over and tested the door handle, finding it locked. It wouldn't stop me if I decided to go inside, take from her what my body craved.

I waited, hating every second I was reduced to this... this... *stalker* in the dark. Lusting after a girl. A girl who couldn't have been older than twenty when I was nearing thirty.

I was no cradle robber. No pathetic creep. And yet I

couldn't seem to make my booted feet leave her front porch, starving for another glimpse of her snow white skin.

It was a few minutes before came back into view, wrapped in a towel, a trail of steam chasing her from a bathroom just out of sight.

She paused for a second then swept her gaze to the left again. A slow smile spread over my lips, thinking I'd been caught, but she looked right through me, the shadows on her porch too deep to see me through their darkness.

I could see her in the corner of the other window frame, hair wet, stuck to her skin like ink on white paper.

She held the towel to her chest. I wanted to strip her down and mark up every inch of that skin so that anybody who saw her knew she was mine. I opened my pants, pulling my cock out, jerking it until it was full and throbbing. I spit into my hand, fucking it as she tiptoed closer, her lips parting in fear as she tried to make out my shape on the other side of the window.

Such a curious little lamb.

It intrigued her, that feeling she couldn't put her finger on. That sense that danger was just around the corner, close enough to bite her.

She might not have been able to see me, but she could *feel* me, unable to shake the sensations making her thighs press beneath her damp towel.

I pumped harder, my cock a stiff rod now. *Drop the towel*, I thought. My breath was ragged, zeroed in on her as I fucked my hand. *Drop it*.

She shifted back slightly, giving her head a shake before releasing her arm from her chest. The thick white fabric fell, revealing every bare inch of her slender curves.

My breath caught in my throat. I fucked my hand

harder, the friction a sad substitute for her hot, wet cunt. Her skin was buttery vanilla. Dusky pink nipples sat on her round, generous breasts. A groomed patch of black hair sat on her mound, right above the place I would have killed a man to bury my face right now.

She was there, and then she was gone, turning to disappear around the corner into the bathroom. I closed my eyes, the image of her seared behind my eyelids. My hand slipped over my cock until I exploded, spilling my seed on her threshold, marking my territory.

I shoved my cock back into my pants and stepped down from the porch, throwing myself to the edge of the woods. Away from her. Away from every dirty, rotten, cruel thing I wanted to do to her.

I wanted to *ruin* her. Ruin her so fucking fully–so completely–that I was the only man who would ever know how to put her back together again.

The crisp night air nipped at my lungs on a shaky inhale.

I wanted her and I was going to have her, it was only a matter of *when*.

A devious idea lit like the strike of a match in my mind, flaring into a burning fire. Her father seemed to need a lesson in submission. Maybe his daughter could help me teach it to him.

# 5

---

## RUARC

I let myself into the back of the mortuary and listened for sounds of life, following the metallic clatter of the undertaker's tools to the cold room. I'd make this quick.

Mr. Snow hunched over a corpse, elbow deep in their chest cavity. Tubes attached to the body led to a tank full of red-tinted liquid.

I knew enough of anatomy to cause pain to the human body without accidentally killing someone during the torture process, but knowing wasn't the same as seeing.

I didn't mess with people after they were dead.

The seedy, white-haired man leaning over the dead body on the gurney seemed almost ghoulish, with his spine showing through his smock and his thin arms pale under the stark lighting.

When he saw me, his eyes bulged twice their size. He staggered back.

"M-Mr. Monroe," he stammered.

"Good evening, *Mr.* Snow. I'm not interrupting anything, am I?"

I came around the gurney and he scurried across to the other side with jerky movements like a rat.

"I've been informed you have something to say to me. Some dissatisfaction with your pay?"

His throat bobbed.

"What? I-I don't know what you're talking about."

I ran at him, causing him to crash into a gurney pushed to the wall. It rolled across the floor, making him lose his balance. He stumbled like a baby deep on legs too long and thin to hold up its frame. I snorted. *Pathetic.*

There was nothing I hated more than a coward.

Mr. Snow wanted to act a big man behind my back, but when it came time to tell me his grievances to my face he recoiled. Searching for anywhere else to look. Someplace else to hide. Tripping over his words.

He was well suited to his line of work. Dead men didn't argue or intimidate. He wouldn't fare even half as well working among the living.

"I was told you had a request for me. Are you saying I'm wasting my time coming here?"

"No, no," he choked out, edging away from me along the wall.

My sneer turned into a grin. His fear was so thick I could practically smell it wafting off of him. He was one second away from begging, bargaining, anything to make sure he didn't end up like the guy on his gurney.

"Then tell me, why am I here? What do you want?" I snapped.

He swallowed, practically flat against the wall.

"Look, I'm sorry. I think there was a misunderstanding."

"Bullshit. Grow a pair, old man."

I slammed my palm down on the metal gurney. He jumped, losing his footing, and fell to the ground. I loomed over him.

"It's the money," he blurted once I was too close for his comfort, "we aren't doing well financially. The mortuary. It's expensive to run. It's a small, family business. Most people go with the big-name funeral homes."

A coward and a shit business man.

"Is it my problem that you don't know how to run a business, Mr. Snow?"

He shook his head.

"You, you have to understand—"

"Do you give orders or do I?"

His chin wobbled. "No. *No*. It's just I can't let this place close down. It's my wife's. It's her legacy. This is the only way I can support us."

I almost recoiled from his admission.

Weak.

Weak men were no good to me.

I wasn't even angry at him, I pitied him.

If his services weren't so conveniently located and accessible, I'd terminate our contract right here and now with a well-placed bullet and the strike of a match.

"When you give me a reason to give you more money, I'll consider it. One of those '*big-name*' funeral homes might be a better investment."

His lip quivered, but something flashed in his green eyes.

*That was where Emily got them*, I thought, marveling at how differently they affected me looking out of his face versus hers. Hers a bright, vivid hue, filled with life and fire. His, a muted shade, too small for his long face.

"You can't threaten me. No one else will agree to this type of arrangement."

His voice finally got a little bass in it. Look at that. Sad sack of shit was *standing up for himself.*

"I don't make threats, undertaker," I crooned, voice low. "I make promises."

"How did you even get in here? You're not supposed to come before midnight. You're trespassing."

I laughed darkly, knowing he would do absolutely nothing about it.

Didn't matter which cop or detective he spoke to within 100 miles of here. As soon as they heard my name, they wouldn't do a damned thing.

My lip curled with scorn looking at the sniveling, sorry excuse for a man crumpled on the ground.

"Are you listening, old man? I need to make sure you hear me."

His throat bobbed again. "You can't–"

"I *can* and I will. Waste my time again and you won't like the consequences. You have a problem? Something to discuss? You speak to Nixon or you have him pass along a formal request for a meeting. Be a man, Snow. I don't work with rodents."

I turned, leaving the mortuary building, my back rigid with annoyance. Though, Snow may not have been worth the trip here; Emily was.

Immediately, her wet, naked body flashed behind my eyelids.

That inexplicable blaze of want flamed through me. I

lifted my gaze, peering through the trees across the property, but her cabin couldn't be seen from the road.

How in the hell did someone like her come out of the ball sack of someone like her father? She had more spine at what I imagined to be something close to twenty-one than her father did pushing fifty.

I floored it back to the house, tearing down the deserted road. I was back in half the time it took me to get to the mortuary.

With a single-minded purpose, I stalked through the house, up the stairs, into my bedroom, into my closet. I searched for a mask, securing it to my face with vivid images of Emily still playing through my thoughts.

Tension flared across my shoulders, in need of a release.

I took the upstairs entrance to the club on the house's second floor, opening via the biometric lock to step out onto the mezzanine. The strong, bass-driven beat rattled through my bones. Sex hung in the air. Predictable roars, groans, and laughs echoed through the hall, bouncing off the high ceiling.

My hands curled around the railing from the mezzanine, staring down at the masked patrons below.

I cocked my head, narrowing my sights on the people fucking on the altar. Three of them.

The woman lay on her back against the solid wood. One guy had her by the hips, jackhammering in and out of her pussy. The other pumped his thick cock between her lips until she convulsed with the need for air.

My own cock thickened as I watched, leaning casually over the rail as they continued. I was already primed, on edge from watching my little lamb. I should've brought her back with me.

The thought of having her in here, showing her my kingdom, was intoxicating, and also... revolting.

I wanted every inch of her to myself. Picturing it now, I could say with confidence that if she were here several clients would be leaving short an eyeball, maybe a hand.

I'd need to collar her.

I bit the inside of my cheek until I tasted blood, frustration clouding my thoughts with hot steam.

I should've taken her at her cabin.

My grip tightened on the railing. I shut my eyes, the thick, seductive energy of the club swirling around me, whispering to me the promise of release. And yet...

The beauty stretched over the altar didn't have hair the color of night. She didn't have skin so unblemished and milky white that I ached to turn it red, taste it on my lips.

Emily Snow would be mine eventually.

Why not sooner?

Why delay the inevitable?

The undertaker would have no choice but to do what I wanted if I had his daughter. The perfect bargaining chip. The perfect hostage.

The woman below gasped as her eyes made contact with me, her purpose shifting from conductor of pleasure to performer in the blink of an eye.

On her back, letting two men use her, she writhed, squealing with pleasure, her moans growing louder as she put on a show for me.

My teeth grated, the need still there, begging to be addressed, but the hard length in my pants was already softening as I imagined fucking the beauty below. Imagined wrapping my hands around her slender neck, binding her hands and ankles. Making her scream.

## Chapter 5

A low growl rose in my chest and I cut my stare away, swiping a palm over my jaw, frustration turning to a manic wonder as the stoic realization dawned.

It was Emily or nothing.

## 6

### EMILY

"Dad?"

"*Hm?*"

I looked up at him from the stiffened hand I was massaging. The body had been dead long enough for rigor mortis to make it heavy and rigid. Dad massaged the other arm, the pair of us working to cut the embalming time in half.

"What happens..." I chewed the inside of my cheek, choosing my words carefully. "What happens to people who die, but they weren't supposed to."

My dad glanced at me, brows low over his eyes with confusion.

"It's kind of hard to die by mistake, honey," he said. "Barring acts of God or some serious foolishness."

"Yeah, no. What I mean is... bodies that aren't supposed to be dead. Like a person who accidentally dies during a hiking accident. What happens to their body?"

"I suppose a rescue mission would follow," he mumbled.

"*Okay*, but after that," I said, my irritation jerking the arm hard enough to move the body on the gurney. I couldn't hurt the guy any more but the body was being prepared for viewing. Decomposition already did a number on the human body, I didn't need to damage it even further with posthumous bruising or denting.

"Then his body would end up at a morgue. Police would get involved. Identification—"

"No, okay, how about this," I said, changing tack, my nostrils flaring with frustration trying to figure out how to ask what I want to without *actually* saying the words that would draw too much suspicion. "Let's say there's this... gang."

*Like that.*

No taking it back now.

"*Okay*," he said, drawing out the word, his focus on the task at hand intensifying, betraying the guilt he tried to hide from me.

"And this gang, they kill someone in a bad drug deal or something. Whatever. Someone is killed who isn't supposed to be killed."

"That's what *kill* means, Emily," he said, his tone accommodating, but growing weary. Trying to put an end to the conversation.

"Okay, okay. So he's dead and they don't want anyone to find out. What happens to *that* body?" I asked, blinking expectantly. I was trying to get him to pick up what I was putting down and either I was doing a bad job or he was too literal for his own good.

He sighed, moving to the body's leg.

"I don't make it a habit to kill people but if I did, I suppose I'd get rid of the body."

"Yeah, so how would that happen?" I asked. Not through a small, unassuming, family-run mortuary, would it? Where the owner was paid off for committing what was probably considered a very serious crime, *would it*?

He huffed another heavy sigh.

"Have you been watching crime shows or something? Where is this coming from?"

My mouth went dry.

The only thing I'd been doing in my free time was reading Tessa's books. I was halfway through the second and worried that I only had one left. They were dark, but the words in those books weren't to blame for my line of thought right now, *he* was.

"I don't know, I was just thinking maybe like the mafia or killers or whoever sometimes use the police and other institutions to cover up their crime," I said, staring at him to gauge his reaction. He deftly worked the rigor mortis out of the body's left leg, not even glancing up at me.

So, nothing.

No guilt? No discomfort? He felt *nothing*?

This was so much worse than I thought.

"Of course, that happens. Corruption is everywhere," he said. I came to join him working on the other leg, sliding my gloved fingers over the stiffened skin.

Swallowing, I pressed on, needing *something* from him. Something more than surface level guilt. Maybe whoever was here was forcing him to get rid of the bodies. Maybe they said they'd kill him if he didn't do it. Or something even worse than that.

But if that were true, he'd be showing guilt, right? He wouldn't be getting annoyed with my questions, he'd be trying to deflect, or maybe he'd admit it outright. Start sobbing over the corpse between us. Tell me he didn't know what to do.

But he wasn't doing any of those things.

"Have you seen anything like that?" I blurted before I could take it back.

He lowered the leg to the gurney, fixing me with an exhausted gaze that made my stomach clench, worried that he'd see the truth in my eyes.

"Let's focus on this body and talk later, okay?"

Later never came.

Embalming took most of the afternoon and I took care of cosmetics before we closed for the day.

I guessed I wasn't really expecting him to admit anything or incriminate himself. What I wanted, *needed*, was confirmation that these things weren't impossible.

Even having seen what I'd seen, I felt like my grip on reality was unraveling little by little every day. Did I really see what I thought I did?

Was that truly what was happening or did I just misinterpret it?

I wanted Dad to look guilty. Scared. To show signs of discomfort when I started asking questions. Anything that said he wasn't a willing accomplice. But he didn't even flinch. If it was true and he explained himself, maybe I'd understand. I'd at least try to but right now, if I was right, I didn't know who that man was anymore. He wasn't the father I looked up to and tried to impress all my life.

He was... a criminal.

An uncharacteristically cold breeze blew down from the road as I walked back to my cabin. I hugged my arms tight around myself. A hot shower before bed was exactly what I needed.

I didn't want to see or talk to anyone to do anything. I just needed to escape into the blissful release of sleep. Maybe I'd finish that book tonight. Throwing a glance over my shoulder at the mortuary, its darkened upper windows and the chimney from the incinerator sent a shiver up my spine.

Ghosts and vampires and ghouls weren't real. My parents made sure I never believed any of that crap. They taught me death wasn't something to be afraid of. Everyone died. That was a simple part.

*How* people died was where it got complicated. Some people died because they were old, some because they were sick, others in horrible–but mostly preventable–accidents.

And then there were others still—those who died because someone wanted them to. I heard the swish of the trees in the wind, and the distant high-pitched chirping of bats. Climbing up the patio to my door, I unlocked it quickly and let myself inside, accidentally slamming it in my haste, throwing the latch to lock it shut.

I fired up the stove to heat the chilly cabin and went to the kitchen for something to drink, stopping dead in my tracks.

The chest that used to be in the main house gaped at me with an open drawer from where it sat next to my couch.

My chest tightened as I approached it.

It'd belonged to my mom. Three drawers with ornate, gold-plated handles. An antique. I didn't know where she got it but when she died, I knew I wanted it.

I didn't keep anything of value inside it. Just chargers, change, random Allen keys and bolts left over after assembling Ikea furniture. I didn't have to open it often which meant I never left it open by mistake.

The second drawer's edges protruded from the drawer's straight face, like it, too, had been opened, then pushed closed but not all the way.

Cold seeped into my gut and spread in tendrils out to my limbs, making my teeth chatter. My feet carried me to the drawers and I pulled them open one by one, expecting the worst.

Except everything was exactly the same. Just as I left it. But...

*I didn't open it.*

I chewed the side of my lip, doubtful. Unless I did by accident? The cold deepened, it burrowed into my lungs, making it hard to breathe. If it wasn't me, then who? Tessa?

No, I would've noticed it open sooner if it'd been her.

I whipped my head over my shoulder, fully expecting to see someone standing there. A ghoul. A *ghost*. Whatever terrifying apparition haunted me.

I swallowed. Ghosts didn't exist.

Plucking up my courage with a mental kick, I straightened back to my full height, checking the rest of the cabin to set my mind at ease.

I scanned the kitchen. Running a palm over the top of my refrigerator, two plate burner, and counter space, nothing seemed out of place. No open drawers. Nothing where it shouldn't have been.

Two forks stood upright in the drying rack. I doubted whether I'd seen them that morning and gave myself another mental boot for my mounting paranoia.

I went up to check my bedroom, anxiety fluttering in my ribcage like a trapped sparrow.

Finding something out of place there would be somehow far worse than in the living room.

This was my space. Where I slept, where I was at my most vulnerable. I winced as I peered inside, saying a silent prayer to whatever gods would hear me that nothing would be out of place.

Or more accurately, that my tired paranoid mind wouldn't see something that wasn't really there. I'd never had an issue living out here alone at the edge of the property and I didn't want to start out.

This cabin was my home. *My* haven. And I'd be damned if I was going to let that be ruined by one tattooed man in a suit and an unidentified body on a slab.

The bed was made, the same way I left it that morning. The nightstands looked undisturbed. The latest book I was reading lay on my pillow where I left it too. Squinting, the memories of my day blurred with fiction and possibility. Did I take the book out into the main cabin with me? I was pretty sure I read it while I had coffee that morning.

No.

Wait, that was wrong.

I was texting Tessa in the morning, so I wouldn't have been reading.

An unsettling tremor ran through the air and the cabin. I sighed, suddenly hyper-aware of my breath, my movements, everything around me. The uncanny feeling that there were eyes on me returned and my brows drew.

"Not now," I whined to myself in the dim, biting my lip.

It'd been happening more and more lately. Sometimes I'd be here, completely comfortable, and then suddenly, the hair on my neck would stand up. The air felt different. The cabin's walls like barricades keeping something out instead of holding me in their warm embrace. I felt naked.

Watched, but with no watcher I could see.

*Who the hell are* you?

*A ghost.*

I shook, insecure in my own fucking house. I was not having it.

*Fuck this.*

I went down the stairs, straight to the kitchen. Sliding a drawer open, I pulled out the longest knife that I had. It needed a good sharpening but it'd do the trick if I needed it to.

I opened the door and carefully locked it behind me. Pausing, I made sure I remembered this moment so I couldn't gaslight myself into thinking I didn't do it later.

The shapes and shadows of the night felt loud and obtrusive as if seeing and hearing them for the first time. I checked both sides of the cabin from the patio platform, seeing nothing.

I tightened my fist around my knife, carefully stepping down off the patio, feeling ridiculous but not enough to stop me.

The forest's tall black trees loomed above with branches like reaching claws, swaying in the wind.

I squinted to see into the abyss of the thick wood. Dark and impenetrable enough to hide anything that I tried to find.

Tugging my phone from my pocket, I thumbed the screen, turning on the flashlight as I thudded down the porch steps and crouched down, shining my flashlight under the cabin. Built on a slight incline, a stone platform supported the front, keeping the floors inside more or less level.

Nothing but cobwebs to be found underneath.

Rising, I spun in a slow circle, looking for the glow of

eyes in the brush or the trees. It would almost be relieving to find them. Little red beady eyes. Even reflective ones. Fuck, I'd take a wolf or a feral racoon over the haunting danger my imagination kept churning.

I clenched against a chill, trying not to shiver.

Outside surrounded by open space, I felt like there was nowhere to run. Nowhere to hide.

Going around the back of the cabin, I gripped the dull kitchen knife tighter in my sweaty fist.

Over the sound of my drumming pulse, I hurried across the back of the cabin, eyes sweeping left and right, until I wound up back at the base of the porch steps.

Nothing. I didn't see anything out there or around the cabin.

My stomach twisted as I watched the calmly swaying trees, heard the soft sounds of the forest at night. Like it was mocking me.

I almost wanted a monster to burst out of the trees. Something, *anything* that told me I wasn't crazy.

Something was out there. I could feel its eyes on me.

"*What do you want?*" I howled into the dark, my voice cracking with the sudden surge in volume. My breaths came heavier, faster.

"I know you're out there!"

A gust of wind kicked up, lifting my hair from my shoulders, but other than its soothing whisper, there was nothing but a deep, calm evening staring back at me from the porch.

My body sagged and I dragged my paranoid ass back inside, slamming the door behind me. I locked it, stalking back to the kitchen.

I barely managed to sit still for a second before the quiet

started to feel too oppressing. Like it could crush me if I let it.

With shaky fingers, I tapped my phone, needing to hear another voice.

"Hey girl, what's up?" Tessa asked as she answered the call and I swayed with relief, stumbling to the sofa.

"Hey, can you talk?"

"Uh yeah, is something wrong?"

My hand tightened around the phone.

*You're being paranoid. You're being paranoid. You're being paranoid.*

"Someone is stalking me."

*And now your BFF is going to think you're insane.*

"I'm sorry?"

"Today, I came to the cabin—"

"Try some lead-up before dropping something like that on me first, *god*."

I sighed, feeling my rattling bones settle back into place, Tessa's attitude giving me some much needed grounding. Taking a breath, I started at the beginning, telling her about the first night I thought there was someone out there. I kept going, telling her about the drawer and how I was certain it wasn't me.

I couldn't risk telling her about the man I saw in the basement of the mortuary, or the cash or gun or doctored envelopes in Dad's office. I wouldn't implicate her. Couldn't make her an accomplice to whatever the hell was going on in there after midnight.

"Have you seen footprints? Heard noises?"

"No. Nothing. I just know... it's like a feeling," I said, realizing how pathetic I sounded but unable to give her any more to go on. I just needed someone to know. I needed her to tell me I wasn't crazy. I needed her to have an explanation for Dad, for the police, if I suddenly vanished in the night.

"Right. Well, babe, it's like I've said since the start. That kind of shit is bound to happen when you agree to live on the same property as a fucking dead-people closet in a tiny ass run down cabin right next to the woods. I mean, you're lucky I even visit. Your place gives me the creeps."

"I've lived here all my life," I deadpanned. "This just started happening."

"Okay..."

I waited. This was the part when she told me I wasn't crazy. The silence continued, then it kept going.

Then it went on some more.

"Oh my god. You don't believe me," I put my forehead in my free hand, sighing down the line.

*Of course, she didn't.*

"I'm sorry. It just sounds so out there. I'm not saying you don't *deserve* a stalker. I mean you're great, you got that whole Snow White thing going on, minus the dwarves, but this came out of nowhere. You don't see anyone but me. You don't go out places, meet anyone. No one would have a reason to stalk you because no one even knows you're out there, babe."

There was the brutal honesty I didn't ask for. Why did she have to call me out like that.

I gritted my teeth, sitting back to sag into the over softened sofa cushions.

"I called to order a little sympathy," I groused. "Not a steaming pile of brutal honesty with a side of bitch-you're-paranoid."

"No, don't be like that. You just need to get out of that stupid place for a hot minute."

I kicked the ground, pursing my lips. "Uh-huh."

"I can get you to Portland on a work trip with me if I ask now. The author requested two assistants but we couldn't find a second on short notice."

Portland wasn't really Hawaii, and it wasn't a vacation, but it was something. It would get me out of here.

Was I really considering this?

I never left.

Dad needed me too much here.

The hairs on my arms stood on end and I whirled in my seat on the couch, giving myself whiplash as I searched for foreign faces in every surrounding window, my heart in my damn throat. I swallowed past the battered lump, finding nothing out there. I pinched the bridge of my nose and took another steadying breath.

"Babe?" Tess prodded.

"Okay."

"Okay? Really?"

"Send me the details. I'll talk to Dad. If he can handle things without me that long, then I'll come."

Tess squealed and I could practically see her clear green eyes crinkling at the edges as she no doubt did a little happy dance in her living room. She'd been asking me to go to one of these events with her for literal years.

"Don't get your hopes up," I warned.

"Too late," she trilled. "Check your email. Deets incoming. And go open a bottle of wine, you need to chill, girl."

The cabin felt a thousand times bigger than it was when I finally ended the call. Like there could be more than one someone hiding in every nook and cranny I couldn't see from the living room. Which admittedly wasn't many since the place was a whopping eight hundred square feet.

I definitely wasn't hungry enough to eat despite skipping lunch earlier and wine sounded like the antithesis of a good idea right now, so I dragged my sorry ass into a shower and straight to bed.

I couldn't bring myself to turn off all the lights, and it took me three tries to get back into the book I'd been reading, jumping at every creak and groan of the old cabin, but once it caught, it fucking *caught*. I tore through the second half of the book and for a while thought of nothing else but the story. The characters. *Their* problems instead of mine.

If I went to Portland with Tessa, maybe I could score a couple more of these things. I hadn't told her yet, because she was going to rub it in my face when she found out she was right, but the books she kept unloading on me weren't just good, they were fucking phenomenal.

The writing itself was good, flowing, easy to follow, but something about the crazy, scandalous things the characters did together was what really kept me turning the pages.

Not that I personally wanted a guy to fuck me with a knife to my throat. Not *really*.

But, I mean, maybe it depended on the guy. If he was like this dude I'd let him do whatever he wanted to me. No questions asked.

Well, maybe not, but it was fun as hell to imagine.

I kept reading from the chapter I left off on, vivid images saturating my mind as the pages turned. My thighs clenched getting into a sex scene and I bit the inside of my cheek, wishing I'd remembered to charge Timmy since I'd last used him.

*She wept,* I read, *partly from the pleasure, partly from the shame. Her body exploded with sensation.*

*"Please stop," she sobbed. She squirmed, trying to escape but there was nowhere to run. Thrashing desperately against him, she only succeeded in sinking his cock further into her pussy. She moaned at the invasion, greedy for more, aching for him to press into her even deeper, and hating herself for it.*

*"Please," she whispered. She was saving herself. She was a virgin. Lust and fear and regret swirled inside her. "Don't."*

*"I'm not the one moving, pet," he snarled in her ear, "you are."*

*He licked the tears running down her cheek.*

I audibly gasped. *Was he...*

I quickly read the next few lines.

He *was.*

And was I...?

I didn't need to reach a hand down there to check, I knew I was. Reading through the rest of the scene, I didn't move my hand, letting it rest between my thighs until I couldn't help it.

I slid my hand beneath the waistband of my panties and found myself hot and wet as I restarted the scene from the beginning. Lower lip between biting teeth, I swirled my fingers in my wetness and rubbed myself as the scene came to life again in my mind.

I moaned, my toes curling as I became her. A girl losing herself to a dangerous man as he had his way with her, taking what he wanted. Completely consuming her.

I swirled my fingertips in my wetness, flicking them faster over my clit as I began to thrust my hips to increase the pressure, to simulate the action of being fucked.

Was it watching? My stalker. My monster. My ghost.

Whatever it was. *Who*ever it was.

The eyes peering over my shoulder. The presence filling the shadow cloaked spaces of my bedroom.

I hoped it was. The thought of it watching as I touched myself sent a bolt of pure pleasure straight to my greedy cunt, making me ache with taboo desire. I threw my head back, letting out a raw cry of ecstasy as I dropped the book to the ground and rode the wave of my orgasm, more turned on than I'd ever been in my entire life.

## 7

### EMILY

*Is it a crime to dispose of a body?*

I typed the query into the search bar and tapped enter. Lines pulled between my eyebrows reading link after link. I mean, of course it was a crime, but how bad were we talking here?

I scrolled down.

*Abuse of a corpse.*

*Desecration of a corpse.*

*Failure to properly intern the deceased.*

*Getting rid of a body 101.*

Each headline was worse than the last. Basically, if he was doing what I thought he was doing, my dad was fucked.

I looked up, my neck sore from staring down at my phone screen. Thinking about my father's office across the property in the mortuary building, my stomach turned.

I still wanted it to be false. I couldn't stand it.

I wasn't young enough anymore to think my father was

this perfect, blameless person who could do no wrong. He was as human as me and all the bodies that came through our mortuary. He could lie, cheat, steal, and apparently get himself involved in some sort of shady criminal business which required him to get rid of bodies.

My neck and cheeks heated. I wasn't young and naive enough to think of my mom somewhere up in the clouds, watching over me, but I was fiercely protective of the legacy that she had built with the mortuary while she was still alive. It was a routine that'd gotten boring and stale, but it fucking meant something.

It made me sick to imagine that after she died, her husband decided to desecrate her legacy with something as messed up as this, whatever the hell *this* was. I didn't care about his reasons or how he had rationalized his way into thinking it was okay.

I needed to get back into that office, but when? Doing it during business hours was too risky.

Sometime between the hours of closing and midnight, then? Which would mean, like, right now, since after midnight was definitely out of the question.

Knowing he told me not to go into the main building after midnight because that was whenever he did what he did was infuriating.

At the heart of every swirling emotion inside, was *hurt*. I spent hours agonizing over this, rationalizing, trying to imagine he had a good reason.

Since I lived here, wasn't I implicated in some way?

I opened my door, stepping out into the cold night. I crossed my arms over my chest, absorbing the small shiver that ran through me. I was getting so used to the sensation someone was out here that it was becoming easier to ignore. Easier to brush off since even though I felt their shadow, they did nothing.

I hadn't been attacked. Or even approached.

A fly on the wall might be a pest but it couldn't hurt me.

It also lent credence to Tessa's theory that I was just being paranoid.

But coming outside, removing whatever space was between me and it, I felt exposed. Inhaling deeply, I almost thought that I could smell musk, or cologne, smell *it*; whatever it was.

I closed the door and locked it, making it to the mortuary in half the usual time. The cold night air nipped at my lungs. I panted coming around the building to the face our clients saw when they arrived. Dad's office was closest to the front entrance and I didn't want him to spot me sneaking in through the back.

Jamming my key in the lock, I looked over both shoulders. To an outsider, the mortuary could seem supremely creepy at night. But the chill in my blood didn't come from the knowledge of there being corpses cooling in the basement. It came from whatever the hell I might find in a much less morbid setting.

I closed the door behind me, locking it up.

Dad never locked his office, trusting me enough not to go inside. To follow the rules that'd been in place since I was a child. I might have broken a rule by coming out here past midnight, but as far as I knew, he was breaking *the law*.

I used the flashlight on my phone, shining it around my dad's office instead of turning on the light. Pointing it toward the bookshelf, I squinted, a harsh reflection of the light glinting off the vase that he used to store all the metal joints that he found in the cremator. Metal knee and hip joints didn't break down in the flame or even melt, they just sat there on the incineration slab when it was all over, a little dusty, but perfectly intact.

Sometimes families asked for them back, other times, they didn't care. So they ended up there. He had had the collection for years and I thought of it as nothing but a banal oddity. It was kind of amusing but now, I couldn't help wondering who all those people were and which ones were illegal.

Everything seemed tainted. Wrong.

I threw the drawer open, forcing myself to snap out of it. It wasn't the time. Checking the lowest drawer where I'd seen incriminating evidence, I found myself looking into a pile of innocent brown envelopes.

*Fuck.*

I balanced my phone on the edge of the desk with the beam of light shining into the drawer as I rifled through the envelopes. Most were empty, some old, all useless.

*Where did you put them?*

A ball formed in my throat.

*Where did you put them?*

I wrenched the top drawer open, and the second, seeing exactly what I saw last time.

They were gone.

For a terrible second, I wondered whether I imagined the whole thing. Over the past week, everything I saw, heard, and touched felt false on some level. Like I needed confirmation, for someone else to experience them so I knew they were there.

I scanned the room wildly, an ache in my chest, squeezing, twisting in my stomach.

Jumping to my feet, I ran to the tall shelf of filing cabinets that stood against the wall. My dad kept paper records like it was still 2003. They had to be in there with the others.

I yanked open the top drawer, barely sure of the method he used to organize these things. I grabbed a handful of paper, and then a harsh yellow light clouded my sight.

"Emily Diane Snow."

I froze, my breath lodging in my chest as my fingers completely immobilized. I froze like I was seven years old and he had just caught me trying to sneak an ice cream bar from the freezer after he had already told me no. This was far, far worse.

I dropped the sheets, every nerve ending ablaze.

"Did you lose something in here?" he asked, the edge in his voice uncharacteristically hard.

My chin jutted out. I wasn't the one who should be under scrutiny here. It should be him.

"Why was there a gun in your desk drawer?"

He cocked his head at me. "I'm sorry, what?"

"There was a *gun* in your desk drawer, Dad, why?"

"For self-defense. We're out here alone," he said, shrugging. his tone was almost mocking, like he was talking to a child instead of his adult daughter.

"Then explain the money. There was an envelope full of money."

"What are you talking about, Emily? What are you doing in here? That's the real issue."

"In there," I almost screamed, pointing at his desk.

"You're going through my things? What did I tell you about coming in here?"

"Now I know it's because you had something to hide. Why was there a false autopsy report in there?" I insisted. His face was so stoic, I felt crazy letting my emotions get the best of me.

"I haven't done an autopsy report in weeks. All our most recent death calls have been cremations and embalmings," he said coolly.

I was so frantic I thought I was going to explode. He was *not* going to lie in my face about what I saw. He couldn't.

"I know you're taking money from someone to get rid of bodies," I said, throwing the grenade out. If he was guilty, I would catch him. I watched his face, his mouth, eyes, anything that would give him away in the light of my phone flashlight.

But then, he laughed.

He fucking *laughed.*

"What's gotten into you, Emily? You've been jumpy and acting weird for days. The only reason I want you to stay out of here is because I don't think it's your place. I work you hard enough as it is. This part is for me. I'm disappointed that you would go against my instructions."

My emotions swirled around me like swamp mud, sucking me down. My vision shook and I couldn't think. His words said one thing, but I knew what I saw. The images in my mind altered, changing themselves to conform to his words.

No. No, I saw them.

"I can't believe you would do that to Mom," I croaked, fighting the doubt. Finally, his face moved. His mouth fell open, and his chest rose, indignant.

"I can't believe you'd ruin her legacy by getting involved in something like this," I continued before he could interrupt, balling my hand into a fist.

His face hardened, rage flickered in his eyes. When he spoke, his even tone was scarier than if he'd yelled at me.

"I was married to your mother for almost fifteen years. I would never desecrate her memory by ruining a business she built from the ground up with her own two hands. How dare you say such things."

He turned his back and walked toward the door. Pausing, he glanced over his shoulder.

"I never want to see you in my office again."

My heart slammed in my chest as I ran across the grass back to my cabin.

It was fake. Everything was fake. All I had to do was go to sleep, and when I woke up, nothing that'd happened in the last week and a half would be real. Everything would be back to normal.

I never saw the ghost in the basement that day.

Nor the gun or files or money in Dad's desk.

I wouldn't feel eyes on me while I slept, anymore.

There wouldn't be—

I stumbled coming up the steps of the patio. The front door of my cabin gaped open like a mouth mid-scream. I stared, willing my vision to shift back to reality, but it didn't, and the door kept screaming.

I closed that fucking door. I *locked* it. I knew I did.

My legs buckled. All the strength flowed out of my muscles as I sat there, crumpled, staring into the shadows beyond my door.

*Take me, then*, I thought. *Just do it, already.*

Nothing emerged from the black. Not a sound eked out

from within. The eerie silence cloaked me until I shivered beneath it.

Shaking my head, I snapped myself out of it, clenching my jaw until it hurt.

I knew one thing for damn sure. I was *not* going back in there.

Retreating back to the grass, I tore my phone from my pocket, dialing Carlos. He wouldn't ask questions, not if I was giving him what he wanted. I needed somewhere where none of this existed. Just for tonight.

I squeezed my eyes shut waiting for him to answer.

*Please. Come on, pick up.*

"Emily?" his voice came through the line.

"H-hey," I stammered, swallowing, my eyes fixed to the door.

"What's up? Everything okay?"

"Yeah. Sorry for—*uh*—calling so late. Are you at home?"

"Well it's almost midnight on a weeknight so, yeah..." He trailed off, tone flat.

We were cordial as far as exes went but off the books, we still hooked up, not often, but enough so that a midnight call wasn't entirely out of the blue.

Usually, though it was him who made these calls, not me.

"Can I come over?"

"Oh. Shit. Like, now?"

"Now," I confirmed.

I heard some commotion in the background, imagining him frantically picking up garbage and dirty laundry before I got there.

"Yeah. Sure. Come on over."

A shock of relief raced over me and I shut my eyes with a

sigh. It was a Band-Aid. A quick fix that wouldn't last more than the one night, but I'd take it. I'd take anything if it meant not being here even for five more minutes.

"Thanks, Carlos," I muttered, jutting my jaw against the shadows on the other side of my door. "I'm on my way."

# 8

## EMILY

My white knuckled grip on the steering wheel eased as the tension in my back and shoulders evaporated the farther I got from the cabin and mortuary grounds.

I barely ever drove into the city but Spokane's urban sprawl had never been such a comforting sight. It took me thirty-five minutes to get to Carlos's condo but it was worth every one of them.

"Hey," Carlos said, opening the door after I knocked.

A wide grin spread over his face. I returned it, even if mine was a little wilted. The relief of being with another person in another place hit me so hard, I felt drugged. Like I'd taken a fistful of tranquilizers after being high on adrenaline for too long.

Carlos pulled me into a hug, kissing my cheek. He smelled like marijuana and cologne applied several hours ago, but he was warm, solid, and familiar.

"I should have brought something," I mumbled. "Sorry."

Really, I should've brought some clothes and a tooth-brush at the bare minimum but even closing the distance between myself and the cabin to shut the door before leaving had taken a Herculean effort.

"Nah, don't worry about it," he insisted, ushering me inside.

"Is Salem home? I should have asked."

"She's not. We have the place to ourselves tonight."

Salem used to be an issue between us. She moved in with him when we were together and I didn't believe him when he said he wasn't attracted to her.

She was a curvy brunette who shared his passions for hockey, poker, and gaming. A guy's girl. The I'm-not-like-other-girls type. The I-can-run-with-the-boys-type. I had nothing against her other than her perfect tits and the way I sometimes caught her staring at Carlos just a little too long.

But that wasn't my problem anymore.

They were under the same roof with more than enough time to bond and grow a connection. He hated staying over at my place because it was allegedly creepy and I wasn't moving so we were practically long-distance right from the get go. Doomed to fail.

At least Carlos and Salem waited until he and I were on the *off* part of the on-again-off-again cycle to start fucking so my insecurities were only half right.

From what he told me, she never wanted anything serious with him and a couple of hookups was all he got out of her and he couldn't bring himself to ask her to leave.

She was always good with rent, clean, and easy to get along with so the awkward tension living together was worth it to him. And now that she had a steady boyfriend, it was only a matter of time before she moved out on her own anyway.

Carlos led me to his bedroom. It was the bigger of the two and had its own bathroom. The air held the smell of the last meal he ate. Tacos if I had to guess. And not good ones.

Yellow light from the lamp on his nightstand made the room feel warm and secure. Everything was just as I remembered it. The wine stain on the carpet from when he'd knocked a bottle over *into my lap*. The crooked curtain rod. The hole in the wall he kept saying he'd fix but never did.

That was one of the better things about Carlos, he was predictable. Static. Walking into his room was like walking into an *Office* episode that I'd seen seven times already. I knew exactly what to expect.

It was one of the reasons I couldn't see myself with him long term, knowing I'd get bored. I'd resent him for making one more part of my life monotonous and stagnant.

Right now, though? I couldn't think of anything more desirable than a boring life.

"Mind if I have a shower?" I asked, biting my lip.

"Yeah, sure. I'll order us some food. Thai?"

"I'm not hungry," I murmured, slipping out of my hoody, loving how the energy in the room didn't feel like it was assaulting me.

"Yeah, yeah, all right," he said, rubbing a hand up his other arm awkwardly. "Take your time, I guess."

"Those clean?" I indicated the clothes piled haphazardly on the armchair by his closet.

He nodded.

"You mind? I forgot my bag."

"What's mine is yours, Em, take what you want."

Thanking him, I gathered a long black t-shirt and hauled my exhausted bones into the shower.

When I came out, Carlos wasn't there but the bedroom had been tidied up, a candle lit on the dresser.

I smirked, knowing damn well the man didn't own a candle and likely swiped it from Salem. I dug my charger out of my bag and plugged my phone into the wall.

"Hey." Carlos shut the door behind him as he came back into the bedroom. The baggy Washington State hoody was off and now, he was in checkered blue boxers and a white t-shirt.

"Hey."

"Tired?" he asked, his brown eyes flitting over my face, no doubt finding purple half-moons and tension I couldn't seem to fully release.

"It's after midnight," I said as if that explained everything.

"I got some of that wine that you used to like. Are you too tired for a glass of that?"

"I'll have a glass," I said, lips tight. When he left, I felt my chest release and I sat down heavily on the edge of his bed.

Why did coming here suddenly feel like the stupidest idea?

Why hadn't I called Tess? Gone to her place. It was only another ten minutes from here, practically the same distance.

I heaved a sigh, knowing the answer without the need to even ask the question. I was here instead of there because Carlos was available and wasn't in the habit of asking many questions. Tessa would ask *too many* questions. Questions I wouldn't be able to answer without telling her everything.

She'd want to call the police. My dad would go to prison. We'd lose Snow's Mortuary.

He walked back into the room with filled wine glasses.

"These are new," I said, fingers catching on the adhesive residue from the sticker still stuck to the base.

"Yeah. Salem got them as a gift," he said, climbing onto the other side of the bed.

"How is she?" I asked, putting my phone down after checking for any missed calls or texts from Dad and finding none. Carlos shrugged, giving me an odd look as he sipped his wine uncomfortably.

"You really want to hear about her?"

"It can't be that bad, is it?" I asked. He laughed sadly, running a hand through his sunbaked brown curls.

"She... *uh*, well she and I gave things a shot when her and whatshisface were on the outs, but... she went back to him, so..."

"Sorry?"

I didn't mean it to sound like a question but it did anyway.

"Nah. It's a good thing. She's a great roomie but that's where it ends."

I drank a sip of my wine, quickly chasing it with a second gulp. Even if it was lukewarm from being kept on the counter over the dishwasher—where I told Carlos *never* to put it—it was still damn good.

His jaw clenched. He finished the rest of his glass, putting it down on the nightstand. "What about you? Have you been seeing anyone?"

I blinked, a stark image of the man from last week, the

ghost in the mortuary basement coming unbidden to my mind, making me almost choke on my next gulp.

"No," I finished the glass. "No one wants to date a girl who works with dead people for a living."

I gave a tight smile.

Carlos looked down at the space between us.

"No one, hmm?" he pressed. "What if I did?"

My eyes rolled and I wished there was still wine in my glass.

"You'd be shit out of luck," I said on a long exhale. "Is there more wine?"

He reached for my glass but put it down next to his.

"Fine." His lips pulled up on one side in a sly grin. "No dating."

He slid a hand over my thigh, watching me expectantly. "We can just fuck."

"Is there more wine? I might need a refill first."

He put a hand to his chest.

"Ouch. Am I that bad in bed?"

"Define *bad*."

He scooted in closer to me, putting a hand around the back of my neck.

"It was good enough to keep you around for a whole year," he teased, cocky now.

"Ten months," I corrected.

"And you're *still* here," he shot back.

He had me there.

Our lips met in a soft but emotionless kiss. His hand, warm, groped up my thigh, beneath the long t-shirt. He shifted over me, pushing me down into the bed.

Was my phone still plugged in?

I opened my eyes, trying to turn my head without

breaking the kiss. His knee knocked into my thigh on its way between my legs, making me grunt.

"Oh, sorry," he said. "I was trying to—"

"It's fine," I said quickly. He smiled, holding my face again, tracing his fingers down the line of my body to reach under the t-shirt, groping toward my breasts.

No life was detected from the waist down. Nothing. Not a tingle, not a spark, nothing.

I resisted the urge to go dead fish on him, he was letting me spend the night after all.

Carlos and I had a lot of sex in the beginning of our relationship but it tapered off, became something more like work, like a performance I didn't want to act in anymore.

Unlike he liked to imagine, I didn't keep fucking him after our breakup because the sex was good. It was because if I didn't, I'd never see a living human being that wasn't my dad or Tessa.

There had been two guys before him; one train wreck when I was seventeen and wanted to just ditch the v-card, and another guy who wanted to *see where things went,* getting boyfriend benefits without boyfriend responsibilities.

Carlos was the only one who met my dad. He appeared responsible and trustworthy, ticked all the boxes, but the sheen on him faded fast.

Carlos pawed my breast, and I closed my eyes, trying to get into it, imaging him as someone else. Someone like the men folded between the pages of Tessa's books.

What if he just...

I reached blindly for his hand, moving it up to my throat. He proceeded to slide it back down to my tit, over my shirt. My eyes would have rolled if they were open. I tried again, bringing his hand to my neck and pressing it down, squeezing.

"Whoa," he said, releasing me. "Are you into that shit?"

*Maybe?*

*Maybe he could help me find out.*

"Are you?" I turned the question around on him, not wanting to admit it out loud.

He pursed his lips, thinking, then shook his head.

"Nah. That's not really my thing. Can get yourself into some shit doing that, you know?"

*Okay but what if I want you to?*

I couldn't bring myself to ask the question outright, finding a bush to beat around instead.

"You wouldn't," I argued. "I mean, it's not like I'm not consenting."

"Consenting?" he repeated, his brows rising.

Any tiny spark of desire I'd been trying to ignite died a quick, quiet death.

"Just forget it," I mumbled, pushing him off me.

He tracked my movements as I pushed off the bed, going for my empty wine glass.

"Are you fucking mad at me right now?"

More like annoyed.

"What do you think?"

"You're mad because I don't want to choke you?"

Well, yes, but that wasn't even the worst part. The worst part was that I wanted him to in the first place. I *still* wanted him to.

And why not?

Why didn't he even try? I fucking asked him to do it. Couldn't he at least attempt something other than missionary and doggy style with very little clit stimulation?

This might actually have turned me on enough not to have to take him dry for the first minute.

"*Em*," Carlos bit out, wanting a response.

"I'm mad because you're always down to hook up but you don't even want to *try* to make it good for me. Like, at least put some effort into getting me wet first."

His eyes traveled up and down my body before coming back to my face, narrowing.

"Who the hell have you been fucking that does that kind of shit to you?"

I huffed, eyes cast toward the ceiling as I ripped open the door and left his room.

The reason why we split up was achingly clear.

Carlos didn't do it for me.

It was harsh and it didn't feel good to think about the almost one year that he got out of me, but it was true. He was fine, but fine wasn't good enough. It would never be good enough.

I mean, fuck, I'd cried harder watching pet reunion videos online than I did when we broke up. Actually, I don't think I cried at all.

I found the wine next to the fridge and sloshed a healthy dose into my glass.

"Can we go back to bed?" Carlos asked behind me, padding into the kitchen.

I swirled the wine in my glass before downing it in two long swallows and refilling it from the bottle.

"Maybe I'll just take the couch."

He visibly sagged, defeated. "Look, you want to blue ball me, *fine*. It's fine. I can tell you're, like, stressed or whatever. Just come back to bed at least."

Wrong again.

This was the part where he should've put his hand over my mouth, held me down over the counter, and smacked my ass so hard it would hurt to sit tomorrow. After that, he'd finger me right to the edge, then refuse to let me come as payback for being such a little brat.

But if I wanted that, I should have just stayed home and read the next book from Tessa.

He waved an arm and I let it go, shuffling after him to his bedroom.

Carlos fell into bed and clicked on the TV, selecting a tv series we used to watch together and choosing a random episode.

I finished my wine and slid into the bed, pulling the covers up high as I snuggled down into the pillow.

It took all of ten minutes before there was a hand on my flank and warm breath against my ear. Carlos' not yet hard-on pressed into my ass.

"Are you asleep?" he rasped.

I shuddered involuntarily, imagining it. Five to seven minutes of uninspired thrusting that would come to a grinding halt when he came faster than he thought he would. After he got rid of the condom, he'd be out like a light.

Was this really all I could hope for?

I rolled onto my back. Maybe it was.

He brushed a palm over my stomach beneath the over-sized t-shirt. "Yeah?" he asked, his gaze heated.

"Eat me out first."

His lips spread into a wide grin before he vanished beneath the covers.

Instead of five to seven minutes, now, maybe I'd get eight.

W e had a breach.
         I'd been in the security office for hours watching silent, repetitive footage.

Part of me still didn't believe it. Delirium was bullet-proof. Security at the gate, more at the entrance, no recording devices inside. We screened members for every-thing from criminal records to proof of funds. Who the fuck got in?

And if it was one of the patrons who'd deliberately broken contract, well, they'd learn that their status meant absolutely nothing to me when put up against the sanctity of my business. Or my word to the other patrons that nothing they said or did within these walls would ever get out.

Since this morning, all the members were being system-atically informed of the security breach. A notification went out assuring the members that we were aware of the issue, but they had nothing to worry about. Measures were being taken immediately to ensure continued privacy. Two grainy photos of the club's interior made it online.

Everyone wore a mask, and the pictures already looked like they were shot with a pin camera. Blown up to print online, the resolution was even worse. It was impossible to make out any identities but it didn't matter. Their existence meant someone got through security with a camera and the reputation of my club, *my* reputation was compromised.

Basically, I didn't need the added shitstorm that Nixon just threw on top of the pile when he walked through that door two minutes ago.

"What did you say?" I demanded, searching Nixon's expression for any hint of a joke and finding none.

His lips flattened. "I said the body was turned around."

"What the fuck do you mean *turned around*?"

His Adam's apple bobbed in his throat. It wasn't often he disappointed me, but right now? Right now I could've severed his artery myself.

"Snow didn't take it. He refused."

The undertaker wasn't allowed to refuse anything. He was processing bodies for us, that was the deal. My peaking frustration surged through my body, making me restless as I paced the length of the security office.

"And you just let that slide?"

Threats, intimidation, break a couple of fingers. There were no shortage of options.

My patience with the undertaker was wearing thin. I wondered darkly whether he knew what the inside of his incinerator looked like when it was on. I'd be happy to show him.

"He insisted on the increase in fees," Nix offered. "Said

he was making a 'formal request' or some other shit and I should bring it to you directly."

Quiet rage simmered through me as I lifted my gaze unseeing toward the wall of screens broadcasting live feeds from every camera in the house.

*Oh he did, did he?*

Beneath the rage at his blatant insubordination, there was something else, because Mr. Snow just handed me the one thing I craved above all others.

He'd wrapped her in a bow and served her to me on a platter.

"Ruarc?" Nixon pressed, following my gaze to the screens, specifically the ones playing a recording of last night's debauchery in the club.

I pulled the collar of my shirt from my neck, hot rage making every little thing annoy me, but I stifled it. Swallowed it. Maintained control.

The undertaker needed to be taught a lesson.

I'd pitied him when we last spoke. Bile rose in the back of my throat. Now I knew I should've just broken his legs like I'd wanted to.

Money problems must be worse than he was letting on.

At this rate, how much did it cost to build my own fucking crematorium right here? Actually, the idea didn't sound half bad. Or better, what if I just bought Snow's? Had his pretty daughter dispose of my sins?

"Who were you delivering?" I asked, calling on the last of my self-control not to lose my fucking shit. I let Nixon handle the day to day bullshit, and I couldn't remember giving an order for an execution.

"No ID. Likely a low level street dealer or a user. Either way, the junkie got in a fight with one of our guys. Got himself dead. It was meant to be a simple cremation, but Snow refused."

Thinking about the long-term consequences of his insolence was giving me a migraine. He wasn't backing down, he was getting bolder. Once again, he had nothing to say for himself in person but he pulled these shitty, sneaky tricks when I wasn't there to put him right back in his place.

Sucking in slow lungful of air, I looked Nixon square in the face.

I'd deal with the undertaker, but it seemed the old creep wasn't the only person in need of a lesson tonight.

Nix knew I was busy as fuck running damage control and he was supposed to be my face when I couldn't be there. Be my voice. Dispense my justice.

He had my trust, but this was below standard, particularly for the efficiency and cold hard precision I was used to from him.

"What have I always told you happens during situations like this?"

Nix's chest swelled with a deep inhale. "They don't have a choice."

"I said *execute*. Whether that calls for a change of plans, an elimination, it doesn't matter. Every task, you fucking execute. No exceptions. Especially not for pieces of shit like Snow."

Nixon's jaw worked, clearly thrilled to be getting the speech again. As my second-in-command, I needed him in cases like this. I still wanted to expand the syndicate through the state. Open another Delirium further south. I couldn't do that when my right-hand-man let things fall through the cracks.

"Yes sir. I understand."

I rubbed my hand over my jaw, feeling how tight it was from clenching so goddamn hard.

"Is there a body rotting somewhere on my property right now?"

I saw him bite the inside of his cheek, stalling. I closed my eyes, not letting the rise of anger get to me. Nixon knew the damn rules. No corpses on property aside from quick transfers.

Whoever said the dead didn't talk didn't know a damn thing.

"Get rid of it. If the undertaker won't take it, get it in the river, take it to the woods. Throw it through the meat grinder. I don't care. No trace."

His eyes clouded, but he nodded. When it came to the undertaker, I was going to have to solve things myself. I could force him to take the junkie, but I had a better idea.

"Anything else?"

Nix shook his head.

"Then why the fuck are you still standing there?"

His jaw flexed as he turned away.

"Nix?"

He stopped, turning back around to face me, the emotion in his face gone. All business between us now. I only dressed him down because I knew he could do better.

I needed him to do better.

"Did you get the name and address I asked for?"

"It's in your email."

I waited until the sound of his footfalls across the parquet floor faded, punctuated by the opening and closing of the front door, before pulling out my phone to find the email.

Attached to it was a multiple-page file highlighting everything there was to know about Carlos Isaac.

Twenty-three.

He attended but never graduated from Washington State.

Most importantly, Emily was at his house two nights ago. She went in, and was still there come dawn when I finally left.

She spent the fucking night.

Nix's notes filled the screen. The dirtbag smoked pot. Had a DUI. Owned the townhouse where he lived and rented out a room. And what's this...

The fucker was on a sex offender registry?

My grip on the phone tightened.

What the fuck was someone like Emily doing with scum like him?

I was at her cabin before she left to go to him.

I thought she was in for the night, but instead she went back up to the mortuary building well past dark.

It wasn't part of the plan but I couldn't pass up an opportunity like that. It was easy to break in, and leaving the door open for her was my way of saying hello.

I wanted to see what she would do. Following every surprise I'd left for her, she stood fast. After an initial freak out or show of strength, she'd go back to regularly scheduled programming.

She hadn't even changed the locks. Didn't install a camera. Didn't get a dog who might bark when something moved outside.

Emily knew I was there but she didn't try to get rid of me. She never ran.

Not until last night.

When she drove off the property, I followed her into the city.

On the file, there were a couple of pictures of him from a Washington State online publication. His bright eyes and wide with toothy grin that made me want to go and pluck out all his teeth.

Not knowing whether he touched her last night made me near mad.

Emily was *mine*.

I closed the email. There were more pressing matters at hand than whoever was keeping Emily warm while I couldn't. He'd have his turn.

The monitor on the desk still glowed with the paused security footage. I watched hours of it. People at double speed filtering into the building. Then hours of nothing before they filtered out again.

I had the list of everyone who was there the night of the breach.

Watching the footage against the list, nobody unexpected could have gotten in or out of the club. I felt my eyes glaze over. It looked like this every night with only minor changes in clientele.

My fingers hesitated over the fast forward button.

Every night looked the same.

I pulled up the leaked club pictures. They were so grainy I couldn't even tell what part of the hall they were taken in.

But more than that...

There was no date. Nothing so much as indicate a time of year. They could've been taken years ago.

My head fell back against the chair's headrest, groaning.

They were smart. With so little to go off of, tracing the

pictures would take time, giving whoever was behind this time to get ahead. I shook my head. I could be grateful no one was identified, but the existence of the club alone would raise suspicion, and online sleuths were already working to clear up the cloudy images and identify the masked patrons just as quickly as my team worked to get every copy taken down.

*Just take her.*

My eyes shot open at the sudden, intrusive thought.

*It's time.*

That swell of desire I felt the first time I saw her returned.

Emily Snow under my roof, the idea alone made me blind with need and I shuddered thinking of everything I would do to her. Everything I wanted to make her feel. The limits I ached to see if she could climb.

I licked my lips, tapping the stop button on the recording. I'd get my guys on this first thing tomorrow. Until there was more to go on, the footage would be all but useless, anyway. Right now, doubling security efforts and assuring our clients a breach like this wouldn't happen again would be more effective.

I'd waited long enough.

It was time to make her mine.

## EMILY

*Just watch it*, she said.

*You'll like it*, she said.

Sucking down my third glass of wine since putting on the movie, I eyed the screen with suspicion. I tried it like Tessa wanted but unlike the books she had been dead wrong with this atrocity of filmmaking.

Whoever wrote *The Paris Hotel* should be taken out to the square and flogged.

The romcom was absolutely absurd.

I was promised sex and passion and angst.

All I got was an absurd romcom about an American girl who took a trip to Paris after her fiancé called off their wedding. Predictably, she runs into a French guy and they fall in love. After some third act misunderstanding, they come back together in a triumphant reunion.

I was an hour in—an hour I would never get back—and there was still somehow another forty minutes of this crap. I could tell you now how it was going to end, with the ex-fiancé realizing his mistake, rushing to Paris to win her back, forcing her to choose between him and her new Paris love.

An obvious choice.

The way Tessa touted it, this movie was just the kind of light, fluffy entertainment I needed. Like somehow it would fix all my problems. Scare away all the bad vibes in the cabin and instead fill the space with unicorns and rainbows and really bad French.

After the third 'Ooh La La,' from the main female lead, I decided I'd rather stab myself in the ears with my dull kitchen knife than watch another minute of it, and clicked the TV off.

The movie was sinking me deeper into despair, not rescuing me from it.

It wasn't even over and I had already taken down close to an entire bottle of wine. That wasn't good.

I'd been trying to pace myself, but then remembered being drunk would be better than being sober. Carlos would be here soon.

If fucking him went the same way it did last time, I *wanted* to be drunk.

Eating me out had predictably been the best part. Afterward, he frantically slammed himself in and out of my vagina while pawing at my tits for about two and a half minutes before coming.

I remembered it being better than that. Really, I did. It had to have been, otherwise, I was sadder than I thought. Settling for that.

It was lost on me why I even agreed to him swinging by tonight when he called earlier. Likely something to do with the fact that I was dead certain I had a stalker by now, but resigned in my ability to do a damn thing about it without drawing unwanted attention to my father's illegal activities.

Besides, the haunting presence never did more than leave a door or a drawer open. Aside from this morning of course, when I found a tall glass of water and pain killers beside my bed. I'd polished a bottle of wine, a habit that I'd have to kick eventually, before going to bed and I definitely didn't have the foresight to prepare for the morning's hangover.

Or at least, I didn't think I did.

Who fucking knew at this point.

Was I really here right now at all?

Would I return from the bathroom to find the TV back on, the movie still playing? Maybe I never shut it off.

What did it matter?

My phone vibrated in my lap and I lifted it groggily to find a message from Carlos. He was on his way.

I grimaced and then mentally berated myself for letting this happen again, knowing I was only giving him hope.

It was worth the shitty lay to not be alone tonight. Did that make me a bad person? Was I using him?

I shook my head. He'd used me plenty. It was my turn now.

I sighed to myself, staring down into the dregs of wine left in my glass.

There were probably people out there who had really incredible sex. Swishing my wine around in my glass, I emptied the entire remaining contents of the glass down my throat.

My head swam as I stood from the couch, propelling me to the kitchen for a glass of water. I emptied it in three long swallows while standing next to the kitchen sink. Spinning to lean against the counter, I looked straight through to the living room, out the gap in the curtains and into the dark.

I hadn't felt it today.

No eyes watching me. No presence just out of sight.

I knew better than to hope my shadow was gone, but the reprieve felt almost cruel.

I eyed the empty wine glass on the counter.

Tessa was always saying I needed more wine in my life. Maybe she was onto something. Maybe it was dulling my senses just enough that I couldn't feel him.

My lips parted at the thought. I'd never really gendered the presence before but there it was. *Him.*

It felt right, and so, *so*, wrong.

*Just a few more days,* I reminded myself.

At the end of the week, Tessa and I would be in Portland.

*You're going to have to work*, she warned, as if that would deter me in the slightest.

I'd be second assistant to the author, whose name I'd already forgotten.

I couldn't imagine why she needed two assistants, but I wasn't complaining. My ticket and accommodation were being paid for, even the meals were a tax write off for the author.

If I thought it would be difficult to convince Dad to let me go, I'd been dead wrong. I hardly got the whole request out before he agreed. No doubt he wanted me out of here for a while just as much as I wanted myself out of here.

Things had been tense since the standoff in the office. I knew better than to ask him about the things I'd seen a second time. When my Dad made up his mind about something he rarely changed it. If he decided to continue to keep me in the dark, no amount of questioning would make him turn on the lights.

A break would be good. For both of us.

It would give me time to figure out what to do. The biggest question–the scariest one—that I kept coming back to was whether or not I had a future here anymore. Could Snow's Mortuary run with only one Snow? Could I leave mom's legacy behind me?

The care she showed with each client... I might've been just a kid, but I remembered. This place meant something to her. It was a culmination of her life's work.

*Tainted.*

*Stained.*

How long before Dad managed to destroy it entirely?

I killed time with snacks from the all but barren refrigerator, making sure Timmy was charged up in case I needed to finish the job myself later. Sighing for the tenth time in an hour, I finally gave up and went back to the couch.

I checked my phone but there was nothing from Carlos.

He should've been here by now.

Begrudgingly, I flicked the TV back on, the horrible movie beginning to play from where it left off.

I watched but didn't watch it, my mind wandering, periodically checking my phone for signs of life as I sank deeper and deeper into the couch.

The voices on the screen dulled to a distant drone and I dragged the throw blanket over myself, blinking heavily as I tugged the little lumpy cushion under my head.

I could stay awake. I just wanted to get comfortable while I waited. He'd be here any minute now.

Something fell.

The metallic *clang* of it hitting the ground had me wrenching my eyes open, groaning, disoriented.

An ache swelled in my skull and I moaned in pain, squeezing my eyes back shut. Dying to fall back asleep quickly, I prayed the headache wouldn't be there the second time I woke.

A shiver rolled up my spine and I froze beneath the thin blanket on the couch.

Wait, something fell in the kitchen. What was that?

I peeled my eyelids back, resisting the urge to hiss as my eyes burned, assaulted by the blue light from the old television and the glow of the lamp I left on in the bedroom.

With a groan, I propped myself up on an elbow, peering into the kitchen, but from this angle I couldn't see much past the little island.

*Carlos.*

I frowned, clearing my throat to call to him, but the silence in the cabin replied before I could ask the question. I was alone. He wasn't here.

Groping into the couch cushions for my phone, I checked the time.

No new messages, and if this was right, Carlos should've been here an hour ago. I thumbed the dial pad, punching in three digits before his number came up, but a second before I could click *call*, the cabin went dark.

The digital hum of the TV cut out with a static chirp, taking the lights with it.

"Fuck," I muttered. "Stupid breaker."

Normally, I called my Dad out to fix it for me, but right now I'd rather sit in the cold dark than see his face any more than I had to.

I could do it myself.

Giving myself a mental pep talk, I forced myself to stand, exacerbating the pain in my head. I stumbled, catching myself on the windowsill as I squinted out into the night, seeing the faint glow of the mortuary security lights still on through the trees. They were.

So, it was just the cabin again. Great.

I almost turned away, but looked again, searching for movement, or any sign of Carlos. I craned my neck to see the side of the cabin, where he usually parked, and found only my old Rav4 sitting there, looking like she could use a good wax.

*Where the hell is he?*

He did *not* stand me up. If he did, that was it. I was fucking done. He could go back to pining over his pretty roommate and jerking off to free porn.

I tried his number.

It rang incessantly until finally going to voicemail.

He couldn't still be driving. Unless he left late. Or stopped to get us some takeout, maybe?

It was 11:15 which meant if that was the case it would be greasy fast food at worst, a pizza at best. I'd take either, I was going to need a handful of pills to kill this headache and it was better to take them with something in my stomach that didn't have an alcohol content.

Hopefully, I could get the lights back on before he got here.

I turned, and there it was.

Settling over my shoulders like freshly poured concrete, cold and heavy.

The eyes I couldn't see. Watching. Waiting.

I scoffed bitterly, chastising myself for thinking whatever it was had gone. A dark laugh left my lips and I tipped my head back, staring up at the ceiling like it had all the answers instead of a bunch of cobwebs I couldn't reach to clean.

"Hello darkness my old friend," I singsonged, trying to make light of a shitty fucking situation, but my voice sounded meek in the shadows, seeming to echo on forever and I swallowed as a fresh frost crept over me.

Where the hell was that fucking breaker?

Kitchen.

*Right.*

I swung my phone light around and stopped still, a scream lodging in my throat.

I blinked, internally screaming at myself to wake up, but the nightmare didn't end, and still he stood, perfectly calm, with eyes that reflected silver in the light like a wolf's.

"It's you."

A slow grin split his lips.

Tattoos and bloody hands.

*The ghos*t.

I staggered back a step and the spell was broken.

He lunged at me. I fell to the ground, my phone knocked from my grasp, scattering to someplace unseen. Going dark.

Blind, I flipped to my hands and knees and dove for the front door trying to wrench it open.

I screamed, but callused fingers clamped over my mouth, muffling the sound. I flailed wildly, throwing feet, elbows, and hands, connecting with hard muscle and bony joints.

He lifted me off the ground and dropped me face down on the couch. I tore at cushions, trying to toss them back at him.

"Come now, little lamb," he crooned.

I slid to the floor, the jar of it should've registered with pain but I felt nothing as I scrambled to get back to my feet.

His hand circled my ankle, dragging me down again. The air left my lungs and I croaked to get it back, kicking with my free leg, trying to knock him off.

With a single strong pull, he had me on my back and I gasped, trying to clench my thighs shut but he wrenched them apart, wedging a knee between them. I protected my face with my arms and he trapped those, too, pinning them above my head with a rough fist.

"Don't!" I shrieked. "Please, *please* don't kill me."

I squirmed against his hold, my whole body shaking, the pain in my head gone, replaced by a ringing in my ears so loud I thought I'd go deaf. This was it. This ghost, this monster was going to kill me and it was all my Dad's fault. I'd seen him that night in the mortuary and now I was a loose end.

I should've gone to the cops. I should've—

"Kill you?"

All the hopeless, chaotic thoughts came to a jarring halt at the sound of him laughing. At the deep rumble I could feel against my chest. "*Kill you?*"

"But—"

He clamped a hand over my mouth, his laughter dying so suddenly it took with it my will to speak.

"No, little lamb. I'm not going to kill you," he said, his eyes roaming my face in the dark, making me feel his intentions like a fire held too close to flesh. "I'm going to keep you."

# 11

---

## RUARC

She got me in the fucking mouth. The taste of blood coated my tongue as I held her to the ground. I had at least sixty pounds on her but she was slippery. Quick, like a cat. I blinked in the dark, the shapes of her face and body barely visible. If I let go of her for a second, she wouldn't just slip away, she'd completely disappear.

I didn't expect her to come quietly but I didn't think she'd be this tenacious.

She sure as hell didn't get it from her father.

The sweet scent of the wine oozed from her pores, mingling with the scent that was uniquely *her*. I'd scented it on her pillows. On the couch. In the clothes she stripped off and left in piles on the bathroom floor after a long day spent with the dead.

Magnolia blossom, honey, and smooth musk.

In baggy sweats and a loose hoody her body still managed to be wired and electric under her clothes. I knew she'd fight me until she got away, or until she couldn't anymore and was convinced she was the only thing truly living and vital in this place.

I held her down, fought her as her body writhed and fought for freedom beneath me. Fear radiated off of her, the vestiges of her resistance, waning with exhaustion but not gone. She shook, the breath coming out of her in small gasps. She was crying.

I gritted my teeth against the hunger.

*Not yet.*

I couldn't have her yet.

I removed my hand from her mouth, looking through the dark into her eyes.

The unnaturally bright green hue was lost to me in the dark but I knew they were wide with fear. My cock filled with blood, throbbing as it thickened, making me grimace.

"Please…" she whispered, trailing off as she ceased trying to pull her arms free, her chest rising and falling so fully, so quickly, that each breath saw her nipples brushing my chest.

Unable to keep control for another fucking second, I dropped a hand to the collar of her loose t-shirt and jerked it downward. Fabric snapped and tore, exposing her to me in the dark.

She let out a cry as I circled her left tit with my hand, drawing it into my mouth to taste her. Emily gasped, bucking beneath me, her thighs pressing hard on either side of my knee between her legs.

*Fuck.* She tasted like honey and salt. Sweet and potent. I ran my teeth along the ridge of her nipple, teasing it, testing it, biting before smoothing my tongue over the hurt.

She let out a whimper, her body pressing into me,

pulling away, pressing in again as I smiled against her breast.

*That's right, little lamb, you want this. You want me. You crave the touch of the monster in the dark.*

I pulled back and she squirmed, trying to get away again, her purpose renewed. I twisted her nipple between my thumb and forefinger, just enough for her to stop jerking, to understand who was in control.

"The more difficult you make this, Emily, the more I'll have to punish you for your insolence. And you aren't the only one who'll pay for it..."

"No..."

"Yes."

"Don't hurt my dad. Please."

I dipped my head, nuzzling into her neck, an addict needing another fix. Her scent so sweet, edged with a sour tang of fear made my fucking chest ache.

The faster I got her to the house, the sooner I'd get to stop wondering what sort of sounds she'd make when I was inside her. How she tasted after I made her come.

She opened her mouth to scream and I pushed two fingers into it, pressing them flat against her tongue, pushing them deep until she gagged on them.

"Do *not* scream," I warned, tugging my fingers free just a second before she clamped her jaw down, trying to bite me. "So feisty, Miss Snow."

"Fuck you."

"Keep going," I purred, pressing the apex of my knee into her cunt. "See where all this defiance gets you."

Taking a zip tie from my back pocket, I slid it over her wrists and tightened it. I eyed her like she was a controlled flame that might flare at any second. The hard plastic strip felt flimsy against her fierce will to escape.

Pinning her arms up above her head, I took my phone out, calling Nixon.

"Ready," I barked, glad I'd elected to bring him.

"Who are you?"

I glanced down at her, only able to make out the shape of her in the dark, regretting my decision to cut the power. I wanted to see her.

For a girl who didn't come easily, I knew it killed her to submit to me like this. She'd spit in my face if she wasn't afraid of what would happen to her father.

"You know who I am."

I let up on her wrists, leaning back to peer outside for any sign of Nixon.

She took her opportunity, yanking her hands out from under mine, ramming her joined wrists into my face. The dull thud of the heels of her hands connecting with my jaw sent a shock of pain through my skull.

She struggled out from under me, clumsily crawling for the door.

A growl tore from my throat as I wrestled her back to me, groping blindly behind myself for one of the cushions that had fallen onto the floor. She swung her joined arms like a hammer, landing shots to my face and head before I finally got on top of her and sealed the pillow over her face.

I didn't want to mark up her pretty face. Didn't want to risk concussion with a blow to the head.

"*Shhh*," I urged her, pinning her between my legs.

The plush material silenced her scream.

Her arms jerked frantically, trying to tear the pillow from her face. She flailed, desperate for air, her body flying into panic. One hand hooked into the collar of my shirt, her fingernails scoring my skin, trying to grab onto something.

I held fast, waiting, counting the seconds.

"Just relax, baby. Sleep."

She jerked and then stilled, the power slipping from her like turning off a switch. I slipped the pillow from her face, bending to hover an ear over her mouth while two fingers pressed to the notch under her jaw, feeling for her pulse.

It was there, weakened, but there.

Soft breaths fanned over my cheek.

She wouldn't be out long.

I prodded my eyebrow and jaw, checking to see whether she managed to split the skin, flinching from the tenderness. I smiled in spite of it, impressed.

She'd still pay for it, though.

I lifted her limp body from the floor, tucking her into my chest, marveling at the feel of her in my arms, at her lightness.

The cabin door opened and Nixon stood there, backlit in moonlight.

"This her?

I handed Emily off to him.

"She'll be waking up soon, and she's a fighter."

Nixon scoffed and squinted, getting a better look at me as we stepped out onto her porch.

"She did that to your lip?" he asked, tilting his chin up in my direction.

"Put her in the trunk unless you want the same."

Nix laughed darkly, underestimating her as I had.

I watched him carry her easily up the rise that took him back to the front of the property where he parked.

I'd have much rather stayed with her, but I had something else to take care of before I could leave. An unforeseen roadblock I'd had to deal with earlier.

I climbed down off the patio and spotted it on the ground. The awkward, lifeless heap that was her boyfriend.

Well, her ex boyfriend now.

The bouquet he brought her had rolled under the patio.

During my attempt to subdue Emily inside, I'd almost forgotten that he was out here.

A frustrated sigh fell from my lips.

I'd been watching her for a little under an hour when his car arrived. Coming down to her cabin with a twelve dollar grocery store bouquet. She deserved better.

I'd brushed the dark hair from her face, my thumb lingering on her lower lip, feeling the warmth of her breath as I watched his headlights bounce over the windows. "I'll deal with this," I'd told her, caressing her jaw in her sleep before leaving.

I did not take kindly to interruptions, and he didn't have a right to touch what was mine.

Carlos froze when he saw me slip from the cabin, straightening my jacket. I padded down the creaking steps, stalking over to him, making his face pinch in confusion.

"*Uh*, hey, man," he said, already cowering, his throat bobbing as his grip on the bouquet loosened. "You a friend of Em's?"

"Not exactly."

His lips parted at the sound of my voice and recognition seemed to flare in his dull brown eyes. He huffed a laugh, throwing a hand through his hair. "Great," he said. "That's just fucking great."

I cocked my head at him, watching him as he tossed the bouquet to the ground. "You're the jackass who got her into all that shit, aren't you?" Another dark laugh, a hand swiped over his mouth as anger heated his stare. "The choking and shit. Yeah. You look the fucking type. *Jesus* "

Heat ricocheted up my back and I clenched my jaw against the swell of violence in my blood, controlling it.

"You need to leave."

I'd give only one warning.

He stared at me openly, shock slacking his jaw until his gaze narrowed, hardening. "Yeah. No problem. You can keep her. Fucking whore."

He turned, but I jerked him back, slamming a closed fist into his face, barely registering the movement until it was done. The worthless skinbag fell to the ground, a hard *knock* sounding as his head connected with a boulder near the base of Emily's porch.

"Get up," I hissed, my fist shaking at my side, thirsty for the breaking of bones.

But Carlos didn't get up, and as a cloud drifted away from the moon, I tipped my head back, rolling my eyes at the heavens.

A rapidly growing pool of blood spread out around Carlos' head where it lay next to the crimson spattered boulder. His wide eyes looked out into the trees, vacant.

Now, I grabbed the body, hefting it over one shoulder, mulling over everything I could have done differently tonight.

I should have waited.

Been better prepared instead of deciding last minute to execute the plan.

I got what I came for and then some, but it'd been sloppy, protracted, and had come too close to failure for comfort.

It would all be worth it, but with her one-hundred-sixty-pound boyfriend on my back, getting heavier with each step, the end goal got a little hard to see.

My chest heaved and my legs burned by the time I got up to the undertaker's house. I dropped Carlos on the steps and rang the doorbell. Why not give him a chance to let me in himself before I took matters into my own hands?

A thrill went through me, picturing Nixon unloading Emily into the mansion. She'd be there when I returned. Waiting for me.

The only thing that stood between me and her now was her greedy father and this corpse.

I balled my fist, slamming it into the wooden door. The light turned on upstairs. Moments later, I heard the lock on the other side of the door. It opened. The undertaker's beady eyes squinted, then bugged out when he recognized me.

"Mr.-Mr. Monroe. Good evening. If-if this is about the money—"

For once, it wasn't. I slammed my hand against the door, wedging my boot against it so that he couldn't close it.

"I have a body for you," I said, motioning over my shoulder.

He was slow on the uptake, frowning at me.

"I paid your daughter a visit. Pretty girl."

He blanched, his frantic gaze searching for the body in question as he barreled past me.

"Oh God."

The undertaker crouched over the young man's lifeless body, hands fluttering just above his bloodied head.

His chin jerked up, intent on Emily's cabin far through

the trees down the path. He stumbled over the body in its direction.

"She's not there," I yelled after him, stopping him in his tracks, a slow grin splitting the cut on my lip.

"What did you do to her? Where is she?"

"If you want to see her again, you're going to get rid of that corpse, *gratis*. And if I so much as hear about another body being turned around... If you deign to demand another fucking pay hike... I'll kill her."

"You took her."

It wasn't a question, so I didn't see the need to respond.

"Please. Please, you can't hurt her. I-I'll do whatever you want. I'll do the work for free. Just give her back to me."

I shook my head. "The price was already settled upon. Four thousand per disposal. No more. No less. And you'll get your daughter if and when I feel you've learned your lesson."

His stark white hair blew in the breeze as he hung his head, his shoulders shaking, sagging with defeat.

He kept his gaze trained straight down as he dragged himself back toward the mortuary, but I could see how his green eyes burned with anger.

The protective fire that men had for their children. There was more life hiding in that shell of a man than I gave him credit for.

"Where is she?" he asked.

I could tell him but it was none of his business, but that wouldn't give me the cooperation I sought. "She's likely arriving at my home as we speak. Being brought upstairs, to a bedroom where I'll visit her later. What you decide to do right now will determine how that visit will end."

"You won't hurt her if I cooperate?" he asked, shuffling

forward. I balked, thinking he might fall to his knees next and beg.

My lips twisted.

"Do your fucking job and she'll live."

The undertaker looked grimly down at Carlos.

"Can you—" he cut himself short when I glared at him. Averting his eyes, he quickly moved around the body, taking him under the arms and heaving him up. I watched, annoyance flaring as the undertaker struggled with the body alone.

I'd be here for hours if I planned to see this through.

I grabbed Carlos' legs, grunting as we hefted him down to the furnace.

"It takes a while to fire up," he said, wiping sweat from his brow as he jammed buttons, turning the enormous furnace on.

I leaned against the wall, waiting. Through the window in the door, I could see the cooling chamber in the room across from this one, imagining slabs of dead bodies, frozen like butchered elk on ice.

"Did she see him die?" the undertaker asked, sliding the watch off the boyfriend's wrist, the rings from his fingers.

"Who? Emily?"

"Did you kill her boyfriend in front of her?" he asked, green eyes muted and cold. He looked shrunken, like someone had wrung the juice out of him.

"No," I replied, feeling generous. "She doesn't even know he's dead."

I'd tell her when I returned to the mansion.

I was curious to know how she would take it.

Truth be told, I hadn't planned to kill the guy. Not yet, anyway.

He didn't have to die for me to get Emily where I wanted her, but he'd put himself in exactly the wrong place at exactly the wrong time and said exactly the wrong thing.

*Don't kill them unless you need them dead.*

Thane's voice echoed in my head.

I learned that a long time ago. Corpses drew attention and enemies were easy to make in this line of work. If someone died by my hand, it was because they *needed* to be dead. I didn't target civilians and it was rare that they ended up in the line of fire.

Carlos' family might mourn him. Emily might mourn him too but the world wasn't going to lose out on much now that Carlos Isaac was dead.

If anything, I might've done it a favor.

The only regret I had was still being here overseeing the disappearance of his body instead of being with Emily.

"How do I know you won't hurt her?"

He didn't, and I would.

Emily would learn things about herself that no man, definitely not the incinerator bound loser, could have taught her. I would make her submit to me in ways she didn't even think were possible. I'd give her the sweetest pain. The greatest pleasure. I'd break her and spend each day laying her shattered pieces back into place, shaping something new. Something made for me.

If Emily returned to this place, she wouldn't be his daughter anymore, not the one he recognized. Already her past was burning to worthless ash.

*I* was her future.

# 12

---

## EMILY

The hum of a moving vehicle vibrated in my ear.

I eased my eyes open, blinking when the darkness didn't brighten. My body sunk heavily into a hard surface and I moaned as a sharp pain sliced through my skull.

I remembered the bottle of red that I'd sucked down in record time, trying to force my aching limbs to move.

Bringing my hand to my face to rub my blurry eyes, I flinched. A hard strip of plastic bit into my bound wrists.

Everything that'd happened tonight came rushing back.

I jerked up and struck my forehead on something hard. Kicking out my feet only for them to hit another hard surface, too close.

"No. *Fuck*." I rolled onto my back, pressing my feet against the interior of a small, enclosed space. It smelled of exhaust and old rubber and must.

A ball formed in my throat.

I banged my bound fists on the roof of the trunk, shouting as loudly as I could, my voice hoarse and cracking.

How long had we been driving?

Where was he taking me?

I shuddered, remembering the tattooed man with the devil in his eyes. The one with bloodied hands in the Brioni suit.

His rough fingers around my wrists. My nipple between his teeth.

Oh god.

There was no way this was happening. No matter how hard I blinked, I wasn't waking up. The hum didn't stop. I didn't stop moving.

How the fuck...

What the fuck was happening?

My heart slammed mercilessly in my chest. My brain short-circuited. I wanted to wake up. I *needed* to wake up.

*Breathe, Em,* I urged myself, squeezing my eyes shut. *Breathe.*

My thoughts slowed, the staticky, frayed edges of them coming into sharper clarity.

I was at home. Drinking, watching a movie, waiting for Carlos.

My throat seized and my eyes flew open.

*Oh my God. Carlos.*

I'd been so pissed thinking he'd stood me up, but now I hoped he did, because the alternative was too terrifying to imagine.

I pulled my knees to my chest, squeezing them tight as I remembered his words in my ear.

*The more difficult you make this, Emily, the more I'll have to punish you for your insolence. And you aren't the only one who'll pay for it...*

My shoulders shook with silent tears. He knew who I was.

*You aren't the only one who'll pay for it...*

That's what this was, then? Blackmail. This monster took me because of my father. Because of what they were doing in the mortuary basement.

Rage burned through me, hotter than the betrayal trying to pump ice into my veins. So, this was *his* fault. If he didn't get mixed up with the goddamned devil I wouldn't be here.

A sob grew in my chest, burning my throat on its way out as I pressed my palms hard into my eye sockets until the tears ceased. They wouldn't help me. Neither would Dad. What could he do? Call the police? *Ha*. Yeah, right.

I'd have to get out of this myself.

I patted down my body on the off chance my phone was on me. It wasn't. I didn't even have shoes on.

Craning my neck, I squinted into the dark, trying to see if there was anything I could use.

A short cry burst from my lips as the car lurched to a stop, making me have to press my bound hands against the solid surface in front of me to stop from hitting it face first.

Footsteps echoed outside. Short breaths flared my nostrils as every muscle braced for attack, my vision sharpening, heart pounding in my ears.

The trunk popped open.

Bright light flooded my vision, blinding me.

"Rise and shine."

A pair of strong arms dragged me out of the trunk. My feet touched the cold floor. Around me, an enormous garage filled with vehicles was only a backdrop to the main event as I whirled on the man, trying to jerk free of his grasp.

But he wasn't my ghost. Not the monster who'd subdued me in the dark. This was another devil. One with dead eyes and a menacing set to his jaw.

"Let go!"

His grip tightened.

"Don't make me hurt you, Miss Snow."

The chill of his tone iced over my resolve, recognizing his words for what they were. Not an idle threat but a promise.

"Where the hell am I? Where have you taken me?"

The man, one hand still clutching my arm, slammed the trunk of the car shut.

"Walk," he deadpanned, shoving me forward.

I stumbled without the balance of my arms, throwing a dirty look over my shoulder at him. At least a full head taller than me, the man was bulky across the shoulders with neatly slicked-back blond hair. Not the ghost, but cut from the same cloth.

There was more than one of them.

He shoved me again and I stumbled forward, shivering at the chill radiating up into my bones from the cold concrete.

The man led me toward a door and I jerked back from it, knowing that nothing good awaited me on the other side.

My gaze darted to the open garage door.

"Don't even think about it."

A loud chirp sounded, making me jump, and the mechanical whir of the garage door shutting behind us stole away my only chance at escape.

The man opened his jacket. The overhead lights glinted off the shining silver surface of a gun holstered on his hip. I swallowed.

"Move."

Inside the door, I was swallowed up by a high-ceilinged foyer, my feet meeting smooth marble floors. A soft umber glow radiated from a chandelier bigger than my bedroom overhead, the crystal shards like jagged stars on a ceiling painted in a mosaic of angels and devils. Fire and frost.

This couldn't be a house.

It looked more like a museum.

...Or Dracula's castle.

Heavy Victorian-style doors and elaborate wooden carvings adorned the space.

"Upstairs," the man barked and I scuttled across the floor with him at my heels.

We passed an endless stream of closed doors and domed archways.

"Where are you taking me?" I asked again, knowing better than to hope for a response.

He said nothing, herding me up another, smaller stair-case until we finally stopped.

The man pointed to the space next to him, bidding me to stand and stay like a dog while he drew out a single brass key, fitting it into the lock on a wide mahogany door.

My stomach twisted, picturing what might lie on the other side.

A prison cell. A torture chamber.

A bedroom?

My lips parted, taking in the space on the other side of the door.

It was huge, with another chandelier dripping jewels over a lush carpet. The walls were flat black edged in gold, and aged paintings hung on every wall. The artworks dark and somehow sensual in their abstract silhouette style.

A four-poster bed took up the majority of the space, draped with lavish fabrics, topped with enough pillows to drown in.

A chaise lounge and other furniture filled the rest of the space, upholstered in a sumptuous plum color that matched the curtains. An enormous gilded mirror sat above the fireplace, reflecting the warm light.

I was stunned silent, the whiplash of my capture and this room warring against each other in my head. Next thing I knew the beast of a man who'd corralled me in here would tell me never to go into the west wing.

What. The. Fuck?

"The bathroom is in there," the man drawled, pointing to the door at the far side of the room. "So is the closet. Everything you need is already here. Meals will be delivered three times a day."

His speech clarified nothing.

"What am I doing here?" I asked, trying again with a question he hadn't answered before. He huffed an exasperated sigh.

"This is your home for the next... well, until he tires of you."

*He...*

"Who?" I demanded.

He slipped something out of his pocket.

"Arms," he commanded, flicking a knife open, rolling his eyes when I recoiled, jerking my arms away from him.

"Fine. He can unbind you himself, then."

He slid the small, compact knife back into his pocket and I was able to breathe again.

"Am I supposed to just wait here until he shows up?"

The man pushed a hand through his hair, clearly wanting to be done with this conversation. Done with me.

"Do whatever the fuck you want until Ruarc gets back."

*Ruarc.* So he had a name. The identity didn't give me anything but something to call him.

"This door will be locked and there are cameras everywhere so don't get any ideas. And we're on the third floor so if you're gonna jump... good luck."

He gripped the door, stepped out onto the landing.

"Wait."

His shoulders rose and fell in a tired sigh.

I swallowed to wet my dry throat and held my conjoined arms up.

"I changed my mind."

His lip curled into a smirk. "I don't make offers twice, pet."

My eyes jumped behind him. He noticed, following my gaze out into the hall. I took the opportunity to bolt, darting around him and into the corridor.

His powerful arms dragged me back, stopping me cold before I could get more than five feet. I screamed, thrashing in his arms. He lifted me easily into the air and I lost the air in my lungs to his hard shoulder before he tossed me unceremoniously onto the bed.

"He warned me you were a fighter," he muttered.

I screamed at him, the sound raw and primal, a roar from a crazed animal that took all my air, all my energy with it.

His brows lifted, watching me with amusement in his eyes as I fought to regain my breath, fists in the embroidered blankets.

"You think I'm taking off the zip tie after that?"

"After what?"

*That voice.*

The temperature in the room dropped. The man backed off of me and I struggled to my feet, freezing when I saw him.

The ghost leaned against the frame in the doorway of the room, his head tipped to one side.

The tiny hairs on my neck and arms rose. The man, Ruarc, looked even more fearsome than he had in my cabin, appearing out of thin air in the dark.

"I'll take it from here, Nixon," he said.

The other man left the room silently, leaving me alone with the monster who took me.

He closed the door behind him, his cold gaze never leaving me as he stood perfectly at ease in the center of the room.

...with dried blood like a river down one side of his crisp white dress shirt.

"How are you finding your quarters?"

"My... my *what*?"

Confusion sparked into an indignant fury at his measured calm.

This devil took me from my home. Held me down. *Suffocated me.*

And now he wanted to ask me how I liked my fucking quarters?

He sauntered up to me slowly, the ghost of a smirk playing at the corner of his mouth, his brow pinched in mock-concern.

Up close, he was bigger than I remembered. With long limbs, wide shoulders, and enough height to dwarf me in size even at five-seven.

"You seem upset."

*I seem upset?* I clenched my teeth, speaking through them, needing him to answer me one thing before I would offer him any level of cooperation.

My gaze dropped to the blood on his shirt. "What did you do to my father?"

I watched him carefully, looking for any sign he may be lying as he replied.

"Nothing. Your father is alive and well."

He caught me looking at the blood on his shirt and glanced down at himself, seeming to notice it for the first time. He pinched the soiled fabric between his fingers with a frown.

"It belongs to a friend of yours," he explained in a chilly tone. "An ex-boyfriend, I believe."

"A what?" My mind scrambled to catch up and I almost choked when I finally understood.

"Carlos."

He smiled then, full lips pulling back over white teeth.

My chin quivered and my eyes burned, imagining Carlos cold and still. In a ditch somewhere. Or worse, buried in an unmarked grave.

My lips parted, registering the ugly truth. Carlos wouldn't be found in either of those places. He'd be ash in my father's incinerator.

"What did you do?" I breathed, my chest aching.

"He's gone."

His casual words fell like boulders.

No. Carlos wasn't gone, he was... he couldn't be.

I talked to him tonight. Just hours ago.

"Why you were with him at all, I'll never understand."

"You killed him."

I lifted my gaze to him, to Carlos' murderer, seeing him through blurry eyes.

"Accidentally, as fate would have it. A waste."

Numbness sept into my bloodstream, leaking out from the marrow in my bones.

He killed Carlos. He said he didn't kill my father but it was only a matter of time. This monster would kill him, too, but not before killing me.

I wouldn't be the next corpse Dad had to load into the cremator.

I made a run at the door, yanking the doorknob violently. It opened and I ran, sprinting down the stairs with my heart in my throat. Trying to retrace the path to the front door.

The ghost stalked after me, the even cadence of his slow, sure steps, somehow worse than if he'd sprinted after me.

I caught myself on the bannister, looking over it to the parquet floor below and the front door, tall with frosted glass panels, *so close*.

Making the mistake of peering back over my shoulder, I found him there, steps away, and threw myself down the stairs. My shoulder ached as I picked myself up from the floor, legs tangling in my too baggy sweats as I struggled to my feet with wrists bound.

Someone grabbed me from behind, lifting me from the floor. I screamed, kicking my legs back, feet knocking against unyielding bone.

I groped helplessly toward the locked door as I was dragged backward.

"Basement," Ruarc commanded from the stairs, the single word cutting through my terror. I thrashed against the man's hold, making him grunt in my ears as he worked to keep his hold on me, twisting a fist in my hair until my scalp burned and I could do nothing but stare up at the ceiling with tears streaming down my face as he led me into the bowels of the mansion.

My soft cries echoed in the dark cavern. A door opened and the fist in my hair released, my body thrown onto the rough ground. Dust kicked up, filling my nose, scratching at my throat, making me cough.

I lay in a heap on the floor, deep exhaustion settling in my muscles, turning them to puddles against sinew and tendon.

Desperate defeat kept silent tears flowing from my eyes as a shadow loomed over me.

I didn't cower as he bent to my level, didn't give him the satisfaction of flinching away as he pinched my chin between his rough fingers, forcing me to look into his cold slate eyes.

"You will live, sleep, and eat here until you can learn to control yourself," Ruarc said.

"Fuck you," the words fell weakly from my lips.

"Once you do," he continued as though I hadn't spoken, his deep baritone expanding in the cavernous room. "You may earn the privilege of returning to the bedroom upstairs. If you're a good girl—"

"Why did you bring me here?"

"You belong to me, now, little lamb," he snarled, his grip on my chin tightening until I whimpered. "Forget about everything outside these walls."

"I'm going to get out of here," I promised him. "And when I do I'm calling the police."

He scoffed derisively.

"Do it. Tell them I said hi. They're not coming to save you. Neither is your boyfriend, and neither is your father. You're *mine*."

I spat in his face, shocking myself more than him. Ruarc barely registered the slight, wearing the pitiful spatter on his cheek like an adornment.

He cocked his head at me, releasing my chin in favor of taking my wrists in his hands.

"I want to make something very clear," he began, rubbing a thumb over my knuckles, making my fists clench. "You will give me anything I want from you. Anytime. Anywhere."

He pulled a small knife from his pocket. Looking into my eyes as he cut the hard plastic, his grip on my hands tightened.

"*Anything*."

The alarm bells in my head rang with deafening volume and my thighs clenched.

"And you will take what is given to you."

My hands came apart, falling uselessly to my lap.

"If you don't, you'll be punished. If you don't learn from these punishments, I will punish someone you care about instead. Perhaps that'll be your father. Or perhaps... Tessa?"

I gasped before I could stop myself, clicking my teeth closed, grinding them together.

His hazel eyes burned dark in the low lighting of my cell, watching me, knowing he struck just the right nerve. He traced a burning path down my body, undressing me with a predatory hunger that stole all the air from my chest.

Without warning, he pressed a palm to my chest, right over my heart, where the fabric of my shirt was torn. I recoiled, but he only pressed harder, bending his head, shutting his eyes, feeling me. Reading my pulse beneath skin and bone.

"Don't pretend it's only fear that has your heart pounding, little lamb. In the deepest parts of yourself, you crave this. You crave *me*."

"I *hate* you."

He opened his eyes, pulling his hand back as he unfurled to his full height, standing over me with the regal grace of a lion mid-hunt. "We both know that's a lie."

# 13

## RUARC

My footsteps echoed back to me as I walked through racks of aging wine to the little cava di vino usually reserved for my enemies.

The guest suite I'd instructed the staff to make up for Emily was a generosity I didn't have to bestow on her. A luxury she didn't yet deserve.

Though, even now, she was being housed next to amarones and cabernets laid down by my predecessor. Many of which were worth more than her car, so really, it could have been worse.

I turned the key in the lock of the door, the old mechanism clanking loudly as it retracted.

On the cameras, Emily was frantic when I first left her a day ago, combing the room for over an hour like an abandoned pet, searching. For what? There was nothing to find.

I longed to punish her for her little show of defiance, but like a good Catholic boy, I was fasting. Starving myself. Whetting my appetite for the inevitable feast.

Twenty-four hours should've been plenty of time for

her to soften up but the precedent was set. Her will was thick and unyielding. I could either pierce it with a knife or wear it down until it was soft and pliant.

My chest swelled with anticipation as I swung the door open.

Having her here the past day, under my roof but unable to touch her was torture. Worse than watching her when she was in her cabin.

Awake, but not alert, Emily sat cross-legged on the floor. Without natural light to mark the passing of time, she could have no idea that it was near midnight.

Being sealed in a glorified tomb with zero stimulation looked to have succeeded in its purpose of subduing her.

Unlike the others before her, I didn't want a momentary outlet for my darkness, a pin prick of pleasure to swallow the bad medicine of the world down. With Emily, I wanted to make it last.

"Emily?"

I watched her warily, but she didn't move. She sat still, eyes down, body slumped heavily against the wall, she looked like a Sim. Lifeless, empty, awaiting animation.

"Have you had time to think?"

Her curtain of black hair hung limp around her face, obscuring any expression. I edged closer. The silent treatment was only going to last so long. Human beings were resilient, but they were social. The worst torture was isolation. At some point, she'd take any scrap I threw at her if it meant hearing something other than her own thoughts.

Perhaps another few hours. Another day? A week at most.

A heavy object sped toward me. I ducked, the heavy chunk of stone grazing my temple, breaking skin.

With spider-like quickness, she lunged past me, flying through the air. I brought my hand to my temple, fingers coming away stained red, and grinned.

I chased, catching her in seconds, my hand grasping the back of her shirt, jerking her backward. She lost her balance with a yelp and our bodies collided, falling to the ground. I climbed over her, grabbing her flailing arms and pinning them to her sides with my knees.

She shouted in protest, enraged, her teeth gnashing as she slung curses at me.

"I see you haven't learned your lesson."

She tried to buck her way off the floor, pushing uselessly against my body.

"If you're going to kill me, just do it," she shrieked.

I laughed, taking her arms from her sides to press them above her head, pushing my knee in between her legs so she was forced to part them. I'd wanted so badly to see her like this in the dark of her cabin and now I knew what I was missing.

Her perky tits lifted with her arms and the hollows on either side of her elongated waist made me feral with need. I settled myself against her, edging her thighs wider despite her fight to clench them shut.

"If I was going to kill you, you'd already be dead."

"*Then what do you want?*"

For her to stop talking. For her to put those lips to better use.

"What I wanted since I first saw you," I said, running a finger down the side of her neck. Her lips parted on a shaky gasp. Fear rose from her body, edged in something far more potent. The intoxicating combination had me hard in seconds.

Taking her right here, right now... I could picture it.

My jaw clenched painfully with the restraint.

"Get off me," she said, thrusting her hips upward, rubbing herself just *there*.

Her face paled at what she felt, a red flush bleeding into the white.

So fucking beautiful.

I brought my mouth to her neck, running my lips over her soft skin, unable to resist. I wouldn't fuck her, not yet. Not until she begged me for it.

But I could taste her.

She was the one being punished, for fuck's sake, not me.

She trembled beneath me, her pulse like that of a cornered mouse against my lips.

"Was it you?" I heard her ask in the faintest whisper. "Outside my cabin... watching me. Was it you?"

I tore my face from her neck so I could see into those wild green eyes.

"You knew."

I slid my hand up her tattered t-shirt, fingers stroking along her collar. She shuddered at my touch.

"You knew and yet you undressed in plain sight of your windows, open to the night."

I curved my palm gently around her slender neck, watching as her breathing hitched.

"You knew and yet you touched yourself, coming even while you felt my eyes on you from the shadows."

Her jaw clenched.

"Why?" I demanded, tightening my hold on her throat, my fingers wrapping around it like a necklace. "To tease me? To torture me?"

## Chapter 13

I released my hold and she blinked slowly, drawing in a slow breath.

She arched her back and I took the invitation, grinding into her warm cunt through her sweatpants as I dipped my free hand beneath her shirt.

"Tell me," I pressed, running my thumb over her nipple, pulling it into a taut, stiff peak. A whimper came from her lips. She liked that. I did it again.

"Tell you what?" she asked with defiance in her eyes.

"Why you didn't run."

I flicked her nipple.

She swallowed her moan, pressing her lips together.

"What?" she snapped as if she hadn't heard me at all, her focus dropping, her eyes glazing with desire.

I smirked, her nerve, her restraint, whatever she was hanging on so she didn't give in to me was giving out. It was intoxicating... feeling her break under my touch.

My cock hardened, restrained by the cage of my pants.

She'd be the greatest reward I ever delayed my gratification for.

Just a little more.

A little longer.

"If you could feel me watching you, if you knew something was out there, *why didn't you run?*"

I abandoned her pebbled nipple, pushing my hand down her sweats.

She screamed, clenching around my knee as I ran my fingers along the edge of her panties.

She gasped, closing her eyes in shame as my fingertips struck gold.

My little lamb was wet.

So wet she was seeping through her panties.

Heat built in my core, rushing straight to my already aching cock.

"What good would it have done me to run?" she asked quietly.

"Admit it,"

I pressed my fingers hard against her clit, making her squirm. "Admit you liked it."

She laughed at me, the sound harsh and short.

"Fuck you," she said, glaring at me through heavy-lidded eyes.

Her mouth said one thing, her body, however, was saying something quite the fucking opposite.

She knew why she fucking stayed. She fought herself, denied her basic instinct. She said she was scared but she didn't run. No. Instead she put on a show.

Even now, she pushed me away, and yet...

I hooked my fingers around the edge of her panties, sliding them along her bare folds, a growl emanating from my throat when I felt it. Her heat. Her desire, undeniable against my own flesh.

"Your body gives you away, little lamb."

I pulled my fingers free of her waistband, twisting them this way and that in the light, watching how her lust glimmered over the surface of my callused skin. She watched as I sunk each one into my mouth, tasting her.

"You're sick," she whispered.

She wasn't wrong.

I analyzed every tiny flicker of movement over her features as I slowly buried my hand back into her, finding no trace of denial. Fear in spades. Anticipation. Anger. But also... *hunger.*

I ran my moistened fingers over her clit, drawing

another moan from her throat that she attempted to block with the dam of her lips.

Sensitive to even the lightest touch.

Fucking her would be heaven on earth, and not just for me.

I hated her ex-boyfriend. I hated any man who had gotten to experience her before I had. Decided I'd kill them all.

I pulled her shirt up, exposing her smooth, lean body. I held my breath, the picture of control as I drank in every perfect inch of her. Her abdomen fell and rose with short, staccato breaths. She watched me warily, awaiting my next move. I wondered if she realized she was no longer struggling. The tension in her arms had gone slack. Her hips beneath me, sat pliant against the cold floor.

"Get a good look?" she asked sarcastically.

Actually, no. Not yet.

I grazed her nipple with my tongue and like a good little lamb she pushed her chest up to my mouth.

"Not so fast."

She let out a sound, something halfway between a whine and a moan.

I held her nipple between my teeth, flicking the hard tip while my fingers danced at her entrance, playing over her slit, touching everywhere but where she wanted, *needed* to feel me.

"Tell me you want me to touch you."

"*No*," she whispered, sealing her eyes shut as I edged closer to the apex of her sweet pussy, the strain in her pinched expression winding me up just as much as it was her.

"Then tell me not to."

Her jaw flexed.

I grinned, sucking her nipple into my mouth as I plunged my finger into her depths. She cried out, back arching off the floor. Her velvet walls stretched as I pushed a second finger into her and began a violent assault of her cunt, using the heel of my palm to keep pressure where she craved it most while my fingers did all the work on the inside.

She turned her face away from me, trying to hide her pleasure even as her hips rocked, desperate for me to shatter her.

My jaw fell slack watching her.

She was exquisite.

Her body deserved worship.

Men should kill and die to have her.

Men had done just that.

I fought the cloud of lust in my mind to remain focused. She didn't control me. She didn't possess me. She belonged to me. Mine.

Mine to touch. Mine to mold. Mine to break.

She bit her lower lip, her body coiling around me, muscles tensing for the inevitable explosion.

I withdrew my fingers, leaving her bereft moan to echo off the walls.

"What are you doing?"

Burning green eyes met mine.

"What do you want, little lamb?" I posed the question a second time. "All you need to do is ask."

She glared at me, obstinate.

I buried my fingers back inside her, jerking them fast and hard. She writhed on the ground. Curling my fingers, I found her g-spot, working her back into a frenzy, right to the edge, before pulling out again.

She let out a cry at the loss, her eyes filling with unshed tears.

A spark of possession zapped through me watching a perfect droplet skate down her cheek and vanish into her hairline.

"What do you want?"

She let her head fall back heavily against the stone floor, panting, her hair stuck to her temples with sweat.

"No," she said, defiant to the bitter end, bent on accepting her punishment like a good girl.

Standing up without spending my erection on that perfect body took every ounce of will I had.

"I don't like that word," I warned.

She swallowed, unable to meet my eyes as she wet her lips to speak. "Is that what you want?" Her voice was so small, so weak and timid, I could barely hear her at all. "To touch me?"

Emily seemed to remember where she was all at once, the austere concrete room jumping back into focus. She covered herself, drawing her legs in close, the tatters of her shirt closed.

I shook my head. Looking at her now I knew it was more than that. Touching her wouldn't be enough. I wanted to possess her. Wanted to twist her into something that could fit against my broken parts. I didn't just want her body. I wanted her heart. Her fucking soul.

"I want it all."

# 14

## EMILY

My eyes fluttered open, squinting at the ceiling light. It stayed on day and night. A cold relentless sun beating down on me without even the apology of warmth.

Every hour down in the stone cell blurred into the next.

Even my feeding schedule seemed chaotic at best. Random dishes with no real indication of meal type, dropped off just inside the door.

*Feeding schedule*, like I was a horse on a farm. At least they got to walk around in the daylight. I had no idea how long I had been down here, but it was too long.

I left my sleeping corner, the one with the most open view of the entrance, walking toward the makeshift bathroom. Nothing more than a barely functioning toilet and a showerhead that only spurted cold water in a stream that was more of a drizzle.

Using the toilet, I tried to ignore the camera perched high in the corner of the ceiling as I finished up and washed my hands under the cold drips from the showerhead.

The room was so empty, my thoughts felt loud and transparent. I hated them. Wanted to force myself back to sleep so I could dream instead. You couldn't be blamed for your dreams, but your thoughts...

Desires...

I shut my eyes, but he was there, too, superimposed on the backs of my eyelids. I knew he wanted me from the surveillance camera. I felt like he could read my mind through the camera feed. See what I was thinking from the barest twitch in my face.

He could come back any second and I'd have no warning.

He could touch me again.

I bit my lips.

This time, I'd let him. I'd let him do far more than touch me if it meant getting out of this room. Did that make me weak?

Did it make me pitiful?

I slammed my closed fists against either side of my head, beating out the thought. No. I wouldn't ask him for it. I wouldn't do what he wanted.

He threatened my Dad. Threatened Tessa.

Fuck, he *killed* Carlos.

I gripped my chest, hating how it felt like his blood was on my hands. If I'd just listened, didn't go into the mortuary after midnight, Carlos would still be here.

I'd never liked his parents much, but the thought of them out there somewhere, searching for a son they would never find, twisted something in my stomach until it was ready to snap.

I tried to bring up some emotion, to grieve for Carlos' loss, but the sob that came to my chest came for an entirely different reason. What was wrong with me? Something inside me had clearly fucking broken because I couldn't bring myself to feel the depth of sorrow I should at knowing Carlos was dead.

There was guilt, a fucking truckload of it, but...

I dated him for ten months. I should feel *something*. There should be more.

I sobbed to myself in the dark, making excuses in the privacy of my thoughts.

*I'm just in shock.*

*Maybe Carlos isn't even dead. Maybe he lied.*

*I'm just in shock. That's it.*

What did he need me to do to let me go? Whatever it was, I was ready. I couldn't stand staying down here alone with my thoughts for another day, another hour. Whatever he wanted, it was his.

I sat in my corner, pulling my knees in, leaning my head against the wall, rolling left and right until I had some semblance of comfort. I closed my eyes, willing all thoughts from my head, begging for the reprieve of sleep to take me.

I startled awake, my heart pounding in my chest at the sound of the door hitting the wall as it was thrown open.

Boots pounded against stone, the sound like bombs echoing in the room as two dark figures swept in.

"Wait," I cried, my behind scraping against the floor as I tried to press myself into the wall, away from them. "No, please, what are you—"

Rough hands yanked me from the floor, dragging me from the room.

I blinked the sleep from my eyes, struggling to regain feeling in my limbs, the stinging needles of sleeping muscles screaming with each stumbling step they forced me to take. "Where are you taking me?"

I whipped my head around, my chest fluttering as I took in stoic expressions on unrecognizable faces. Did the ghost know they were here? Did he know they were taking his little lamb?

"Where's Ruarc? I want to see Ruarc!"

They shoved me through a door and a hot wall of lavender scented steam slapped me in the face. I slipped on a slick floor, eyes clouded, and caught myself on the rim of a wide copper tub.

The door shut behind me, locked.

I stared down into hot, milky bathwater.

Oh my god.

Unable to help myself, I stuck my hand in and sighed at the comforting warmth of the silky water.

Flipping around, I checked the door, the room, for any signs of life, expecting to see *him*. Waiting in the corner, hidden by the steam.

But I was alone. The windowless room held little aside from the massive tub in the center of the floor. A high-backed wooden chair with some towels atop it stood next to the tub. The deep purple walls seemed to swallow up most of the light from the small chandelier over the tub.

I pulled my lower lip in between my teeth, running my fingers over the surface of the water.

My mind raced trying to figure out what this meant, but the visceral need for warmth, cleanliness, and comfort ultimately won out over logic and scorn. I stripped down to nothing, leaving my soiled clothes on the floor as I clutched the rim of the tub and stepped into the water.

I sucked in a breath at the near scalding temperature,

but forced the other leg in, too, sinking myself into the satiny bathwater. The tub was so big I could stretch my legs out all the way and still have my shoulders beneath the surface. I sighed to myself, hating myself for how my nose burned with the sudden, inexplicable urge to cry.

Folding my arms across my chest, I slipped beneath the surface of the water, my hair swirling around my face.

I let out some air, the sound of the bubbles racing for the surface loud in the water. I let out some more, wondering darkly if I shouldn't let it all out. If I shouldn't breathe the water instead.

End myself before the bastard who took me could be the one to do it. See him try to blackmail my father with a corpse. There would be no reason to harm Tessa then, either.

No more time spent in a cold, dank cell underground.

No more guilt.

Just... nothing.

I forced out the last of the air from my lungs and opened my eyes beneath the surface, bracing my hands on either side of the water warmed copper tub to keep myself underwater.

*Breathe. Just breathe.*

I opened my mouth to suck in a lungful of water, but as soon as it filled my mouth, I shot up, water sloshing over the tub's edge as I spat it out, gasping for breath.

What was I doing?

I couldn't even *die* properly.

Angry tears filled my eyes as I fell back against the copper, resting my head on the rim.

The water hadn't even begun to cool when the lock turned and the door opened, the two men from before swarming the tub. I stood before they could haul me out, shoving their arms away as I went for the towels on the chair, uncaring that I was completely naked.

"Don't fucking touch me," I hissed, wrapping the towel around myself, wringing my hair out onto the floor

The taller one reached for my arm again but I pulled away, glaring at him. "I said don't touch me. I'll walk myself."

The two silent men shared a look before the shorter of the two waved an arm toward the door, indicating that I should leave.

I scooped my soiled clothes from the floor on my way out, turning back toward my cell with leaden legs.

"Other way," the tall one said and my brows furrowed.

Were they taking me back to the bedroom?

Fuck. I was going to cry again.

I swallowed against the wall of emotion building in my chest, too wary that at any moment it could be shattered beyond repairing.

The two men fell into step with me, one in front, one behind, corralling me like a wayward sheep back to its pen.

Striding through a glass door, the sky opened up above us. A velvety midnight blue brightened by the moon and stars was clearly visible through an open roof.

The man in front of me moved to join the other man behind, the pair of them leaving without a word.

My mouth dried. Something was wrong. I'd been desperate to leave the basement, but this didn't feel any safer.

Lamps stood on perches, scattered throughout lush greenery and winding pathways. The hedges in some areas looked so high not even the tallest of men could see above them. A maze?

I spun around, gasping at the rise of an imposing gothic spire against the night sky. I could see more of the bath side of one wing of the grand mansion, all of it dark and sharp and hauntingly beautiful. Something out of a twisted fairytale.

Casting away my curiosity, I tried the knob on the glass French doors I'd been brought through.

Locked.

No surprise there.

*Break it,* I thought, spinning to find something, a stone, a brick, anything to smash through the delicate glass and twist the lock on the other side.

Like a shot of lightning through the dark, a deafening blow sounded through the air.

I fell to the ground, my hands over my ears.

My mind blanked. My ears rang.

I knew what it was and wished I didn't.

As the shock subsided, fear engulfed me. I was stuck, frozen where I stood.

Do something. Run. *Run.*

Adrenaline pushed me to my feet. I pivoted, making for the tall windows I'd seen on the other side of the space, praying for an unlocked door.

There he was.

Ruarc.

My stomach dropped to my toes along with the pile of soiled clothes. I clutched the towel tight around myself.

"Run," he commanded, the barrel of the old looking gun still loosely clutched in his right hand smoked at its mouth.

"What?"

I blinked, my mind scattered.

He raised his arm, pointing the gun in my direction.

*Run.*

I bolted as a tall cement vase shattered behind me, raining dirt onto the flagstone.

I screamed, rushing through the bushes, arms tearing to get through, my heart pounding in my throat. Tears running down my face. I whipped my head around in the dark, but he was gone.

No. not gone. I could feel his eyes on me in the dark. A predator stalking his prey.

I pushed into the maze-like garden of hedges, rushing around bend after bend, the *tap tap* of his measured steps behind me spurring me forward.

A bench sat in a lonely corner of hedge, overgrown with vines.

"*Little lamb...*" Ruarc called, his rough voice a dark melody to the violent rhythm of my heart.

I dove for the bench, tucking myself beneath it. I sealed my lips shut, silencing my breath. My throat ached, burning and raw. My lungs withered in my chest.

All this just to shoot me now? It didn't make sense.

His steps drew nearer and I slapped a hand over my mouth, holding my breath.

"There you are."

The garden went still with deafening silence. I waited. *Waited.*

Tentatively, I withdrew my hand from my mouth, peeling one eye open.

He grabbed my leg, dragging me out from under the bench over the cobbles. I screamed, kicking.

The gun clicked. I froze.

"I thought I told you to run," he mocked, hovering over me with a curious glint to his eyes.

I stared up at him, up into the barrel of the gun pointed squarely at my face, unable to move.

He tipped his head to one side, as if considering me in a new light, liking what he saw. The flush in my cheeks. The bright burn of fear in my eyes.

"Fear is your red lipstick, little lamb, though it suits you more than that shade ever could."

My lips parted, trying to make sense of his words in the riot of my pleading thoughts.

"Do you remember what I told you?" he asked, moving closer, wedged between my legs.

"Wh-what?"

"What did I tell you, little lamb?" he asked, his voice low, almost a purr, starkly in contrast with his actions.

I struggled to regain coherent thought. He expected a reply. I didn't want to think about what he might do if he didn't get one.

"You told me to run."

"What *else* did I tell you?"

There was more?

A cold sweat broke out over my chest and I fought to swallow.

"Everything," I stammered, the memory like a whip cracked against bone. He wanted my everything. For me to do whatever he asked. For me to ask *him*.

"Good," he admonished. "Now strip."

He reached out a hand to help me stand, but I recoiled from it, standing on my own.

Ruarc let out a chuff, watching my every movement as I

gripped the towel still around me, now covered in nettles and dirt.

"*Now,* little lamb."

Static rang in my ears. Desperate, rote obedience activated somewhere deep inside the recesses of my brain and my limbs moved almost as though of their own accord. Like a watcher in a dream or a nightmare, I distantly was aware of the towel coming apart, of the kiss of air on my still-damp skin, the feel of it falling in a puddle on my feet.

I wouldn't lift my gaze to find the expression he wore, but it had to be smug. It had to be glee. Twisted joy that I was his puppet to control.

"How many more nights do you need in your dungeon?" he asked.

I pressed my lips tight, not knowing what else to say. *None,* I wanted to scream. *No more.*

He moved suddenly.

I flinched, instinctively trying to move away from him, backing into the spiky hedge. Ruarc crowded me, pressing the cold metal barrel of his gun to my neck, drawing a fractured whimper from my lips.

"How many?"

"N-none," I croaked, helpless.

I was paralyzed, completely at his mercy, my fingers gripping the foliage at my back, needing something to hold on to. Something solid. Something to remind me that this was real.

"Is that so?"

Whatever he wanted, he was getting it. I felt his thigh press between the apex of my thighs, but this time he didn't force them apart, he waited, an expectant gleam in his eyes, until I opened them for him.

His lips feathered against my cheek, moving as he spoke into my ear. "Good girl," he crooned and I closed my eyes, a heavy breath escaping my lips before I could snap them shut.

The cool hardness of the gun moved down my body.

I stiffened as he dragged it over my collarbone, lower to graze one of my nipples on the way down. Lower still until the barrel bumped over my hip bone, pressed into my inner thigh.

Sirens more urgent than the gunshots he'd fired went off inside me, awakening every nerve ending, breathing life into my hollow soul.

"What are you doing?" I whimpered.

Fear made me jump at his slightest touch. I could barely string two thoughts together, but the gun between my legs sent panic flowing out of every one of my pores.

"Anything I want," he rasped, barely above a whisper.

And then something touched me. Hard and cool. It brushed over my mound and slid down to my clit. I gasped, my legs sealing together.

"*Please*," I whispered, my nipples hardening, core tightening.

I squeezed my eyes tightly shut against the wave of traitorous arousal striking sparks over the fresh gasoline in my veins.

No.

*You could* die, *Emily.*

"*Uh, uh,*" Ruarc scolded. "Open."

My lips parted but I had no words for him. None that I would dare speak out loud.

Don't touch me.

*Don't make me like it.*

It was like prying apart metal to force my thighs open for him a second time. He took his time, running the side of the smooth metal barrel up my thigh until it pressed flat against my cunt. I shook, my back arching as the pressure awakened something I didn't even know I had inside me.

Ruarc lifted the weapon to the moonlight, finding the evidence of my arousal on the sleek barrel before returning to its lethal work.

He rocked the butt against me, slowly, up and down, a controlled pressure that was enough to stir something in my core. My body knew what I wanted him to do, but my mind was running blind, fighting the dark at every turn.

Ruarc drew the smooth body of the gun over my clit. I groaned, feeling the hard weapon on my softest flesh.

"Please," I whispered. "I don't... I don't want..."

Why couldn't I finish that sentence?

He laughed darkly while I stewed in a vat of my own self-loathing, biting back a moan as he swirled the quickly warming metal against my nub.

"Stop fighting it," he demanded.

I was so humiliated I could have died as he reached between us, his fingers plunging into me.

Ruarc thrust two fingers hard and deep into me, searching out all my ugliest secrets, my most vile sins, taking them for himself.

This monster had me in the palm of his hand, teasing out every sick desire I had, making me face them. He pumped his fingers hard and fast, curling them into that spot, the one no one else seemed to be able to reach, all the while keeping the heel of his palm against my sex, mounting rhythmic pressure there until I was seeing stars.

I didn't realize I was rocking into his fingers until my hazy eyes snapped sharply into focus on his knowing smirk.

No man I'd ever been with elicited such a feral response from me.

My body surrendered to him, hurtling towards orgasm, a quickening clenching in my core, squeezing, building...

...but he withdrew.

A sob escaped me. My body ached for release.

"Tell me what you want."

My throat tightened, and my pussy pulsed with an ache I knew could only be properly sated by one thing. One dirty, deviant, dominant man.

"*Tell me.*"

"Don't..." I trailed off, two sides of a battlefield struggling for triumph.

Don't touch me, I thought.

"Don't stop," I said.

Hot shame crawled up my neck as he brought his fingers to my mouth, pushing them past my lips. I opened for him, tasting myself on the digits.

Staring into the abyss of his reflective eyes, I trembled against him, sucking them clean.

Below, the smooth gun was back between my legs. Ruarc gripped my jaw, his fingers still in my mouth, pressing down on my tongue, holding me in place with a makeshift muzzle.

He restarted his assault on my clitoris. I moaned, the dull pressure not enough. Not nearly enough. My hips jerked wildly, the friction teasing my desire, holding release just out of reach. Frustrated tears stung my eyes.

"You want more?"

I tightened, feeling the barrel against my entrance. I

stiffened, the muscles and tendons in my thighs stretched taut as I fought the urge to snap my legs closed. Any rapid movement, any jerk of my body, could see that trigger pulled.

Ruarc groaned, gritting his teeth as if he shared my pleasure as he slipped the tip of the barrel into my dripping, greedy cunt. I threw my head back in a silent scream, bucking my hips. His fingers left my mouth, smoothing down my jaw, around my neck.

He squeezed, jerking my head back down to look him in his lust-filled eyes.

"Fuck yourself on my Glock, Emily."

My pussy clenched around the firearm. Its irregular, hard grooves pressed lewdly into my yielding flesh. I cried, overwhelmed with terror and shame and lust. My walls shuddered as I sucked small breaths through my lips, Ruarc's hand on my throat tightened and black spots danced at the edges of my vision.

Lust, stronger than my fear, moved my hips.

I writhed and twisted for the sensation, every movement assaulting my flesh. I felt light-headed. My body bathed in heat.

He barely moved the gun, letting me fuck myself on its hard barrel. I bucked wildly, afraid he would withdraw again. I felt like I'd fucking die if I didn't come this time. Like I'd spontaneously combust from all the pressure with no outlet for its escape.

Desperately, I released the foliage behind me, rolling my clit under my fingers. The added stimulation blasted me over the edge. I screamed without sound, coming so hard on the gun that my vision blackened. My cunt shuddered and throbbed, electricity shooting through my core, curling my toes, coiling up my spine.

The gun, Ruarc, the garden, everything disappeared. I drowned in my release, the pleasure giving way to shuddering, broken exhaustion.

Every bit of energy in my body drained away as the weapon slipped from me and I drew in a full lungful of air. Ruarc's grip on my throat loosened, but not gone as he stroked a finger down my carotid artery.

I tried to hold myself up when he finally released me, but it wasn't necessary. My ghost's dark shadow covered me, arms lifting me with ease from the flagstone.

Too weak to fight him, I slumped against his chest, my feet swinging with each step he took out of the maze.

"Where are you taking me?"

I winced at the thought of returning to my cell.

I'd done what he wanted.

Just like he wanted.

With my face against his chest, his warmth and the steady beat of his pulse was strangely soothing. His smell, like warm sandalwood and smooth musk filled me, soothing the spikes of fear still sharp in my blood.

Just minutes ago this man held a gun to my head and put his hand around my throat. Just minutes ago he made me beg for him to let me come and pushed a weapon into me.

And I didn't try to stop him.

I didn't fight him.

I came on his gun like some twisted whore with a death wish.

Silent tears filled my eyes, but I forbade them from falling. I wouldn't cry for this monster. I'd already given him too much.

No more.

*No more.*

My eyes fluttered open and closed as we went from outside to indoors, the cloying talons of sleep too persistent to ignore.

Soft fabric greeted my sensitive skin, disorienting after the harsh stimuli I'd endured downstairs. I opened my eyes to a warmly furnished suite, the same one the other man, Nixon, had brought me to when I was first dragged into this salacious nightmare.

I opened my mouth to say something but Ruarc walked out without a word over his shoulder or a look in my direction. I resented his silence but it felt like a peace offering. A reward. I'd earned my way back upstairs, and now he'd leave me to pick up all the pieces of me he'd shattered in the gardens.

# 15

## RUARC

"How long are you keeping her?"

A plume of white smoke rose from the cigarette in Nixon's hand.

The entrance to the club waited in silence for the night to begin as my staff readied everything inside for another night of debauchery.

Hiding in plain sight.

Whoever had taken those photographs and posted them online was hiding in plain sight.

It had been all I could think about since the security breach.

When it wasn't that, it was *her*.

Truthfully, my little lamb had been more of a distraction than anything, but one I couldn't seem to keep away from, even while my kingdom lay under siege from an unknown enemy.

Nothing seemed amiss.

Everyone who attended was vetted and approved by the same rigorous standards as they'd always been.

The club had been swept for recording devices and came up clean.

I'd checked the escorts I had working the floor. From the outside looking in, it was as though nothing happened.

I was hesitant to open up to guests but that was the only way to figure out where the leak was. Draw it out. Set a trap. Kill the rat.

"Until I'm done with her," I said, giving Nixon the reply he seemed intent on getting, staring at me intently.

"The undertaker will want more of an answer than that," he replied.

I narrowed my gaze on him. "The undertaker will *want*..." I trailed off, repeating his own stupidity back to him. "What's gotten into you, Nix?"

"I just don't see how this ends. You took her to control the undertaker. If you let her go, then what?"

"Then hopefully the jackass will have learned his lesson and won't want me to take her a *second time*."

Nixon pushed the toe of his fine leather boot into the hard packed dirt, rolling a reply around in his mouth, too much the coward to spit it out.

"Get on with it."

He shrugged his shoulders with the comfort of someone who knew they were allowed to speak freely in my presence.

"If you want to teach the undertaker a lesson, returning her defeats the purpose. He gets what he wants. No doubt he'll squirrel her away somewhere, someplace far beyond our reach, and then what?"

My chest tightened and a rueful laugh escaped my lips.

This was why I kept him around.

He was wrong in so many ways, but he made a point.

Since getting her to the house, I forgot about her father and the reason, well, the main reason why she was here in the first place.

He was forgettable and insignificant but his daughter was something else. She had a way of climbing into my thoughts, appearing when I least expected. After I touched her, her essence clung to me like perfume that I couldn't wash off.

And even though Nix did have a point, a swell of defensive anger rose in me.

"I'm not killing her, Nix," I deadpanned, putting the full weight of my authority into the words, feeling the truth of them like a sling to hold up the weight of a decrepit heart. Sturdy and true.

"Why not?"

He was looking at me, his gravel-colored eyes dead serious. He didn't see it. See *her*. Not the way I did. "You never fuck them more than once anyway, boss. Use her, do what you will, and then dispose of her. Or better, send her in pieces back to her father."

Why did I get the sense he was testing me. Prodding at my resolve. Feeling for cracks.

"She's more use to me *alive*."

My fists clenched. If Nixon wasn't careful, he'd be the one meeting the hard edge of my knuckles tonight.

But on closer inspection, I could admit my anger wasn't only at his apparent desire to murder someone who belonged fully to me. It was also because in bringing Emily here, losing myself in her, her father became an afterthought. That made her dangerous. The kind of distraction that could allow a leak at the club to go unnoticed. A spy to slip in between the cracks.

*Don't get involved,* Thane's words echoed in the darkest recesses of my memory. I couldn't count how many times he repeated those words to me. When he fired the third housekeeper I'd stuck my cock in more than once, reminding me that all women were a means to an end and nothing more.

When he killed the man I spared because he told me he'd just had a baby daughter the night before and he needed to bring formula home to feed her. Thane made me watch as he turned out the dead man's pockets, finding them filled with nothing more than lint and the heroin he bought instead.

Or the dog I saved from a cougar, the one I called Opie, who later got rabies and almost tore my left ear off before Thane put him down.

*Don't get involved.*

"I can't fuck her if she's dead," I muttered, taking a flask from my inside jacket pocket for a swig of smooth bourbon.

Nixon laughed, crushing his cigarette butt underfoot, and lighting up another.

"Nah. Necrophilia ain't your jam, but I wouldn't recommend keeping her around either."

I was going to do whatever I wanted in the end but Nixon's statement interested me.

"You don't like her."

He nodded, shrugging as he puffed smoke from his nostrils.

"You've got a whole fountain of pussy, Ruarc. Why fill only one cup?"

I scoffed, appreciating the analogy.

"You haven't had any other women since you brought her here. Actually, for weeks before that, too."

I didn't have to hunt. Women found their way to me all on their own, but I wasn't looking. Didn't see them.

Emily was the first woman I'd ever gone out of my way to possess. In my defense, I hadn't even fucked her yet, how could I get rid of her already?

Maybe when I finally had her, my obsession would relent.

No more obsession meant no more need to keep her. No more distractions.

"You seem a little too preoccupied with what *I'm* doing, Nix. Do you need another project, something to keep you busy?"

He exhaled another plume of smoke, smirking. "Nah, you run me ragged as it is, boss. I just don't see the appeal."

"What? She not your type?"

He lifted a brow. "Not *yours*," he corrected. "I thought you liked them a lot more... submissive."

My hand went instinctively to my eyebrow. Everything was all healed now, but Emily had not come quietly. I didn't just *like* submission from a woman. I needed it.

I used their bodies however I wanted, and then afterward I never saw them again. I was already breaking one of those rules for Emily. The other one, she was breaking, and I was letting her.

She must've felt that she had to fight me, tell me no. If she gave in to her darkest desires, it would mean I won. It would mean every vile thing she thought about herself was true.

I'd been right about the things she craved, whether or not she was being honest with herself.

No. Emily wasn't going anywhere. Her utility against

her father was secondary to my desire to keep her. Now that I had her, she couldn't leave. I wouldn't allow it.

A muscle in my jaw ticked, the need to go back inside, check that she was still there, rushed through me like a live current of electricity.

I wasn't naive enough to think my little lamb wouldn't leave if she was given the chance. If I didn't have eyes on her at every moment, if there was an unmanned window or an unlocked door, she would run for freedom.

I couldn't give her that option.

An icy heat filled my core as I drew out my phone, tapping shakily over the screen to log in to the app with the live feed of her bedroom.

My mother's face flashed across my eyes and I furiously blinked her away, hating how even now the memory of her face made something in my gut sour and twist.

She was still young the last I'd seen her. Close to my age, but haggard by a life of drugs and street prostitution. With guarded eyes from so much betrayal.

Always adorned with bruises, split lips, and new marks on her body given to her by her johns or pimps.

I sat in a puddle of my own refuse for days before wandering out from the hovel we called a home, knowing even in my adolescent naivety that she would not be returning.

I should thank her now.

She taught me a valuable lesson the day she decided to let herself be bought and packed like cargo on a ship bound for Europe.

Nothing was too precious, too beloved, to stay.

If I wanted something bad enough, I had to hang on. I had to fight, destroy all other alternatives.

The feed of Emily's room came into focus on my phone screen, showing sitting on the bed, her gaze on one of the paintings in the room.

"Emily will come around," I told him.

I passed through the club on my way back through the mansion. Closed and quiet, it seemed almost benign. You could pass it off as an avant-garde performance or exhibition space. That might have been what it was in essence. My mind went to Emily, upstairs.

Three days since I was with her in the courtyard...

Since she let her lust win, using a deadly weapon for her pleasure.

A throb of desire started in my core. I'd never forget the way she felt, her cries, her racing pulse under my fingers.

I couldn't remember the last time I'd fucked my hand so much. I barely made it from laying her in her room to my own quarters before I had my cock out, thrusting into my own palm to find release in a pent up roar that had me spurting ropes of cum over my Persian rug. Clutching the mantle to keep myself standing as dark spots crowded at the edges of my vision.

In the control room, I dismissed security before setting into the man's seat, bringing up the feed of my little lamb on the largest screen.

Her room and bathroom were fully covered with cameras. I saw everything. She was laying on the bed now, wrapped in a towel, her cheeks flushed from a hot shower. She showered or bathed daily, sometimes more than once.

I had to assume it was a way to pass the time besides sleeping and reading. The books in the room had been placed there mostly for decoration by the staff. Tomes of dry philosophy, history, and a few rare editions of fiction.

If I had my way, I'd lock myself in that room with her and not come out for a week straight. She was already a distraction but going to her whenever the urge struck would be catastrophic. My empire would burn to the ground while I lay buried between her thighs.

Emily licked her lips as she flipped the page on the weathered book in her lap, moving to lie back against the pillows.

Propping the book up with one hand, she reached between the flaps of the towel, pushing her hand between her thighs.

My cock jerked to attention against my thigh.

*What did you find, little lamb?*

I leaned into the screen as she bent her legs, getting a better angle, her fingers playing between her folds. The towel fell to one side and I toggled the camera view, finding a better angle of my own as I watched her swirl her dainty fingers over her opening.

Her wild eyes flicked to the camera across the room, meeting mine through the screen.

*Naughty, naughty little lamb.*

I admired my restraint so far but I'd only be able to keep it up so long. She was holding back too. She had needs, dark desires, almost as dark as mine. This proved it.

Just look at her, asking, *begging* for me to come to her. Taunting me. Teasing me.

I clenched my jaw, watching her head tip back as she pushed her fingers into herself, rubbing her juices over her greedy cunt.

With a growl, I undid my pants, plunging a hand inside to ease the want. My hunger for her lingered just below the surface, restrained enough for me to keep back but I was only so strong.

I'd never tire of watching her.

Emily was *mine* and mine alone.

How far would I have to bend her to make her into someone capable of loving a monster? I knew, watching her watch me as I spit into my palm and fucked my own hand, gripping the edge of the console, that her body wouldn't be enough.

Not even owning a piece of her soul would settle my own.

When I told her I wanted everything, I didn't realize how deeply the meaning ran. I wanted her whole heart. I wanted her to love me like she would never love another person on this vile planet.

When I was finished with her, I'd hand her the key to her freedom and I wanted her to drop it at my feet.

I wanted her to *stay*.

# 16

## EMILY

At least this place had books.

I ran my fingers over the spines lining the bookcase. The selection wasn't optimal but I'd give any of my vital organs not to go back to the basement.

The variety of books I hadn't read yet was dwindling, but I had an interesting crop to pick from. Old leather bound histories, yellowed page philosophies–those I mostly ignored–but then there were also romances and adventure stories.

Jane Austen and Emily Bronte. Jack London and Conan Doyle.

I plucked a hardback of *Brave New World* from the shelf and cracked it open to the copyright page. Its pages were yellowed and fragrant, the edition published in 1933. I slipped the book back into the lineup and kept looking. The collection altogether told me exactly nothing about the people who owned them or lived here. I had a feeling though that the building had not been constructed or lived in by anyone who knew who the Kardashians were.

The books made me think of Tessa. I had no idea what day it was anymore but I was supposed to be traveling with her.

I wondered what tall tale had been concocted to excuse my absence.

Was someone out there with my phone, tapping out replies to my friend, keeping up appearances? Or was my face on a milk carton somewhere?

There wasn't a goddamned thing I could do about it either way.

My mind wandered to the books she gave me, how much I'd rather be reading one of those right now.

If I told Tess what was happening right now, she'd never believe me.

Whenever I saw Ruarc, I needed to stop, take stock, and blink a couple of times to make sure he was really there. Corporeal. Not a nightmarish fiction made flesh.

But ghosts didn't have warm skin. Hallucinations couldn't give you the best orgasm of your life.

My eyes flew to the door. The last time it opened, it was meal time and someone brought me a large plate of spaghetti and chicken parm. The next time it opened, I'd probably be asleep, the used dishes cleared away. The sun set four times through the barred windows since I'd last seen him.

Had I done something wrong? Something to upset him? If he didn't want to touch me anymore, what would that mean for me?

I could only think of two things. Either he'd return me to my father, unlikely, or he'd kill me to send a message.

My teeth dug into my lip as I flipped the book's pages, too distracted to read more than a couple lines at a time.

Footsteps padded against the hardwood floor somewhere not far from the door to my luxurious prison and I held my breath, thighs clenching only to deflate as they faded away.

Was that it? Was I just... horny? Was that why I didn't fight harder to stop him?

*Jesus.*

If it was true, what did that make me?

Because my hands worked just fine and I'd been using those to get off since I was fifteen.

Was I so starved for human contact that I'd take whatever weird, crazy shit he wanted from me, or was it *him*?

I had no reason to *like*, let alone desire him. He fucking kidnapped me.

Ruarc was the reason I had no idea whether my dad was okay. The reason Carlos was dead and Tessa wasn't safe.

He'd terrorized me and used my body like a toy.

I should have been disgusted by him. I should loathe him.

...and maybe I did.

But I also...

My eyes fluttered back to the door, watching it again as if that would somehow encourage him to appear.

If he escalated every time we saw each other then what would come next? It scared me to wonder what the depths of his depravity were. It was worse to imagine whether I'd meet him at his level or whether he'd finally push me past my limits.

Was the gun he'd fucked me with loaded? Was the safety off?

I gulped, looking around the fairytale room. My padded prison.

Beautifully furnished and comfortable.

With clean clothes in the walk-in and sanitary supplies in the bathroom. Light, medium, *and* heavy tampons. Like a hotel. Just one you couldn't leave.

It wasn't unbearable.

And in the moments I allowed myself to imagine I was here by my own will, I would almost say it was comfortable. Without Ruarc here to turn it back into a nightmare, it felt more like a dream. A vacation from my mundane existence.

Aside from the predictability of it.

That was stifling in its comfort and sameness.

Read, sleep, eat, bathe, rinse and repeat.

I looked back down at my book, the words on the page blurring together as rage filled me with heat. Hating myself for my own thoughts.

How fucking dare he make me feel grateful for being in this room instead of the dungeon?

How dare he make me so starved for human interaction that even the thought of him walking through that door made me feel something akin to relief?

Fuck him.

Righteous indignation rose in my chest and I threw the book across the room, my gaze zeroing in on one of the three cameras in the room. Was he watching me right now?

I'd put on a show for him yesterday, attempting to draw him out. The sooner he got everything he wanted out of me, the sooner this could be over.

One way or another.

"Hey!" I shouted into the camera. "How long are you going to keep me locked up in here?"

No reply. Nothing but the incessant blink of the red light on the base of the lens.

Was this all he wanted from me, now? To watch me on his cameras like some sick personal reality show?

If he wanted a show, fine, I'd give him one.

I dragged the high backed cushioned chair from the corner of the room, its legs scraping over the polished wood floors, leaving deep gouges.

Grabbing it by its wooden arms, I lifted it as high as I could, throwing back to the floor. The heavy piece of furniture landed noisily on its side, sliding along the floor before getting caught on the edge of the carpet and stopping.

I tried again, picking up and driving the chair into the ground as hard as I could. This time I was rewarded with the sharp *crack* of splintering wood.

One of the arms shook loose. Picking it up by the high back, I slammed it into the floor legs first. Two of the back legs buckled and one of them cracked, a few more blows against the floor and it came free.

Panting, arm straining, burning as I caught my breath, looking to the window. Back at the chair, sizing it up.

It wouldn't do anything to the bars, but still...

Heaving it into the air, I ran headlong into the window, smashing it. Glass shattered, a shower sprinkling onto the floor by my feet.

I laughed, exhilarated.

The chair lodged in the space, blocked by the bars.

My heart pounded with excitement. Destroying the beautiful room sent thrills of adrenaline coursing through me. Starved of contact, excitement, and stimulation, the juvenile rebellion felt euphoric.

Letting the chair fall to the ground, I flipped it around so I could push it out back first angling the legless seat until I could shove it through the bars.

Leaning through the hole, I watched it crash to the ground below with butterflies in my stomach. It smashed on the verdant lawn, the back breaking off from the cushioned seat.

The wind blew against my skin and through my hair The air fresh after so much time spent breathing in my stale recycled oxygen.

I closed my eyes, breathing deeply.

I shivered, invigorated, my world seeming to blow up into something bigger than just this room. I curled my hand around one of the iron bars, giving it a shake, judging the space between it and its twin to the left. The gaps were wide. Wider than they'd appeared when the old warped glass was still intact.

Swallowing, I gripped the bars tight, avoiding the broken glass at the base of the frame to lean out the window for a better view.

A forest grew beyond the property in a dense, lush patch of green. I'd stared out at it for hours before but I'd never properly seen it until now.

There didn't seem to be neighbors close by but they were there, somewhere. The whole world was there, moving along without me like nothing had even happened.

A crash behind me made me jump. I spun around, stopping stiff when I saw him.

"What the fuck are you doing?"

Ruarc stood in the doorway, eyes wild, shoulders and chest heaving.

I puffed my chest out, proud, triumphant.

His stance was tentative apprehension, but his eyes were crazed, quivering as he regarded me.

It was fear, I realized with a sinking in my gut, and it had no right to be on the face of a monster.

I lifted my chin, wishing I could take the same gratification at seeing his fear as he did eliciting mine.

Before he could come any closer, I climbed onto the sill, bracing myself between two of the bars.

His heavy steps barreled toward me as I balanced myself on the window frame, a shard of glass slicing along the edge of my right foot.

I barely felt the sting as I looked down, my heart jumping into my throat.

*Let go,* my own voice shouted in my skull. *Let go!*

I let my feet slip from the ledge, closed my eyes.

Ruarc's arm closed around my waist and yanked me violently back into the room. He panted, throwing me to the bed. My head knocked into the ornate headboard and I blinked as blackness and bursts of light flared momentarily across my field of vision.

"What the fuck?" he shouted, bearing down on me, hands gripping my shoulders.

"Let go of me!"

I kicked out at him, hitting him in the stomach, making him grunt as he struggled to maintain his hold on me.

"What the fuck were you doing? *You could have killed yourself,*" he bellowed.

He panted harsh, short breaths, his arms, and shoulders tense, watching me like he was afraid I'd try to get around him and jump again.

"What the fuck do you care?" I screamed in his face.

His breath hissed through his teeth. His lips sealed, darkness hardening his gaze as he released my shoulders with a shove, sitting back heavily on the mattress.

His shoulders shook in silent laughter as he pinched the bridge of his nose. His expression told me he was wondering the same thing I was.

"You're the worst idea I've ever had." He shook his head. "Resorting to dangerous games to get my attention..."

"But it worked."

He snapped his attention back to me, his clear slate eyes burning into my soul. His upper lip curled, seeing my outburst for what it really was. The thing I wouldn't admit even to myself.

Ruarc curled rough fingers around my ankle, eliciting a yelp from my lips as he dragged me to the floor, jerking me up onto my knees with a bruising grip on my shoulder.

I pushed against his hold, but he shoved down on my shoulder, keeping me there as he used his other to pop the button on his neat black pants, freeing his cock.

My mouth snapped shut, watching it harden before my eyes, growing to a length I thought reserved only for porn stars and horses. A thick vein pulsed, running up one side before it vanished just shy of the perfectly domed tip.

"Open your filthy mouth," he barked.

I pressed my lips together, turning away petulantly.

He gripped my jaw, forcing my face forward.

I protested in angry moans against my sealed lips as he pried my mouth open, pushing his cock between my lips, thrusting his length into my mouth.

He hardened further, lengthening, overwhelming the already filled space. I choked, my mouth struggling around his size.

Devious satisfaction pulled his mouth into a smirk watching me struggle. He was bigger than any cock I'd put into my mouth. His head touched the back of my throat and my eyes stung as he began to move. Every punishing thrust making me gag.

He fisted a handful of my hair, forcing me to take him deeper, pressing past my limits, having his way with me.

I pressed my thighs together, feeling a powerful throb in my cunt, denying its existence.

His raw power fell over me like a spell.

This was what no man in the past had been able to give me.

Potent, undeniable domination.

His presence was so strong I buckled underneath it.

Ruarc cupped either side of my face with his hands, pistoning in and out of my mouth, fucking my tight little throat until I saw stars.

I moaned around him, feeling my own wetness soaking through layers of fabric between my legs.

"You like that," I heard him say, his voice light, almost amused as he pulled my head forward, pressing himself past the dam of my throat, making it burn.

"I've watched you in here," he said in a low voice that was almost lost to the rush of blood in my ears. "You touch yourself when you're alone. I know you're thinking of me. I know you wish your hand was my cock, making you come."

I choked and spluttered as he pulled out, catching my breath for only an instant before he began his assault again, the salty taste of his precum awakening my taste buds.

I fisted my hands in the luxe fabric of his tailored pants, pushing him back, pulling him close, holding on for dear fucking life as he fucked my mouth, the staccato sounds of his breaths edged in the husky groans of his own pleasure sent liquid fire through my veins.

Ruarc held my head in place, his hands on either side of

my face pressing tighter as he drew nearer his release. He let out a feral roar, arching his spine as he poured himself into my mouth.

He withdrew and I gasped, ready to spit him out when he fell into a crouch, pressing a hot palm over my lips, sealing them shut as his other hand wrapped around the back of my skull. "You'll take what I give you and you'll *like* it. Now *swallow*."

I gagged, a muffled burst of air against his palm as his fingers dug into my cheeks, his eyes never leaving me. My gaze narrowed on him, and I hoped he could see the depth of my hatred for him, even as I worked my throat, pretending to swallow down his bounty.

"Good girl," he praised, his hand slipping from my mouth as he rose to his feet. I spat his load on his polished leather shoes, swiping the back of my palm over my lips.

He clucked his tongue and I didn't dare raise my eyes to his level, keeping them trained on the floor as my nails dug deep half-moons in my palms.

The fabric of his pants whispered as he stuffed his cock back in, adjusting the zipper.

"As you wish," he said curtly. "If you can't respect the furniture, then you'll have none."

Without another word, he turned and walked toward the door.

Hot rage seared through me. That bastard. That fucking son of a bitch. I jumped to my feet, racing to the scattered glass on the floor to lift a loose shard the size of a dagger.

It bit into my skin as I rushed at him, a savage cry tearing from my throat as I swung at him wildly.

Ducking back as if he'd already anticipated the attack, Ruarc grabbed my arms, knocking the glass from my hand, immobilizing me with my back pressed against the floor.

"*Get in here,*" he roared.

Two men appeared in the doorway.

"Chain her up." He hissed the command to his men but his attention remained focused on me. "And then take every scrap of furniture, every *book* out of this room. Leave nothing."

I screamed in his face as the men took me from his grasp, dragging me toward the wall. I thrashed against them, fighting with every ounce of energy I had left as they shoved my bed out of the way to reveal an iron bolt in the wall, a chain hanging down to the floor with a manacle on one end.

"No!"

I knew what downstairs meant. The dungeon. My throat stung, becoming hoarse as I screamed, thrashing uselessly against them as they manacled my ankle. I ran at them, jerked back by the restraint, only making it across half the floor. It would be enough slack to reach the toilet in the bathroom, but not enough to get back to the window. Or to the door.

"You bastard!"

The two men began dragging my bed to the other side of the room, out of reach, along with absolutely everything else. I seethed, anger rippling over my flesh like a thousand tiny ants were milling just under the surface, and all the while Ruarc watched, emotionless. Withdrawn.

"*I hate you,*" I shouted at him, my voice cracking trying to maintain the volume.

His jaw ticked and he nodded. "This time, I believe you."

"What happened to your face?"

The question came from a tall man in a minotaur mask. Shirtless, his body and the uncovered half of his face gave his age away as somewhere in his late forties.

"My girl attacked me with a piece of glass after threatening to kill herself."

The statement was incredulous enough to be both a lie and the truth.

He pursed his lips, nodding like that was sometimes how these things went.

"She got you pretty good," he said.

Yeah, I'd noticed.

Her strike was too haphazard to leave a wound bad enough to need stitches, but she got me right above the mouth. The cut was still red and scabbed. Another mask choice might've hidden it, but oddly, I didn't want to hide it. I wanted to show it off. Wear it like art.

If nothing else, I wanted to leave my mark on Emily. It was only fair if she returned the favor.

A tremor of discomfort rattled through my limbs thinking about her.

She'd needed three stitches in her palm after that episode with the broken glass. My men had to sedate her to tend to her wounds properly. Not something I wanted to do. I'd have rather stitched her myself, without sedative, without anything for the pain.

Just me and her, a needle and thread.

That would teach her to defy me.

But I couldn't trust myself around her at that moment. Didn't *want* to see her.

That moment... the brief second where I thought she might jump through the crack in those bars over her window... I'd felt...

I don't know what I'd felt, but it wasn't something I *ever* wanted to feel again.

The furniture and the window were no problem. The window was fixed the same day she broke it, and the chair would be back in a week, good as new. That wasn't the point. She was trying to enrage me. To push me. To test my limits like a child.

She didn't fucking quit. She was relentless.

"I deserved it," I told the minotaur.

"Is she here?" he asked, looking around the crowded club, trying to find her amid the writhing bodies and tailored suits.

A possessive fire sparked in my chest. I bit my tongue, stopping my initial response before it came out.

*No.*

He couldn't touch her.

No one else could touch her.

She was *mine*.

The thought of her in this place, with other men looking at her or worse, another man enjoying her filled me with animalistic rage.

I cleared my throat, remembering this particular client was one of my upper tiered members. A supreme court justice I needed to keep on my good side.

"She's not here."

I turned my attention back down to the scene on the first floor of the club. Bodies, semi-clothed and naked milled around the space, some wrapped up in each other already though the night was young.

The heady musk of debauchery lingered on the air. Masked couples, throuples, and more engaged in all kinds of play as the ambient thrum of music beat through the concealed speakers, peaked by the rhythm snap of a whip on tender skin somewhere deeper into the club.

"That's too bad. Bring her next time."

I didn't say anything, lifting my nearly drained glass instead.

He took the hint, leaving with a nod.

Emily would be popular if I brought her here. New faces, *women* particularly always were. Some men got off on the idea of their woman's sexual desirability to others. I wasn't one of them.

Though, having been chained in her chambers for a couple of days now, I knew she'd be starved for activity. What would she make of my domain?

Tonight the crowd was a mixture of longtime members and a couple of recent additions. Plus ones couldn't be first-timers, they had to be previously vetted visitors. After coming up with a list of possible high-risk attendants, I curated the guest list to narrow down possible suspects.

Some members, knowing about the breach had elected not to show up on their own. As of yet, nobody had canceled their membership and I wanted to keep it that way.

The loss of one or two members, even ten wouldn't be the worst financial hit. The worst thing that was coming out of this no matter how fast it was resolved was the hit to our reputation.

Discretion was what our members paid for, more than even the experience. The black mark on our perfect record pissed me the fuck off.

I watched every passing individual below like they were a possible suspect. The club had been swept again, top to bottom for recording devices just before tonight's opening. For our guest's privacy, cameras inside the club were prohibited and I would only use them as a last resort, which meant my presence and the presence of several of my most trusted men was the only thing that might lead to finding the culprit, and stopping them before any more photos leaked online.

My thoughts coiled in on themselves with no end in sight. I gripped the ledge so tight, my knuckles turned white. My lips pressed together, tugging the scab from my skin, pulling my thoughts right back to Emily.

She had seen some of it now, the dark parts inside of me that sunlight never touched.

I was foolish to think I could strip back her layers without shedding some of my own.

An idea formed, and before I could change my mind, I

exited the club. Two men guarded the door upstairs even though the house was virtually impenetrable.

"Have her dressed and brought to me."

Silently, one of the men left.

Instead of going back to the club, I cut away, heading to my room.

The promise of her was so close, I could practically taste it. I picked a white and silver mask from my collection. Stylized to look like a crescent moon, it would cover her from her cheekbones up and curve down to cover half of her face, leaving her mouth free.

I clenched it in my grasp, gaze tracking to something else in the drawer. Grabbing it, I hurried downstairs to the foyer.

"I'm walking, get your hands off me," I heard coming from the stairway.

Strange warmth filled my chest hearing her complaints.

She and the guard appeared in the foyer, his hand grasped around her arm while she obstinately tried to get away from him.

"I thought you'd be grateful for a little freedom."

They both stopped. Shock crossed her face before it was replaced immediately with anger. Her narrowed eyes told me just how happy she was to see me, but curiosity lingered just beneath the surface of her stare as she took in the dark mask concealing most of my face, and the items in my fist.

"Whatever you brought me out for, you might as well take me back."

Her stubborn chin and the obstinate set of her jaw would've set me off if she was anyone else. But this was *her,* and she infuriated me beyond fucking measure.

Forcing me to realize she'd become more than just a woman, just my captive.

We were eye-level, she and I.

When she met my gaze, she didn't look away. She didn't blink.

Most men didn't have the balls she did.

I held the mask out to her.

"I'd like to show you something," I said, putting away the urge to demand her to do as I bid in favor of a little test.

Her brow furrowed.

"Will you come?"

Her arms crossed, face blank like I was speaking Russian.

"I have a choice now?"

"Tonight you do."

She seemed like she was mulling it over, her eyes going from the mask, back up to my face.

"If you'd prefer, I can have Josef return you to your chains."

She gave Josef a dirty look, ignoring what I said to point at the mask in my hand.

"What's that for?"

A slow smile spread across my face. I had her. I pushed the mask into her hands.

"Masks are mandatory. But clothing's optional."

"What is it you want to show me?"

I tsked her, wagging my finger back and forth. "You'll ruin the surprise."

With shaking hands she lifted the mask to her face and I stepped behind her, fastening the supple satin strands into place over the low bun knotted in her dark hair.

"Just one more thing."

There was only one way to ensure no one else touched what was mine within the walls of Delirium.

I tugged the collar from my pocket, feeding the leather strap around her neck. She put her fingers to the choker, running them over it as I fastened it into place, and latched on the matching short leash.

"There. You're perfect."

PUSHING THE DOOR OPEN, I LET HER WALK IN FIRST.

The darkened corridor concealed inner workings of the club from view, but I knew she could hear them. Their pain. Their pleasure.

She pulled gently against the leash, eager to see what she could only imagine from here.

As the corridor opened into the main atrium, I tugged her back against me, curling a hand over her shoulder to speak in her ear.

"Welcome to my wonderland."

Emily gasped, walking as though through a dream into the space.

Her steps slowed as she took in the scene in the grand atrium. Writhing bodies on low leather couches. Mouths on pierced nipples. Whips and chains and collars and floggers.

Her gaze went to the airtight woman at the center, each of her holes filled by cock, her body used beyond measure.

My little lamb didn't cower. She didn't hide. I kept a couple of steps between us so I could gauge her response; see how she took it.

I had punished her more cruelly, showed her darker and more twisted than this, but my hackles were raised. I pushed her limits all the time, but this time, she was in control. Within these walls consent was paramount and I wouldn't break the rules I forced each of my clients to follow.

In here, Emily could say no, she could say stop. She could push me away and I would let her.

My hands started to sweat. An uncharacteristic lump of anxiety forming in my throat wondering why the fuck I'd decided to bring her here.

She threw a glance in my direction.

"Where are we?"

"It's my kingdom. Politicians, CEOs, athletes, priests, anyone with heavy pockets and something to lose; I provide them experience. Discretion."

She looked over the room, her lips parted in perhaps in shock, perhaps wonder as she allowed me to lead her further into the hall.

Male gazes strayed from their night's distractions, lingering on Emily just a little too long, hungry for fresh flesh.

I growled as we passed, sending each pair flying back to where they belonged.

"*Mine*," I hissed, tightening my grip on Emily's collar, my shoulders trembling with the injection of testosterone into every muscle.

Even in the plain robe she wore, barefoot, there wasn't a woman in this room who held a candle to her and every one of them knew it.

I jerked her back.

I shouldn't have brought her here.

"It's time to leave."

She spun, grabbing the cord of the leather leash in her

hand, tugging it back. "No," she protested. "I... I want to stay."

The one cheek I could see for the covering of her mask flushed pink. She swallowed. "Show me," she urged. "Show me more."

I pried her fingers from the leash and she let me, not fighting back. Her breath caught as I trapped her hand in mine, running my thumb over her knuckles.

Was that lust in her green eyes?

My jaw tightened. I nodded, jerking my chin in the direction of the opposite corridor. "That way."

Her head swung left and right, passing the semi-private rooms filled with writhing, naked bodies. Passing one, a line of masked men, five or six, stood around a table as another man plowed a woman in pink lingerie lying on her back. They were taking turns.

In another room, a woman screamed against the Saint Andrew's Cross bolted to the wall, chained, her flesh pink from flogging, her juices running down her thighs as a man buried his face between her legs.

I led Emily up the stairs, coming to the mezzanine where she could look down from above. She put her hands on the railing, leaning over.

"What is this place?" she murmured just under her breath.

"Delirium," I replied and she nodded to herself, as if that made perfect sense, before her gaze strayed to me, the silver of her mask making her eyes brighter than they had any right to be.

She was looking at me, not with confusion or fear for once, but with something more like curiosity. Or was it understanding?

"So what do you think?"

I had never cared so much about what anyone thought in my entire miserable fucking life.

I wanted her acceptance. Her approval.

Backed into a corner with no option but to say yes, she couldn't refuse me. But here...

"I think it's..." She trailed off, leaving me on the edge of a goddamned cliff.

She shook her head. "I don't know what I think it is," she admitted, her gaze falling back to the scene below. "I've never seen or experienced anything like this."

"Most people haven't."

"Ruarc?"

I choked, my name coming from her lips enough to send a bolt of white hot flame straight through me. I wanted her to say it again.

And *again*.

"Yes?"

"Why haven't you..."

I followed her gaze to the couple engaged in passionate sex on the long couch pushed to the far wall.

"Why haven't I fucked you?" I guessed.

She nodded gravely.

My nostrils flared, unsure how to respond, because I *would* fuck her. And I really doubted she'd deny me whenever I decided to have her, but in here, she held the reins and I wouldn't take them from her, not until I dragged her back through the door.

I'd wanted her to beg me for it, I still did, but maybe this would be better. If I could have her submit to me willingly, give herself to me openly, freely, I...

My cock thickened to a hard rod against my thigh just thinking of it.

"Within the walls of Delirium, all adults must be *consenting*. At the very least, they must sign a waiver for *consensual non consent* if that is the fantasy they wish to fulfill prior to entering."

I let my words linger in the air between us, watching her reaction, the working of her jaw, the pinching of her brows.

"And you follow those rules? I mean, *in here*?"

The edge of spite was not missed in her words.

I gave her a nod.

"So if I tell you you can't touch me..."

"I won't touch you."

"And if I ask you to touch me?"

My lips parted in surprise, meeting her intense stare. "Then I will touch you, little lamb."

I wrapped the length of leash around my fist, reeling her in closer, but not touching her, not without her giving me the command.

"Are you asking?"

Her throat bobbed.

"I am."

Without another second's hesitation, I led her away from the mezzanine, down the gilded black corridor toward the rooms reserved for the most elite members.

We passed rooms filled with specialized gear and equipment, and one with a spinning table, all the way to the back. To the room not often reserved for its eye-watering fee of fifty-thousand a night.

Everything in the room was entirely replaced prior to the paying client entering. The furniture. The bedding. The chest full of every manner of toy, bondage, or accessory a person could desire.

Most clients requested special additions for this room, but as it stood, it was simple in its elegance, but not so simple that Emily didn't audibly gasp as we pushed inside.

Lush in furs, silk, gold, and crystal, everything dripped with luxury.

The sandalwood and amber aroma diffusing into the air was a favorite scent of mine, and it seemed my little lamb was a fan, too, her pupils dilating as she breathed it in.

I shut the door behind us and crowded her against it, drawing her attention back to me. Her lips parted and I felt the sudden visceral need to taste them. I couldn't remember the last time I kissed a woman, didn't see the appeal... until now.

A hum, low in my stomach, had my upper lip curling back, guarding myself against the swell of foreign emotion.

Emily's gaze traveled to my lips, her green eyes hungry but restrained, resistant to her own desire.

Did she hate herself for how I made her feel?

The bass-heavy music thrummed through the door, vibrating the warm wooden pane as I lifted her arm from her side, placing it over her head. With an award-worthy level of restraint, I ran the backs of my first two fingers down the length of her arm, to her neck, to the curve of her breast beneath her shirt. Her breathing hitched there and when I met her eyes a second time to find them still on my mouth, I gave in.

Curling my fingers around her neck, I drew her face to mine, crushing my lips to hers. I shuddered, groaning into her mouth as I kissed her. Emily let out a low whine, her fingers tangling in my hair, twisting. The pain awoke the beast sleeping deep within and I growled, prying her lips apart with my tongue, taking everything she was willing to give.

She opened for me, moaning wildly as I claimed her with my mouth, our frantic breaths mingling as heat like liquid fire charged through my blood.

Emily began unbuttoning my shirt and I gripped her wrists, breaking the kiss.

"On the bed," I ordered. "Now."

She nodded, such a good girl, and brushed past me, heading for the ornate mahogany four poster draped in swaths of lush burgundy fabric.

She sat on the edge of the bed as I popped my cufflinks and unbuttoned my shirt, taking it off along with my mask.

Emily did the same, removing her mask before sitting erect to marvel at my bare, muscled, tattooed skin as I drew nearer.

Coming up to the bed, I reached for her, lifting her hair out of the way in a clenched fist to unhook the collar around her neck and let it fall to the floor. Next, I hooked my fingers in the belt of her robe, tugging it free. She let me, lifting her hips to make it easier for me to pull it all the way off, revealing her perfect tits and nothing else save for a pair of silk panties.

She leaned back and I reached for them only to have her stop me, her hand roughly grabbing mine.

I flicked my gaze upward, my jaw clenching.

She knew I didn't like to be told no. She also knew this was the one place in the entire world I would allow it. This was a test. Would I pass it?

I waited, and her grip loosened.

"Do I have your permission?" I asked, each word a bitter pill on my tongue.

"Permission to do what?"

"Anything and *everything* I want."

The rapid rise and fall of her chest halted as she considered.

"Consensual non consent," I reminded her. "If you give it, you're *mine*. There is no 'no.' There is no 'stop.' If spoken, I won't hear those words, do you understand?"

*Please,* I thought, a mixture of shock and disgust erupting at the silent plea. I didn't beg. I didn't plead. I took what I wanted.

But this once. For her...

*Do not deny me, little lamb.*

*Do not deny yourself.*

"You have it."

My heart punched into my ribcage, sending a ricochet of primal desire racing through me, going straight to my cock.

"I need you to say it, Emily. The whole thing."

She licked her lips, the fear in her eyes so vibrant I could almost taste it.

"You have my permission," she elaborated. "To do anything and everything you want to do to me, no matter what I say. No matter what I do."

I moved forward, ready to fucking pounce.

"But," she added, the word a bullet in my gut. "I want all my furniture back. And my books. No, better books. I'll make you a list."

"Bargaining?"

She nodded astutely and a swell of pride grew in my chest.

"Done."

A flash of terror brightened her wide eyes as I tore her panties from her flesh, tearing them to ribbons as I dragged the tatters from her legs and shoved her back onto the plush covers.

I hooked her left leg over my shoulder, going to my knees on the carpet. I jerked her forward, marveling as she opened for me like a flower.

"Ruarc!" she cried out as I descended on her, dragging my tongue wickedly over her clitoris, teasing her opening with my fingers before plunging them inside her, giving her no time to adjust.

She arched into my mouth, every one of her broken moans got me harder with every pulse, every roll of her hips as she fucked herself on my tongue.

Emily writhed and whined, giving herself over to me. In seconds she was panting, making wild grabs for the back of my head as her orgasm threatened.

She shattered, coming around my fingers, gushing on my tongue with a cry that echoed off the walls. She bucked and pulsed around my fingers before attempting to seal her legs closed from the stimulation. I forced her to remain open for me, continuing my assault until, compelling her to wring every drop of pleasure from the orgasm until she was shaking, begging me to stop.

I didn't let up until her hot core unclenched, only then did I crawl over her on the bed, lifting her higher onto the pillows before wrenching her legs wider.

I covered her body with mine, sealing her parted lips with my own, swallowing her moan.

Feeling the press of my erection through my pants

against her wet cunt, she flinched back, pressing herself into the mattress.

I pushed a hand beneath her lower hips, pulling her hips up to join mine with a growl, forcing her to feel how hard she made me.

I fisted her hair and jerked her head up, countering the hard gesture with a deep sensual kiss. Agitated moans started in her throat.

She had jagged edges, hard and rough like mine. That sting of pain intensified the pleasure. Made her feel it deeper, more keenly.

I parted our lips, hovering just the hair's breadth away from her. Her eyes flickered open, searching mine for the reason why I stopped. I ran a finger down her neck dipping it into the notch at its base, then I enclosed it in my palm and clenched.

Her eyes turned to hot pools of lust.

I released her hip, snaking my hand between us to her clit, working her flesh in long, focused caresses, before firmly tapping it with my flattened fingers. She jerked at the sudden jolt.

Tightening my hand on her neck, I plunged two fingers into her. She moaned, bucking and riding as I finger fucked her. Just before her orgasm, I loosened my fingers, letting a deep inhale of oxygen into her lungs as it overcame her. She shuddered violently, her cunt convulsing around my fingers.

It was a marvel, watching her come undone for me. I'd never tire of it.

Her unfocused eyes blinked, long lashes batting against the ridge of her arched brows. Fuck.

I couldn't wait. Not another fucking second.

The fierce urge to claim her seized my throat as I unbuckled my belt and snapped it free of the loops, tossing it to the floor. Emily helped me work my pants low enough to free my cock, her movements just as frantic as my own.

For the briefest moment, I considered a condom. I used one with every woman I'd ever fucked, but I couldn't imagine purposefully putting anything between my cock and that sweet, sweet cunt.

My patience fully spent, I took her in one smooth thrust.

She cried out in surprise, and I cursed, her tight channel choking me. I couldn't be slow. Withdrawing, I pistoned into her, grabbing her throat as I savaged her pussy. I grunted, her pulse pounding against my fingers as I fucked her. Her legs wrapped around me, keeping me close. She wanted this. Needed it.

Emily clawed at my arms and shoulders, desperately searching for something to hold onto as I gave her the ride of her fucking life. I bent, drawing one of her pebbled nipples into my mouth, keeping up the slaughtering pace between her thighs. I rolled her nipple over my tongue, again and again, flat and flick, flat and flick, corralling her to orgasm as rapidly as her gorgeous cunt was prodding me to mine.

When her moans turned short and her body began to clench around me, when her fingernails in my forearms were at the point of drawing blood, I bit her nipple, throwing her from the cliff she clung to.

She gushed on my cock and I roared, coming powerfully into her, milking myself dry in her pussy.

Our breaths came in heavy pants as I kept myself anchored in her pussy until every drop of me was deposited inside. Only then did I pull out, rolling onto the bed next to her, sated, but not for long. Already, I was ravenous to have her again.

Unconsciously, I found myself reaching for her, wrapping a possessive hand around the top of her thigh, caressing her warm skin.

She turned to me, watching me with guarded emotion in her eyes as she ran her fingertips over the ink on my chest, and up my neck, to my jaw, my lips. She gently touched the scab forming there. The one she gave me.

"I'm sorry about this, by the way," she said.

"No, you're not."

"You're right," she said, her lips quirking up on one side in a cheeky smirk. "I'm not."

## 18

### EMILY

I pressed my face into the pillow, the last of my sleep draining away as I breathed in the scent that was unmistakably Ruarc.

Vignettes of the previous night came filtering into my semi-conscious thoughts, making my thighs clench and a deep ache form low in my belly. The echoes of Ruarc's monstrous cock pounding into me still remained, making little aftershocks shiver up my back and down my arms.

The soft sheets and comforter of the bed cradled me as I stubbornly refused to open my eyes.

Groping my arm across the bed, I expected to feel him but there was nothing. Cracking my eyes open as wide as they would go, I squinted across the room.

Curiosity piqued, I bid my heavy eyelids to open wider, taking in the foreign room. Vaguely, I remembered leaving Delirium. I'd been, well, delirious... as Ruarc guided me back through the throng of naked bodies and into the main house, up the stairs, and into this room.

*His* room.

My eyes adjusted, seeing more in the light of day than the darkness of the previous night had allowed.

The bed was larger than a king, the sheets a shimmering black silk softer than anything I'd ever touched in my life.

The walls were a deep slate gray, but the upholstery on the bed, sofas, and the curtains were in shades of navy and midnight black. I rolled onto my back, in awe at the elaborately molded and carved ceiling and the twisted chandelier that seemed to be welded from wrought iron to look like a gnarled thorn bush.

The mantle over the tall fireplace held fine vases and other sculpted art. The light was off, letting dawn light filter in the room, giving it a warm glow at odds with the vibe of its owner.

I sat up, feeling oddly bereft as I ran my hand over the vacant silk covered pillow next to my own.

Was it wrong to wish he was there?

Since I'd arrived here, this gothic estate felt like an elegant prison. A lavish imposing structure that would bite, chew, and swallow if I dared attempt to escape it.

It suited its owner.

But now, it felt less like a prison and more like...

Not a home, but a dwelling at the very least. A place where I resided. Like a rented villa. One you couldn't leave.

I lacked the correct words for the twisted, trusting, yet apprehensive relationship between me and this place. Between me and the man who ruled it.

Ruarc had me twice more in this bed before both of us succumbed to exhaustion, my pussy so beaten, so thoroughly destroyed that I doubted I'd be able to sit properly for a few days. Add to that the bruises on my ass from his death grip as he pummeled into me from behind and yes... sitting was decidedly uncomfortable. I twisted, slipping from the sheets to place my feet on the warm floor and stand on wobbly legs.

I walked around the room, my feet padding over soft, almost velvety carpet, and polished hardwood. Last night, he'd been something other than the beast I'd grown to expect. He was still that, but he was more.

He'd given me a choice and I chose him. Something about having the power to say no and forfeiting it, giving it to him willingly...

It felt so right in its absolute wrongness.

Ruarc showed me he could be cruel. Terrifying. *Monstrous.*

But he'd also shown me thoughtfulness. That beneath the shadows cloaking his soul in a blanket of impenetrable darkness, he possessed the ability to feel.

Biting my lip, I padded to his bedroom door, hesitating before trying the handle. It opened with one turn of the smooth filigreed handle. My lips popped open as I pulled the door inward, peering out into the hall.

On this level of the house, there were rows of doors to either side of me and stairs leading both to the upper and lower floors. I pushed a foot out before remembering I was completely fucking naked. Right.

Quietly, I twisted the handle, pushing the door back until I heard the solemn *click* of the latch taking.

Rushing back across the floor, I used the fancy toilet in his massive bathroom before tip-toeing beneath the archway that opened to his massive walk-in. In the middle of the closet was a glass-topped console with drawers running down its height. Underneath the glass was a collection of blindingly bright watches nestled in soft fabric.

Heading for the racks instead, I ran my hand over the line of hanging button-down shirts, plucking one from its hanger and slipping it on.

I clenched my teeth against the smile trying to worm its way onto my lips, smoothing the shirt over my body. It reached well past the apex of my thighs, covering the bits that needed covering, rendering the need for pants obsolete. I opened one of the drawers in a smaller unit set in the wall, finding ties and silk napkins and little slips of cloth. I used one to bind my hair into a knot at the base of my neck, getting it out of my face.

I PEERED OUT INTO THE HALL AGAIN, SURVEYING THE CEILING FOR cameras.

Ruarc told me the entire house was filled with them. He told me I would never get out, locked door or no.

The worst part was I believed him.

No, the worst part was that even though I believed him, I still wanted to try.

Ruarc was steadfast in his principles.

Depending on what I did, how I acted, I was either punished or rewarded.

Either way, *something* happened and the drudgery of my identical passing days was finally broken.

What was another couple of nights down in the basement if that was what he wanted to give me for my insolence? I could take it. Though I doubted I'd ever see the inside of that stone cell again.

Every time I pushed him, his limit moved.

He gave me that little bit more of an allowance.

Creeping from his bedroom, I found my way to the staircase and padded down, running my hand along the smooth wood of the banister.

I took in the beauty of the mansion.

Every other time I had been outside of the basement, or my room upstairs, I didn't really have a lot of time to look around.

Eventually, I came to the foyer at the foot of the stairs where the front door loomed across a vacant expanse of parquet floor.

My heart beat uncomfortably hard and out of rhythm as I clutched the banister.

*Just a little more.*

I wanted to see just a little more before I left.

I recognized the entry to Delirium from the night before, and across from me in the other direction, the tucked away garage entrance. But there were other hallways branching off from the main atrium like veins from a heart.

Picking one at random, I wandered through a tall archway and went down a couple of steps into a beautifully furnished living area. I wandered through it, running my fingers over the lacquered surface of a grand piano before pushing through to an adjacent hallway.

The hall opened up further down into what looked like a grand library. A thrill went through me, my steps picking up pace before stopping suddenly.

A familiar voice echoed from the room to my right.

I slipped into the space, finding the man standing at open glass French doors with his back to me, talking on his phone. Wind blew the wispy curtains inward, making them billow around Nixon like restless wraiths.

"...then we just have to go higher on body disposal," he said into the receiver.

I froze, not wanting him to hear me.

"What do you mean it can't get higher?" he asked.

*Body disposal?*

If he was talking about body disposal then... was he talking to my Dad?

A ball formed in my throat.

"Tell him... then tell him again," he was saying. "He doesn't have choices, why don't you understand that? You have the bargaining power here, not him. He needs you, not the other way around."

Nixon paused and his hand came up to his face, rubbing over his eyes. His shoulders tensed. Rage rippled through his body.

"He's not going to—look, I'll make sure he doesn't," he said. "Just do it, old man or I'll see to her end myself."

He ended the call.

I backed away, but Nixon turned around on a dime, his cold gaze locking on me, registering surprise before suspicion took hold.

"How the hell did you get out of your room?"

I lifted my chin, holding my ground. "Ruarc left the door open."

Apparently, that wasn't the right answer.

Nixon came at me, toppling a tall side table in his haste, spurring me to run. He chased me, catching a handful of my hair to yank me to a shrieking stop.

"What? Did you think you were going to escape?" he taunted, releasing my hair in favor of twisting my arm up behind my back with a firm grip on my wrist. He pushed me, walking fast enough that I lost my footing trying to keep pace.

"What are you doing?" I hissed, struggling against his hold. "Let me go. I wasn't doing anything!"

"Why'd you run, then, *huh*?"

I winced at the pain in my shoulder. "Because you were *fucking chasing me*, asshole."

"Move!"

He walked us back into the foyer.

"Nixon."

He stopped cold. I looked around for the source of the voice. Ruarc was on the stairs, looking down at us, his head cocked to one side, eyes blazing on Nixon with the wrath of a thousand suns.

"She got out. I found her by——"

"Release her immediately."

"Ruarc?"

"*Now*, Nix," he growled, his presence thundering like a fucking hurricane, making me recoil back from the violence in his eyes.

Nixon let go of my arm and I stumbled forward, clutching it to my chest, wincing at the sharp ache in my shoulder.

"She almost escaped. If I hadn't——"

Ruarc's gaze tracked to me. "Did she?"

I didn't give an answer, shuffling away from Nixon, putting myself an equal distance between the two men.

"Because I was tracking her every move on the cameras just now. She had a wide open opportunity to walk out that front door," he pointed to it, stabbing his fingers through the air like a blade. "And she didn't."

The men stared at each other, the air between them heavy with tension.

"Ruarc, you can't trust—"

"Emily is free to move about the house as she pleases," Ruarc said, seeming to make the decision on the spot, his words carving a hollow in my gut.

Nixon was first to drop his eyes, nodding. "As you wish," he muttered, stalking away, a black cloud following in his wake.

"Where *were* you going?" Ruarc asked me when we were alone, coming the rest of the way down the stairs to meet me in the foyer. My skin pricked, singing with anticipation as he drew my arm away from my chest into his hands, checking for injury.

He was shirtless, wearing nothing but loose pants hanging low over his hips. He'd been home all this time? Watching me from the camera feed. So, his not being there this morning was a staged test to see if I'd try escaping.

...and I'd passed his test.

"What if I did intend to leave?" I asked.

He smirked, looking younger than I'd ever seen him. Playful, almost.

His hard, sharp features softened as he languidly massaged my shoulder, his demeanor so relaxed it was hard not to feel at ease.

"You wouldn't have," he argued, that smirk turning from cute to infuriating in the breath of a single second.

*Oh yeah? Wanna bet?*

I gently pulled my arm from Ruarc's grasp, my throat dry.

"So, where were you going?"

"I was looking for you," I admitted, realizing it for the

first time myself. I'd gone down that hallway under the guise of exploring, but really, around every bend, in every room, I'd been hoping to find him.

"You picked Zegna," he said, his tone almost appreciative, as he rolled the shirt's fabric between his fingers. Did I? I thought I just picked a shirt. Something told me that I'd have a stroke if he told me how much it cost.

"Do all your shirts have names?"

Ruarc laughed before his eyes cut sharply to mine, panicked as if the sound coming from his own mouth startled him. His jaw clenched tight, cheekbones flexing as he cleared his throat.

"It looks better on you than on me," he said, eyeing me appreciatively. "Now, go back upstairs. I'll bring you something to eat."

He pushed a stray lock of my hair back from my face before brushing past me to stroll down a narrower hallway I had to assume led to a kitchen.

My lip caught between my teeth, watching him go. It was jarring sometimes when he was warm. Making me think unsafe thoughts. Treacherous things like maybe he was just misunderstood. Maybe he wasn't so bad. Maybe... maybe I could love him. Each thought like a path leading to an ever darker part of a gnarled forest. If I wasn't careful, I'd get lost, never able to find my way back.

And yet I knew in the marrow of my bones that Ruarc was the most dangerous thing in the room, and with him, I'd never be more safe.

How fucked up was that?

Once the sound of Ruarc's footfalls faded from earshot, I rushed to the front door, my breaths unsteady as I shakily threw both wide open to the day. Sunlight bathed me in its warm glow and I shut my eyes, allowing it to paint the backs of my eyelids in gold.

I blinked into the brightness of the early afternoon, staring my freedom dead in the eye. Down at the bottom of the grand staircase there was a gravel drive, it curved around the front of the gothic mansion and spread out in two directions, winding out into the trees toward the road.

A cloud passed over the sun, suffusing the warm glow of the sun into a cold hue. I wavered, flinching back from the sudden chill in the air. He would only drag me back...

With shaking hands, I stepped back. Back again. And shut the heavy doors, uncaring that the sound boomed through the house.

Hot tears pooled in my eyes and I blinked them back as I ran back up the stairs, down the long hall, up onto the next floor and straight to my bedroom.

I buried myself beneath the covers, shivering despite their warmth.

By the time Ruarc came in, a tray balanced in his hands, the shaking had stopped, replaced by a ravenous hunger growling in the pit of my stomach like a starved animal.

He slid the tray onto the covers next to me.

On it there were two cups of coffee but one plate of food. Pancakes, with bacon and sunny side up eggs.

In a shot glass next to the tall glass of orange juice was one small white pill.

"What is that?" I asked, though I thought I might already know.

"It's... just in case."

"An emergency contraceptive?"

I shivered at the reminder of him inside of me.

He nodded. "If you're not avoiding it, you're asking for

it. Take this and then we'll start you on a regular course of pills tomorrow."

The thought of possibly carrying his child bent my mind out of shape. I took the pill, throwing it to the back of my throat, chasing it down with hot coffee. Thank fuck one of us was thinking clearly. But the promise of *more* between the lines of what he said made my core tighten.

A regular course of pills.

I'd only need that if...

I cleared my throat. "Are you leaving?"

"Not yet," he said, his eyes narrowing on me. "Why?"

I watched him take a sip of his coffee. A simple, totally benign action that every single adult human being on this earth did, and yet somehow he did it in a way that was superior. Like a king. Or a fucking *god*.

*I am so fucked.*

It was like learning who someone was in reverse. Getting all the bad, all the dirty, all the ugly, out of the way before glimpsing all the things that were pure and true and *good*.

Like the fact that he liked cream in his coffee. Or that he had a dimple in his right cheek when he smiled.

"What is it?" he pressed, setting his coffee back down on the tray while I picked at a piece of bacon.

"I think I heard something I wasn't supposed to hear today."

A vein in his temple jumped. He pushed the tray closer to me.

"Eat something."

I obediently ate a forkful of pancakes drenched in syrup.

"How long has Nixon worked here?"

"He doesn't work here as much as he works for me," he

answered, his eyes watching me intently over the rim of his coffee cup. "Why?"

I looked down, using the plate to distract me. I split one of the strips of bacon, biting into it.

"When I ran into him he was on a phone call. I heard some of it."

I hazarded a look up at his face, which was still calm so I kept going.

"He was talking about body disposal."

"He would be. Coordinating that is one of his duties."

Look at me, having a perfectly normal conversation with a man who had 'body disposal' on his resume right next to 'stalker' and 'sadist.'

I nodded, coughing to get control of a rogue laugh at the ridiculousness of it all.

"He was arguing about the cost of body disposal. I think he might've been talking to my dad."

His stubbled jaw clenched almost imperceptibly as he lowered his cup from his mouth.

"You learned all that from what? Hearing half a conversation?"

I swallowed, putting down my fork.

"I said I *thought* I heard something I wasn't supposed to hear. I'm telling you just in case you know more about it. I don't want my dad to get hurt."

His jaw clenched harder now, its already sharp line firming even further. There was something there. He wasn't giving anything away, and his suspicion was clear, but there was something he wasn't saying to me.

"What did your father tell you about the disposal service he offered us?"

"Nothing," I answered truthfully. "I found out what he

was doing, what you were doing by mistake, that night I ran into you in the basement. If he had it his way, I still wouldn't know."

"I see. So then you have no idea what you might or might not have overheard during Nixon's call."

I rolled my eyes. He was right, I didn't know the bulk of what he did or what he talked about with my dad, or what Nixon was talking about on the phone; but I knew what I heard. I knew for a fact that he brought bodies to my father to process off the books. I knew that much. I wasn't in the know, but I wasn't clueless either.

"You can ask him if you want. He said that the cost needed to be higher, that he–my dad–had the power or something like that."

Ruarc's expression went blank, a mask pulled over any emotion he might've been feeling just under the surface.

"He's my right-hand man, he tells me everything." His tongue was sharp, dressing me down with his eyes. "If you want to make claims like that, you better have the proof to back it up."

I bristled at the harsh edge to his words, the meager amount of food I'd manage to ingest souring in my gut.

"Forget I said anything. I just... thought you should know."

His lips flattened and he sucked his cheeks in, emphasizing his already sky-high cheekbones.

"There are things you don't know or understand about me or my business, Emily, and it would benefit us both if you remained ignorant of them. Don't get involved."

"Okay," I almost snapped, hating how he was talking to me like I was some naive child who wouldn't have a chance of understanding him or the violent things he did. "I just thought the conversation was weird and maybe you should know. Don't believe me, I don't really care. I don't have proof, like you said. Ask Nixon. Or better yet, ask my dad. That's who I think he was talking to anyway."

He discarded his empty coffee cup on the tray with a clatter, pushing tattooed fingers through his dark hair.

His silence was worse than when he spoke.

"Do you have any more intel for me? Conversations you weren't supposed to hear? Things you weren't supposed to see?" he asked. I ignored the sarcastic edge in his voice, sipping my quickly cooling coffee before responding.

"No. But if you're taking requests, any chance I could get my hands on a phone?"

"No."

His answer was so flat, I almost laughed.

"Thought so. Can't blame a shooter for shooting," I said, shrugging. I looked up, spotting the smallest smirk on his face.

"This house has three libraries. You'll die before you read every available book. If you're bored, start there."

"About that. Any chance you could order something that was published in this century, this decade would be even better. Something... *spicy*."

His smirk grew, he smiled and then he laughed.

Warmth exploded in my chest. I couldn't explain how absurdly happy it made me that I could make him laugh. It disarmed me, presenting an ordinary, approachable version of himself I never knew I'd be able to access. His handsome features became beautiful when he smiled. He brushed his hair back.

"Am I not enough for you?"

It was my turn to laugh and shrug. "I need something to keep me company when you leave me for days at a time."

"*Hmmm,*" he purred, the treble of his tone making my skin prickle. "Suppose I'll need to rearrange my schedule then."

He rose, stretching, before heading to the door.

"Was that a yes?"

"Yes, little lamb, I'll order your filthy books."

Ruarc moved to close the door behind him, but then released the handle, leaving it open.

# 19

## RUARC

"I'm sorry, they do what?"

Emily laughed, running her hand over my chest.

"*Leak*. Like the body is sixty percent fluid, right?"

"But they're dead. Why would they leak? Doesn't it all harden in there, or something?"

"They leak *because* they're dead," she explained. My hand ran through her hair as we lounged under the covers. I could have sworn we were talking about something else before this. How exactly had we come to leaking corpses?

"Emily, that is disgusting."

"I thought so too, in the beginning. After a while, it's very... you know. Normal. I mean, I don't think I've dealt with any more feces or urine than the average mother or sanitation worker," she said. I felt her shoulders shrug, using the most clinical terms to refer to human waste.

"So what do you have to do? Drain them?"

Generally, I got rid of them *before* they could start decomposing. She shifted on my chest, getting comfortable, tucking herself under my arm.

"Kind of. It's called aspiration. Getting all the fluid out or at least most of what's in there. It really only matters if the body is going to be displayed or stored for any amount of time. At some point, you just stick a diaper on them."

"You're fucking with me."

She tilted her face up to look at mine. There was something catlike about her. It was the green eyes and the sharp eyebrows, her small nose and plush lips. It was that smirk she had on her face when she told me shit like this that she knew grossed me out.

"The leakage is involuntary and that region of the body has a number of... openings, so it's just practical. Sometimes we plug them."

"Stop it."

"It's not often that we've had to do that. Just sometimes. There are those bodies that just don't stop."

"Emily."

"H*m?*"

"That's the most disgusting thing I've heard in my life."

She giggled, pressing her face into my chest.

"Well, someone has to do it."

She had a point. It was because of people like her and her father that I was able to quickly and efficiently dispose of bodies that didn't need to be found. Getting to spare myself from the knowledge that dead bodies leaked and purged liquid seemed a bonus.

The stuff she'd shared in the last ten minutes alone would've made a weaker man ill. I'd never met anybody so comfortable in such a dark, morbid topic. Imagining her working with the dead. Cutting them, draining them, painting them...

I started to wonder if I shouldn't be more afraid of her than she was of me.

"Can't imagine it was your dream job, though," I edged the statement in a question, leaving her room to respond, absently trying to remember the last time I talked like this with another person. Not giving orders or going over the merits of shibari versus traditional bondage...

I couldn't remember.

"You'd be surprised." She laughed.

"How so?"

There was a pause before she spoke again.

"It was what my mother did. She opened the mortuary. I was always around that stuff so it never scared me, and after she died, I became sort of obsessed. I read all her anatomy books, the ones about embalming, all of it.

"I just needed a way to connect with her, I think. So, in a way I guess it was my dream job. At least for as long as I can remember. Was this yours? Doing whatever it is you do?"

I couldn't say that it was.

For the first ten years of my life, there was nothing I wanted besides a safe place to sleep at night. One where I couldn't overhear the things being done to my mother in the next room. There were so many nights I wished I could stick my fingers into my ears deep enough to make myself go deaf, just so I wouldn't hear it anymore.

I considered her question, but I barely thought of the future back then. I didn't have the presence of mind to think about whether I wanted to be an astronaut or the President of the United States. I just wanted to get to tomorrow.

Once Thane chose me, it was natural that I took over from him. It wasn't my dream initially but it became that. It became my path and my duty so I didn't question it. It offered safety, not just from scum like the johns mom fucked, but from anyone who might dare try to harm me or take what I'd rightfully earned.

I was the king and this was my throne.

"It was a succession," I replied finally. "Didn't really have a choice."

I didn't. Not really. But if I had I would've chosen this for myself anyway.

I left out the details telling her the simple facts of my trade. She knew the broad strokes of who I was and what I did, enough to have an idea.

We talked a little while longer until she stopped responding, falling asleep in my arms.

I never shared my bed with anybody.

My fingers ran through her hair, strands of black silk that hung around her face. She was particularly beautiful when she was like this. Calm, comfortable, and not telling me the gritty details of body decomposition.

She didn't have any secrets from me. She didn't have a reason to lie to me either. Tension stiffened my muscles remembering what she told me about Nixon. The quiet serenity of my sanctuary was broken by my thoughts.

I'd known this woman for mere weeks, a pitiful fraction compared to how long I'd known Nixon. There was over a decade of trust and brotherhood between us. I would never choose a woman over him. I couldn't because no woman worthy enough existed. My words felt hollow feeling Emily's warm body rising and falling against mine.

She wouldn't say something like that for no reason. Nixon didn't like her, and she had no reason to like him, but she did care for her father, which lent credence to her admission.

...making it impossible for me to completely ignore.

I slipped carefully out from next to her making sure she didn't wake up.

It was 11 o'clock, he should still be awake.

I got dressed quickly and went down to the garage, taking my Aston Martin to speed up the road to the mortuary. It was nothing personal. If the undertaker stopped being an efficient, clean way to get rid of bodies, then I had to do something about it. I didn't want to think about what that meant if Nixon was involved, but it needed sorting.

I'd barely slept since Emily told me what she overheard, regardless of whether I actually believed there was any truth to it.

The lights in the mortuary were off but the lights in the house wedged off to the right of the property between the trees were on. I banged on the front door, waiting for him to answer.

The door opened and he halted, seeing me. The color drained from his face and his mouth fell open. In a second, he crumpled, falling to his knees.

"You said you wouldn't hurt her."

"What?"

"Where is she?"

"Calm down. She's not here. Your daughter's fine."

...couldn't say the same for her pussy, but that was another matter.

"Where is she? Where did you take her?"

My annoyance peaked. I wasn't sure how he worked my last nerve, but his daughter had managed to work her way under my skin and live there since we'd met. I didn't have the energy for his dramatics.

"I'm not here to talk about Emily."

His bottom lip shook but he dragged himself back up to his feet.

"If you hurt her—"

"What are you gonna do? If I hurt her and brought back her body, ready for the oven, what would you do?"

His face clouded over again. Yeah, that was what I thought. He didn't have leveraging power here, I did. I wasn't going to hurt Emily. But if he thought I was going to, that would make him more amenable.

"Let's keep the disruptions to a minimum and maybe one day I'll send her back to you."

"One day?"

I said the words without thinking. I had no immediate or future plans to say goodbye to Emily.

I liked having her around the house.

I liked talking to her.

I liked fucking her more than I ever liked anything else in my miserable life.

And she wasn't actively trying to run anymore. There hadn't been a locked door to stop her in days. Nearly a week now. But she was still a prisoner. Still trapped. Not a fully willing participant of my twisted devotion.

The hair on the back of my neck prickled as I beat the intrusive thoughts back.

"Promise me you're not going to hurt her," the undertaker demanded.

If I ever hurt her, it was because she enjoyed it.

"She'll be safe as long as you cooperate," I deadpanned, finished with this arm of the conversation.

"I got rid of the boyfriend's body," he said.

That loser was the furthest thing from my thoughts and I didn't appreciate the reminder.

I hadn't thought about the guy since I'd told Emily he was dead. Come to think of it, Emily hadn't brought him up either.

"When did you last see Nixon?"

"Nixon?" he asked. His eyes became comically large, bugging out of his head pretending not to know what I was talking about. Or maybe I was overthinking it.

No. I was never wrong.

"Every second of my time that you waste is a second you won't get back with her," I warned.

"I…" He faltered. "He's only been here once."

Ice ran down my spine.

"When?" I demanded. He shrugged.

"It was a while ago. I don't know. He was alone."

"Three days ago, on the phone, what did he tell you?"

His eyes shifted until he broke eye contact completely.

"He didn't say anything. He just wanted," he sighed. He was stalling. Hesitating. There was something there, he was just afraid to say it. Trying to make up something else that would fit the narrative.

*Fuck, Nixon, what did you do?*

There was history with Nixon but Emily owed me nothing. She had nothing to gain by sharing what she heard.

I slammed my fist into the doorframe.

"What did he tell you?"

Snow jumped, his will crumbling like a piece of burnt toast.

"He wanted more money."

"From you?"

"From *you*," he countered. "He wanted me to ask for more money."

He was staring at the ground, showing me the top of his head.

The realization was slow, taking a while to settle in. Like acid eating away at open flesh.

"When did he start asking for a cut?"

The undertaker's eyes shifted. "Please..."

"Answer me."

"S-since the beginning. It was his idea."

Shadow darkened all the interactions I had had with Nixon since the first fee hike request came. It was slow, creeping, that bitter taste of betrayal as it coated my tongue.

"You didn't make the requests for your own greed," I said, more a statement than a question.

"Please," he tried again. "Mr. Monroe... he's threatened Emily. He said if I didn't push for a higher increase in the fee he'd—"

I lifted my hand to stop him right fucking there.

He. Threatened. Emily.

I blinked, trying to keep composure despite the column of fire rapidly growing in my core.

"You'll protect her from him, won't you? I swear I'll get rid of as many corpses as you need. I'll even take a lower fee, just... she's my only child..."

The betrayal hung heavier now. It'd seeped into my muscles, making me want to crawl out of my own skin.

"He will not harm Emily."

It was the only promise I could make as I turned to leave.

"Wait, what are you going to do?" he called after me.

To Nixon? I didn't know yet.

To him? Nothing.

To Emily... I didn't want to think about it. I'd taken her because of the undertaker's greed, to teach *him* a lesson that wasn't his to learn. My right to keep her just turned to dust, seeping between my fingers.

"You don't report to Nixon anymore. Only to me. Do you understand?"

"I do."

A venomous shudder rolled down my spine.

"And my daughter?" he called, louder now, realizing what I'd just realized a moment ago. That I no longer had a legitimate reason to keep her.

I ignored him, my feet heavy in my boots as I stormed back to the car.

Nixon couldn't get away with this.

If he did, it would send shocks of dissent through the ranks of my other men. A king dealt with insubordination swiftly.

My mind rattled, still struggling with the truth.

*Don't get involved.*

Unlike the others, I'd let Nixon in. It wasn't only orders and payment with him. I talked to him about things I'd never spoken of with any other people on this planet. I talked to him about Emily. Considered him the closest thing to family I had left.

I looked out in the direction of Emily's cabin, not able to see it in the dark. For a while now, keeping her had nothing to do with keeping her father in line. My stomach sank, reckoning with the next hard revelation. Cold desolation hit. My hands idly held the steering wheel, unable to move.

Dark thoughts swirled, vying for attention from the furthest recesses of my mind. If Nixon could betray me like this, it was only a matter of time before Emily would do the same. Before I got so twisted up in her, with her, that pulling her roots would hurt me just as badly. Or worse.

*Don't get involved.*

*Don't get involved.*

*Don't get involved.*

This was what I'd earned myself for breaking the rules.

There was only one solution.

They both had to go.

## 20

---

### RUARC

I'd never been to Nixon's apartment.

I had to call back to the house to get the address from the security staff, and parking the car on the side of the road outside his building felt like arriving at a stranger's home.

Unsettling in more than one way.

I'd never even thought about coming here. Over a decade of working together, of friendship, and I'd never seen this building.

Granted, he hadn't lived in this building the entire time we'd worked together. He just moved into this place a few years back. And he spent so much time working for me, in my home, that he had a room perpetually made up there for his use whenever he should need it.

To my knowledge, he used it often.

Nixon called me 'brother' and yet I didn't even know where he laid his head most nights.

I took the stairs to the top floor of the lavish condo

building, a ball of iron in my gut. I needed to draw it out, use the exertion to clear my mind before I got to his suite.

The penthouse.

I paid him well. Always had. But perhaps not penthouse condo *well*. Not in this area of the city. Where else was he skimming off the top?

Why couldn't he have asked for more. For him, I would have given it freely.

I had waited five years before I wore the crown. It had been that long with Nixon already. I had been in his shoes and succession wasn't always so cut and dry. It was certain, but only as certain as the king's life. An accident killed Frank. If that hadn't happened, I would still be in Nixon's position.

Did he wish me dead? Did he think I'd had enough time sitting on the throne at the Monroe Estate?

Did he fancy it his turn?

I was getting ahead of myself.

I needed proof. Something more than words from an old man and clever girl.

Nixon's door had been left unlocked after the cops designated it a *scene of a crime*.

I organized the arrest, wanting him out of the way, and without warning.

He was too much of a flight risk to allow free rein and if he was compromised, it was hard to say how many of my other men were too.

He had to be cut off completely.

I pushed into the condo, feeling slow where I used to feel sharp. Sluggish.

When Thane died I remembered losing hours daily, just staring into space, blank. His loss had carved the hole in my chest just a little wider. Made the edges jagged again after years spent smoothing them into something sufferable.

When the empty feeling wasn't there, dragging me down like the bony fingers of a skeleton from the grave, there was anger. Red-hot, it burned in my chest, giving me a hair-trigger temper that I'd spent a decade learning to control.

The emptiness happened when my mom left, too. Once I came to terms with the fact she'd never return.

This felt like that.

Like Nixon was dead. Like I was fucking burying him.

A chill ran over my skin as I looked around the open living room and kitchen area.

It was sparsely decorated, and furnished with simple, elegant dark wooden pieces and leather furniture. Even in that austerity, I could feel him, see his touch in the orientation of the TV remote, tucked between two couch cushions right next to where he probably liked to sit.

All those years of friendship, brotherhood and I felt like I was crossing a line entering into his space without his knowledge.

I tightened up, determined not to let the familiarity that I had with him cloud my judgment. Proof would be the final nail in the coffin but thinking about finding what I looked for made me want to shed my skin like a snake.

A lurking uncertainty still tingled around my ears. I was trained to be ready for the worst and so I was, at all times. It's what had made me the feared and respected king of a multi-statewide crime syndicate.

I found my feet carrying me into the kitchen instead of somewhere more obvious. I was stalling.

In the sink, there was an empty mug. On the marble countertop, a full pot of coffee. Cold and untouched.

He was in here when they came to get them.

I walked out of the kitchen past a couple of bedrooms, finding the biggest one, the master. Pushing in, my pulse thudded in my ears. A brown leather bag lay on the bed. Next to it facedown was his phone.

I picked the phone up, finding it code-locked. This was his personal phone, the one he always used. If *I* was doing something I wasn't supposed to be doing, I would have a secondary phone. I didn't approve of it, but if that was his game, I hoped he was at least playing it smart.

I picked up the bag, emptying its contents onto the bed and sure enough, another phone fell out of its depths.

His burner. An older flip model cell.

I went directly to the messages, seeing chats with only about five different people. None of the phone numbers were saved, but a quick search of the term *body* turned up the chat he had with the undertaker.

Seeing the words he typed, and phone calls he made hardened his betrayal into crystalline fact. Listening to the most recent voicemail from one Gerard Snow just cemented it.

*Don't. Get. Involved.*

I never should've trusted him. Never should've...

*Fuck.*

Rage simmered over me, raising the small hairs on my arms, my neck, making my breaths come so hard and heavy it was a fucking marvel they didn't smoke.

I searched the other chats, scrolling furiously to see what else he had done. Wanting to flay the open wound of his betrayal wider, get all the cutting done at once.

Satisfied that I'd examined everything to be seen in the ancient mobile, I tossed it to the feather down comforter and rifled through the other items from the bag

A white sheet printed with lines of small text caught my eye. It was folded tight, small. One of those electronic manual leaflets. I picked it up, about to throw it in the trash can by the wall when I saw the box resting there atop the pile of receipts and bottle caps.

The words *wireless Wi-Fi camera* were printed in prominent black letters along its side, striking me like a slap to the face. I snatched the box from the trash bin, wondering how long it'd been there.

Reducing myself to a fucking dumpster diver, I fingered through the papers, finding a receipt for the camera not far down into the pile. It was bought weeks ago. Over a month.

The breach at Delirium.

No.

He wouldn't.

I fought not to see it all coming together.

The pictures leaked online. The security breach.

It had to be someone who frequented the club. I thought it was a client, but why not the muscle? Nix had free rein in there. He came and went as he pleased, some nights as the hired muscle when we needed an extra man, other nights just to walk through, being my eyes and ears, representing my interests. Showing my patrons that though I wasn't there myself, my eyes were everywhere. All seeing.

I crushed the box between my fingers.

The next hour passed in a blur. I turned his apartment upside down looking for more. Footage, notes, fucking anything that would implicate him.

There was no more room for denial. Now that the ship

was going down, I would make sure it sunk into an abyss deeper than Mariana trench.

My feet dragged, weary by the time I'd had my way with every pillow, every drawer, every nook and cranny.

I jammed the elevator button, Nix's computer tucked under one arm for processing. The whole thing was fucking decrypted, way beyond my skill to unravel.

My jaw clenched so tightly I could hear the protesting of my own teeth as I waited in the vacant corridor as the elevator soared up all thirty floors.

Why, Nix?

*Why?*

Fucking bastard.

He made this choice for me.

He acted, knowing the consequences.

His fault. *His fucking fault.* Not mine.

It had happened once when Thane was alive and he dealt the killing blow himself. I remembered it clearly. Thane pulling me out of bed, dragging me to the front foyer, where one of his confidants, a man named Toby, knelt on the parquet floor. He was beaten to a bloody pulp and looked nothing like the same man who fetched bones for Opie and brought me candies from town.

"This is what a traitor looks like, son," Thane had said. "Wearing the face of a friend."

Toby had begged then, but not for long before Thane planted a bullet between his eyes.

He'd knelt in front of me afterward, staring into my watery eyes long and hard. "We don't cry for traitors, Ruarc. We shed tears for *no one.*"

I'd held them in, forcing the burning in my throat to abate until it was gone entirely.

## Chapter 20

"Now, tell me how traitors should be dealt with."

"Swiftly," I replied, even toned, reciting the words he'd drilled into me for the last three years.

"And..." he prodded.

"And without mercy."

## 21

**EMILY**

W hy did people stop building houses like this? I felt like a time traveler in this place, a character out of a Gabaldon novel.

I walked up a narrow darkened staircase, eyes up to see when it would end.

Around another bend in the worn wooden railing, it opened into a room.

Dark wood shelves held rows of books, but this one was smaller than the other libraries. It looked more like an office with a heavy wooden desk placed centrally in the room. A freestanding gold lamp with a red shade on it stood next to the desk. It was furnished in bold jewel tones like the rest of the house; red, oxblood, blue, and jade.

The windows were large, reaching up towards the impossibly high ceiling. A telescope stood by one of them.

Ruarc lived alone but every place I'd explored in the house was always clean, dusted, and beautifully maintained. I'd spied a few maids here and there, but they were the sort not frequently seen or heard. They had to work in the nights for the house to remain this clean without my running into them more frequently.

The mansion held no sign of neglect or disrepair, everything maintained as if time hadn't touched this place while it ravaged the rest of the earth.

The walls were gently curved in the circular room. Orienting myself with a glance out the peaked stained glass window, I put myself in one of the two turrets.

A soft laugh pressed against the inside of my lips.

Turrets.

*Jesus.*

I hadn't believed Ruarc when he told me they were functional and not just decorative. He hadn't been lying.

Like a lot of the other rooms, there was a fireplace in this one. It was too hot this time of year, but the thought of cozying up in front of a lit fireplace with a book when it was cold enough to do so had me grinning.

Would Ruarc still be keeping me here when it was cold enough for a fire.

I bit my lip, choosing not to think about the future, it never led anywhere good. Not anymore.

My errant thoughts dampened my excitement exploring the room. I didn't know what was going on anymore.

There had been a week when we barely left his bed. With no sense of time passing or whether it was day or night. We ate when we were hungry, slept when we were tired, and feasted on one another when we woke.

For a while, we only talked about me. He said he preferred it that way, and even though my existence must've seemed horribly mundane to him, he never seemed bored.

It was like pulling teeth at first, but one night, after half a bottle of whiskey, he told me about his life. Offering me little glimpses of himself, always stopping just shy of going too deep.

Ruarc told me about the dog he'd rescued, though he never said what happened to it. About Thane, his father for all intents and purposes. About all the situations he and Nixon got themselves in when they were younger.

And then he stopped.

He stopped talking to me. Coming into the room to fuck me stupid and then leave, muttering about having some things he needed to attend to.

Now, for days I've woken up alone.

The days were starting to drag.

I could do anything I wanted, provided I didn't leave.

I was... comfortable. But lonely.

Ruarc still held out on that Netflix subscription and my books hadn't arrived, but even if he left the front door open and dismissed his guards and turned off the cameras... I wasn't sure I'd leave. That had to be the most terrifying thought of all.

That I might *like* being a monster's captive. That I might choose this over what waited for me back home.

*Home.*

I shivered thinking of cold nights in my cabin beneath the covers. With only the moaning of the walls to keep me company.

I went to the telescope to see whether I could make anything out. It was dark but the sky was overcast. I carefully maneuvered it, trying to focus on the world outside. Distant footsteps started quiet, then got louder and faster, coming up the stairs. I turned and jumped, starting when I saw him even though I heard him coming.

He filled the wide frame of the door, his shoulders flexing with every heavy breath, every bit the shadow from the cabin again. My ghost come to collect its soul.

Something was wrong.

A tremor rattled down my spine. "Ruarc?"

Did I do something?

He said I could move around the house as I pleased. I didn't leave the house. The furthest I went were the balconies and the enclosed courtyard. My heart beat wildly, fear I hadn't felt this strongly for weeks filled my chest.

"Ruarc, what—"

He barreled toward me.

I didn't run, too stunned to move.

My mind blanked, bracing for impact, but then he was kissing me.

Our teeth collided, his mouth hungry and hard. My body awoke to him, a moan clawing from my throat as my toes curled and my thighs clenched.

He lifted me from my hips, bringing me to the desk. I wrapped my arms around his neck, twisting my fingers in the hair at the base of his neck, but he wrenched me away with a growl.

I gasped as he flipped me around, shoving my head down into the surface of the desk.

"Ruarc," I gasped, to no response.

He held my wrists together behind my back. I heard his zipper, then he was tugging my shorts down my legs.

I screamed as he pushed roughly past my entrance, my body stretching uncomfortably around him. My eyes closed, holding my breath against the sharp bite of pain.

Tears threatened as he withdrew only to slam back into me, my body jerking hard against the unyielding surface with the force of his thrust.

He knocked my legs apart from behind, adjusting his angle to bury himself into me deeper as he fucked me, hard and fast. His violent thrusts rammed my hip bones into the carved edge of the desk, making the items atop it rattle, some of them rolling over its edges.

The repeated blows were in stark contrast with the gathering pleasure in my core.

I panted, arching my back into him as he pressed my cheek harder into the surface. I cried out as he hit something deep inside me, a spot that pulsed with both pain and pleasure with every one of his relentless strokes.

He roared with primal desire, the sounds of his pleasure provoking my own, making my core quicken, nerve endings like tendrils coiling tighter, *tighter* for the release.

I came with a teeth baring shout, my vision going out for a few seconds before it came roaring back with the hard *slap* of a hand on my rear.

Ruarc carried on mercilessly between my legs, drawing out my orgasm while I weathered the assault until he suddenly stopped.

My tender flesh throbbed and my arms fell from his hard grip.

"Ruarc, what's going on?" I asked.

Nothing.

He jerked my bicep, turning me back around, pushing me up onto the edge of the desk, making me catch myself on my palm as he jerked my hips forward, burying himself back into my pussy.

The invasion hurt less this time, my already wet core

ready to receive him. Ruarc fucked me wordlessly, his face a mask of desire and anguish as his shadowed eyes flicked to mine.

My heart shook seeing him.

Every thrust was a fervent plea.

Something happened. Something was wrong.

I embraced him, wrapping my arms and legs around him as he rocked his hips into me, letting him take what he needed from my body, no matter how brutal.

Despite myself, my orgasm hit again, making me seize, pulling me away from him. I fell back against the desk, hanging on to the ledge for dear life as he continued his relentless thrusting until he came, swallowing his groan and gritting his teeth. His head tipped back in ecstasy, every vein in his neck bulging. Every sharp angle defined. A phantom backlit in shades of royal blue, red, and yellow from the stained glass window at his back.

He didn't move for a moment, remaining like that, with his cock in my pussy, warm around him. Neither of us moving.

I pushed up on my elbow, reaching to put a hand to his chest.

His head fell forward, bent to shadow his expression from me.

Finally, he pulled out of me, stuffing his softening erection back into his pants, tucking in his shirt, adjusting his collar. Putting himself back to rights.

Why wouldn't he look at me?

My stomach twisted as I tugged my shorts back up my legs, ignoring how his seed spilled out onto the soft fabric. I could clean up after.

He walked to the stained glass window, bracing a hand on the frame to look out over the property.

"Do you want to know how I ended up with this house?" he asked finally, his tone an emotionless droll that only served to increase the tension in the room.

"You said you grew up here."

"I came here when I was twelve or thirteen. The man who owned this house, Thane Monroe, became a father figure of sorts to me. He owned the syndicate that I control now. It became mine when he died and so did the estate."

Caught off guard by his sudden openness, I ventured a question, desperate to know more about him. Where he came from. How he was made.

"What about before then? When you were a child?"

He paused, drawing air deep into his lungs before speaking.

"My earliest memories are being sat in front of the TV while my mom led a parade of different men into her bedroom by the hand. I think the TV was supposed to be loud enough to drown them out, but it often wasn't."

My throat constricted. "Was she..."

"A prostitute? Yes."

"I'm sorry, that must've been difficult to understand as a child."

...and suddenly some things started to make sense.

"What was awful was when they hit her," he added, his knuckles turning white as his grip on the window frame tightened. "Watching her cry, seeing her bruises fade from black to purple to yellow. Seeing her stuck in the pattern of prostitution and addiction, unable to get out of either. It was almost a relief when she left."

"She left?"

A nod. "When I was eleven. Weeks before, one of the johns attacked me. He was trying to—" He cut himself off but I could fill in the blank. My heart sank.

"I fought back. Used a bat. I wasn't very strong then, but apparently I was strong enough to knock him down. The painted cement statue Ma kept near the front door did the rest, cracked open his skull."

"That wasn't your fault. It was a mistake. You did it in self-defense."

"No," he argued, the word blunt and honest. "No, I wanted him to die and he did. My mother helped me bury the body the next day in the woods. She told me the man was my... my..."

My hand flew to my mouth, covering the pained gasp there.

...his father?

His own father had tried to rape him?

He *killed* his father.

"Ruarc..."

I rose to go to him, but he stiffened and I stayed put.

"And then weeks later," he continued, as if he was telling a story that belonged to someone else instead of the one that shaped him into the man standing in front of me. "I woke up to find a hundred dollars on the kitchen counter and she was gone. Just like that. I didn't know what to do. Where to go. She had no family here. I had no aunts or uncles. No cousins or even friends."

My heart bled for him, withering in my chest like a prune.

"A few years back, I found out where she lives and what she does now. She's an entirely different person. Doesn't even look the same."

"Ruarc, that never should've happened. Every child deserves a mother—"

"Who didn't leave? Yeah, that would've been preferable."

He tapped his palm against the wood. Still, he wouldn't look at me and I got the distinct feeling I shouldn't approach him. Not yet. Not right now.

"It was easier when Thane died. There was an accident so it was a shock, but he didn't leave me the way she did. He didn't *want* to leave, but he was still gone."

"I'm so sorry, Ruarc."

He shook his head, dismissing my apology, finally turning around to face me. His drawn expression unsettled me, the hollows beneath his eyes dark and deep. His skin pale, drained of color.

"Why do you think I have so many cameras in this place, so much security?"

His pause made me think he wanted an answer.

"Because you need to keep yourself safe."

He shook his head. "No, Emily. I had cameras for Delirium before you arrived. A few for the property."

That didn't sound right. There were cameras everywhere. In almost every hall. In my bedroom. My bathroom. The wine cellar turned prison in the basement. Even in this room.

"These," he said, waving an arm at the two cameras in the library office. "Are here because I couldn't let you leave."

He paced, short angry steps, brushing past me to rip one from the wall and discard it on the floor. The *crash* of it shattering against the hardwood made me jump and my breath catch. I gripped the edge of the desk to keep myself rooted to the spot, not wanting to flee. Not wanting to show fear.

He whirled on me, his dead-eyed gaze suddenly blazing with life.

"I was obsessed with you from the moment we met," he all but shouted. "I knew I had to have you. Bringing you here, I knew it wasn't what you would want. I knew you would try to escape so I did everything in my power to stop that. I wanted you for myself."

He paused again, taking a shallow breath, regaining control.

"Your father gave me the perfect excuse to take you, bring you here, make you mine."

He threw a hand through his hair. "But you were right. Nixon was in on the price hikes, harassing your weakling of a father into asking for higher disposal fees. Fees that Nixon got a handsome cut of."

"I-I don't understand," I muttered, more to myself than to him.

I was right? But if Nixon was the one to blame for my father's so-called greed then...

"I wanted to teach the undertaker a lesson, remind him who he was dealing with, but he had nothing to do with it. At best, he was Nixon's pawn."

I didn't like where this was going. A hollow cavern opened in my stomach.

"I'm sorry you had to find out that way. I hoped I was wrong."

He cocked his head at me, brows lowering over narrowed eyes that watched me for a long, silent moment, analyzing.

He stalked toward me suddenly, without warning. I

held my ground as he yanked open a drawer next to where I stood and plucked out a familiar gray bag.

"Where did you get that?" I asked.

He held the purse out to me and I took it, feeling weight inside. Unfastening the silver clasp, I found my phone, wallet, and a change of clothes folded neatly inside.

"You need to leave."

His words hung in the air for a long time before I could process them.

"Why?"

"Because I don't want you here."

The rejection stung like needles in my eyes. My tongue was a useless lump in my mouth. Numbly, I shook my head.

"If Nixon's the problem, then why do I need to go?"

"Get the fuck out of here, Emily," he snapped at me. "We're ten minutes west from the mortuary. You can walk if you want or one of my men will drive you."

Frantic thoughts tumbled over each other in my head, words still failing me. He was... he was letting me go?

No. He was kicking me out.

"What if... I want to stay."

"No." He glared sharply at me and something within me crumpled. "I got what I wanted, little lamb." He sneered. "Now it's time for you to go home."

"I'm not leaving," I said, my shaking voice giving away my hurt.

He laughed mockingly, pushing a palm over his mouth. "Let me make this easy for you, Emily. If you're still on my property in ten minutes, I'm going to kill you."

My mouth popped open, his cruel words like the twist of a knife, wringing scalding tears from my eyes.

I was so stupid. So fucking foolish to think...

What? That we were a couple?

Was I exempt from his cruelty because we had fucked a few times?

I was his captive. He was my jailer.

I was his pawn on his chess board and he was moving the pieces.

My body caved in on itself, shocked betrayal burning in my core.

Ruarc walked out, leaving me in devastated silence.

I dried my eyes and stood, legs shaking as something that felt more like rage than sorrow fought for dominance in my core.

My monster had returned.

"Fuck you!" I shouted after the sound of his retreating footsteps.

My menace.

"*I hate you!*"

My *ghost.*

## 22

EMILY

I painted more makeup on dead people's faces than I'd ever painted on my own.

At this point, I wondered if the skill was even transferable.

Just because I could make a dead person look not-so-dead anymore, didn't mean that I'd have a steady hand putting on my own winged eyeliner.

It wasn't like I had many places to wear it, anyway. The place I spent the most time was at work and there was no reason for me to put it on just to come in here and do this. The dead didn't care what I looked like and neither did my dad.

The family of the deceased asked for a rosy-cheeked, bold-lip look that'd really suited her when she was alive. I examined the variety of reference pictures they gave me to work with, showing the woman in varying stages of aging through her life from her early twenties until the present.

She was in her early forties now, and died from complications of a congenital heart condition that threatened her health on and off all her life.

In each photo she had that bold lipstick, the one the family dropped off with her body, but the rest I'd have to use my best judgment to mimic.

MY HANDS WERE STEADY, GUIDING THE NEEDLE UNDER HER SKIN and shooting the formaldehyde-laced filler into the places that disease, age, and death had hollowed in her face. Sometimes, the only time people had their makeup done was when they ended up here, at the end of their life, not even able to look in the mirror to see whether they liked the results.

I scrutinized the picture of the deceased. Blown up and printed, it had lost some of its quality. I always went easy on the filler because it was easy to blow past the *rejuvenated* look to an over-filled pillow face disaster that completely distorted the features you were trying to preserve in the first place.

My steady hand trembled, recalling the needle Ruarc's men had threaded through my skin, stitching the cut in my palm from when I'd run at him with a shard of glass.

*No. Stop.*

I withdrew the needle, gripping the shaking hand in my other one, squeezing it tight to will the trembling to end.

*Was any of it real?*

The thought came like a conspiratory whisper in the silence of the room.

Would I ever leave this place again? Or would I remain here, a permanent fixture, not five miles down the road from *him?*

I never had FOMO, not in the traditional sense. I didn't care that I had never been to Coachella or New York City. It didn't really move me that weekend after weekend went by and I spent all of them right here, working. If not working, then in my cabin, just letting time go by until I had to work again.

It never bothered me before. Not like it had in the days since I left Ruarc's gothic mansion, straight past the car with the open door, walking home barefoot down the lonely backroads outside the city.

My place was *here*, doing *this* with my father. Some people had varied, interesting lives. I didn't.

But I had, briefly.

The room suddenly felt tight. The walls seemed to list and shift, pressing in. I eyed the door like it was about to fly open. Like I could feel him there, just on the other side.

Except, I couldn't.

I hadn't felt his presence since I left. It was like he was a figment of my imagination. A ghost in earnest now, Ruarc would forever haunt me in memory alone.

My stomach dropped violently.

The room spun and I winced, putting my tools down on the stainless steel tray with a clatter, pressing a sterile gloved hand to my chest.

The whiplash of being back was so strong sometimes, it knocked the wind out of me, made it so hard to breathe that dark spots crowded at the edges of my vision.

The wave passed slow, dragging me back out to calmer waters where I could catch my breath.

Being back in my normal life was absurd. It felt wrong after what I'd been through with Ruarc. The familiar rooms of the mortuary, my routines, the things that used to be so normal to me felt wrong and stifling. Fake. Like my whole life I'd been living in a cardboard cutout and it took me until now to notice.

Now that I had, I couldn't unsee it. I couldn't unfeel the things he made me feel.

I had finally counted the days I'd spent with Ruarc.

Thirty-seven.

After flinging me into a world I couldn't even comprehend existed, much less so close to the one I lived in now; Ruarc discarded me like trash. Wrung me dry and moved on like it was nothing.

My hands shook as I tried to rearrange the tubes and pots of mortuary makeup and tools. Just because he gave me something didn't mean I couldn't have it myself. I was gone for over a month and the mortuary didn't burn to the ground. That meant I could leave if I wanted. I could do more than that. I could travel, go skydiving, find a fucking sex party and screw twenty different people in one night.

My teeth ground together as I fought against the haze that came over me thinking of him. I was free. I could do anything but when would I finally stop short-circuiting when I thought about him? My life had become foreign. *I* was foreign.

Going back to work, I repeated the mantra that'd gotten me out of half a dozen panic attacks since my return.

I belong here.

*I belong here.*

Darkening the corpse's eyelashes, I looked at her face, examining the makeup I'd applied, but seeing more than that.

Her husband was a wreck when he came to make arrangements for her. On his face was the profound loss of someone he didn't know how to live without. I didn't know her or their relationship but his world shifted on its axis when she died; that was the impact she left.

Even dead, she still meant something. There was a difference between being alive and feeling alive and currently, I was only one of those things.

How could I be the one grieving if I was also the one who was also dead inside?

I hadn't cried all day which was an improvement over the past three since I returned home but the waves of anguish still came. They were small sometimes, swooshing around me like a breeze that made me squint and stung my cheeks. Sometimes it engulfed me, suffocating until finally, mercifully, releasing me back to numbness.

There was more than the anguish though, there was rage, too. A bitter regret at having ever met him. At having ever allowed myself to feel anything for him but disgust and loathing.

Work was the only thing keeping me on my feet, out of my cabin. If I didn't have work, I could truthfully say I'd be fucking catatonic. Letting the wave pull me under just because the effort of beating it back was so exhausting.

I finished working on the body and transferred it back into the upper-level cooling room. She wouldn't be transported until the next day and before the family came to collect the body, I would have to do one final inspection to make sure it hadn't continued to purge.

After cleaning up and disinfecting, I went downstairs to the basement. I found my dad doing the same thing I'd just done; disinfecting and cleaning up after an autopsy. He noticed my entrance before I said anything.

"I'm done. Just wanted to say I am heading out."

He straightened up from the autopsy slab that he was bent over.

"Great. Thanks. Are you having an early night?" he asked, voice light, pitching higher than necessary, like he was talking to a puppy or a child. Even with his question, he carefully didn't ask what he really wanted to know. *That* silence was loud.

I'd collapsed into his arms when I first dragged myself back onto the property. The overwhelm was too much to contain and it'd spilled out of me in waves of broken sobs so loud and so ragged I didn't recognize myself in the sound of them.

Dad helped me into the house, up into the room I had when I was a little girl, where he put me to bed.

I slept for a day and a half before I woke and he never asked me what happened and I never told him. He poured me some orange juice and told me he understood if I could never forgive him but that he would do whatever he could to make it right.

The next day, I went to work. There was a backlog of requests for post-mortem makeup applications, many of which had expired, but I took every one I could, eager to drown out the buzzing in my head with anything else.

"I might," I replied.

It wasn't like I had anything better to do.

He waited in patient silence for me to say something more. I didn't. "Well, 'night, Dad."

"Any chance you're hungry?" he asked.

No.

Thinking about food for the first time all day, I made the belated realization that I hadn't eaten.

I wasn't big on breakfast, and I worked through my midday break.

I felt like I was on battery-saving mode. Like all of my body functions were working at half speed to preserve energy, leaving me feeling only half-charged. Half alive.

"I don't think so. Thanks, though," I said.

The corners of his mouth fell, giving away his disappointment.

There was a surge of discomfort in my stomach. After being gone the way that I had been, I wasn't the only one who was affected. So was he.

I didn't doubt he'd worried every day whether or not I was still alive. If I was hurting or scared or hungry.

He ran this whole place alone in my absence. Had to tell people what happened to me if they asked, making up a tale that was passable enough to obscure the truth.

Really, I tried to empathize with him, but every time I did I hit a brick wall.

This was on *him.*

*He* disposed of Ruarc's sins in the basement. *He* brought the monster here. *He'd* given in to the whims of Ruarc's right hand man, trying to gouge more money from the monster himself.

It was his fault I'd been taken.

His fault I would *never* be the same.

I didn't know how to talk to him anymore.

The tension since I returned was tenable in every conversation. In every room when both of us were inside it.

"Go and get some rest then," he said.

I nodded, my arms crossing over my chest. "Yeah, thanks. Have a good night."

I turned around and walked toward the door, heading up a couple of stairs before my feet stopped and I went backward instead. I couldn't stand this anymore. We needed to get some shit out on the table. He needed to know that I wasn't the same Emily that was taken from here forty days ago. He needed to understand that I would work alongside him to preserve this place in Mom's memory, but that I didn't know if it could ever be the same between us again after what happened.

"I saw him that night," I said and my Dad lifted his head, surprised to see me returned.

His lips parted, but his brow furrowed in confusion.

"*Ruarc*," I said when he didn't respond.

I hadn't said his name out loud in days and hearing it sent tingles over my skin and carved a fresh well in the hollow of my gut.

"What night was that?"

"Months ago. That night when Tess came over. We came out here—after midnight—and I ran into him."

His eyebrows bunched together.

"These days it's like I don't even know who you are," he said in a low tone, surprising me. "You went through the things in my office which was bad enough but now you're telling me you'd broken my other rules before that?"

Indignance rose in my chest, forcing out a bubble of dark laughter. My dad took it like the slap to the face I'd intended it to be.

"*That's* the part you want to focus on?" I asked. "Not the fact that he was here illegally disposing of a corpse, paying you for your service and silence?"

He averted his eyes and flattened his hands on the table.

"I'm not going to apologize for doing what I had to do for us to stay afloat."

I faltered slightly, losing some of my nerve. We'd never discussed things like this openly before. Certainly not his arrangement with the crime lord, but neither did we ever speak about finances. I only knew money was tight, but not the extent of it.

Our relationship was clear; I'd always be regarded as the child and he as the adult. He didn't expose me to the *real world* and until now, I never asked for access.

"THOSE BODIES YOU DISPOSED OF; DO YOU EVEN KNOW WHO THEY were? Do you know why they died? *How* they died? Do you even care?"

"That's none of my business," he snapped before controlling the level of his voice, his nostrils flaring as he exhaled to collect himself. "They aren't good people, Emily. They're pimps and drug dealers and sex traffickers. People who stepped on Ruarc's toes. People who tried to betray him or hurt him."

A monster killing other monsters.

Wait?

"You said, *aren't*. Are you still cremating corpses for him? Has he been here?"

The edge of mania in a voice couldn't be missed and Dad rushed to shake his head, lifting his hands in a placating gesture, not understanding that the reason I sounded so distraught wasn't for fear, but for something far worse.

"Don't worry, Emily. Your security has been assured. You're safe now. He won't take you again.

My eyes burned.

"Before all of this," he continued. "You never knew. I'd

been working with Mr. Monroe's men for years and nothing like this ever happened before. We'll go back to how it was. As long as you follow the rules, you won't even know when he's here or anything that happens in this building after midnight."

I blinked back tears, carving half-moons into my palms.

Once, I'd felt insulated here, tucked away from the worst horrors of the world despite Ruarc and his kingdom existing practically on my doorstep.

But my eyes were open now.

There were darker things than I could imagine existing in the most unexpected places. There was a darkness within myself, too. One that my ghost awoke in me and that I would never be able to put back to bed.

Had he been here since I returned then? Was he in this very room with my father while I slept not two hundred yards away in my cabin, oblivious to him being here?

Dad sighed deeply, his eyes down.

"This place was your mother's dream, and she is the reason why it was a success. When she died, things changed. I wasn't her. I couldn't do for this place what she did. I tried, but it got away from me. Year after year, the bills started piling up but our income wouldn't cover them."

His fists clenched on the autopsy table and it was like I was hearing him through glass, his voice muffled through the cotton stuffing in my ears.

"I wouldn't get involved with someone like Ruarc unless I had to. The extra income insulated us. It meant that this place could keep running."

"Is that what you told yourself? That you did this for Mom?" I spat.

His eyes cut to me sharply, their color cold and empty.

"You were never supposed to know about him or what was happening. I worked so hard to keep you out of it, you have to believe that."

*Yeah and look how that turned out.*

His eyes narrowed on my face, on the tear I forbade from falling gathering on the rims of my eyes. I sniffed, looking away.

"Did he hurt you?"

"No," I said in a strained whisper.

*Not in the way you think he did,* is what I didn't say.

"He only used me to try to control you," I said.

*He didn't care about me*, is what I didn't say.

My chest swelled with a bone-deep ache and I shuffled uncomfortably, trying to swallow a sob.

"I'm sorry you became part of this. I should have done better."

I sniffed.

"It's over now."

I didn't want to talk anymore. I just wanted to pull the covers over my head and wallow in the dark beneath them.

"That bastard won't ever touch you again, I promise."

I flinched, unable to meet my father's eyes because that... that wasn't what I wanted at all. But he wouldn't understand. No one would. Especially if they knew the truth.

Ruarc and I weren't wrong. Whatever fucked up thing we were, we weren't that, because if we were, then I didn't want to be right.

"Right," I said, voice tight as I turned to leave, not trusting myself to stay composed for much longer. "Anyway, goodnight."

"Wait, I have something for you.

"*Hmm?*"

"I don't know whether you want it, but there's no one else to give it to."

He disappeared briefly and came back with an urn. The cheap, plain piece was one of the urns that we used to keep unclaimed ashes. We stored them for a number of years in case of collection but eventually disposed of them. I stared at the plain ceramic vessel until a powerful realization forced the air from my chest.

"Because of the circumstances, I couldn't return it to his family," he said. Tears sprang to my eyes and I gasped. My father's face dropped.

"Emily, I'm sorry. I didn't mean to upset you," he said. "Ruarc said you knew about Carlos."

I shook my head, swallowing hard.

"No... no," I said through my sobs. *Carlos.* Whatever was left of his physical body; the crushed remains of his bones left over after the cremation process... he was in there.

"I can keep it if you'd rather—"

I held my hands. Not wanting to keep it but needing to. A blind sense of duty forced me to take them. He placed the urn in my hands and I mumbled a quick thanks.

Rushing out, I hugged the urn to my chest.

Tears flowed freely down my cheeks. It was my fault that it had come to this. My wild adventure with Ruarc had been like sleeping as I was awake. The things I did, felt, and saw, didn't feel real sometimes, even now. This didn't feel real. Ruarc telling me that he killed Carlos were just words.

Now, this, right now, this was real. A life was ended and all that remained of it were the ashes in this urn.

My world had always felt like a place where I belonged. Now, it felt tight and ill-fitting. I suffocated at the constricting pressure of it, trying to cram myself back into a box where I no longer fit. The tears came harder the farther I got from the mortuary, coupled with a bone-gnawing guilt. Because I wasn't crying for the loss of Carlos...

I was crying because *still* I felt virtually nothing when I thought of never seeing him again.

I was crying because instead of grieving the dead man in my arms, I grieved the loss of the one who killed him.

## RUARC

Dark bags hung beneath Nixon's eyes accentuated by the bad overhead lighting.

It wasn't doing his skin any favors either, his sallow complexion resembled something out of a Burton film. His hair clung to the top of his head, oily and flat.

His cheeks looked sunken like he'd dropped fifteen pounds while he was in here.

"I didn't think you'd come," he said, coughing as he slid into the seat across from me at the table in the small interview room.

The dull drone of the fluorescent lights on the ceiling filled the silence as seconds ticked away, none of them bringing me any closer to recognizing the man in front of me.

"Neither did I," I admitted after a minute.

His lips twitched at one side, a sad smirk twisting them upward.

"I'm honored."

His light, unaffected tone grated on my nerves. Did he

think for one second that I wouldn't snap his goddamned neck just because of where we were?

I'd do it.

I'd do it even if the man outside this door couldn't be bought and the action bought me my own sentence behind bars.

The syndicate's hierarchy had to be reshuffled and dealt out after cutting him loose. The bad eggs weeded from the masses. Co-conspirators dealt with.

Nixon Vandermoor had already wasted enough of my time.

"You requested this meet," I said in an even droll. "Start talking."

His eyes widened. If he thought asking me to speak to him in person would affect the outcome here, he was painfully mistaken. There was only one place he was headed and I'd see that he got there myself when the time came.

He nodded, coming to the understanding that from here on this would be business and absolutely nothing more.

"I know you've taken everything. My phone, my computer. I know you searched my place," he listed, counting them off on his fingers. "I can assume you've also spoken to the undertaker."

He edged that last bit in a question, but I didn't do him the kindness of a reply, leaning back in my stiff plastic-backed chair to see if he'd openly admit to anything more.

I watched him across the nominally short distance that the table covered between us. When he offered nothing more, I ground my teeth.

"Why did you do it?"

He scoffed, throwing his hands up. "Why not? The undertaker was an easy target and I was due for a raise."

A nonchalant shrug lifted his shoulders and I wanted to break both of his arms.

"You know what this means."

He swallowed, his Adam's apple bobbing in his throat.

"I was counting on it being too late for you to find out," he said. "I just needed a few more things put in place and people in much higher places would've seen to your end. The job done for me."

"You mean from your little camera stunt at Delirium?"

He didn't answer me, pressing his lips in a taut line.

"What was your plan? Continue to leak footage until the club went under? Until the fucking supreme court justice or the mayor or the archbishop decided to slit my throat?"

I could see the truth of it there in everything he wasn't saying, his eyes glimmering with malice.

"It was her, right?"

My head cocked. "*What*?"

"Emily. She's the reason you found me out."

A shard of defensiveness sliced through me hearing the accusation.

"You get her name out of your fucking mouth you gutless coward," I snapped, leaning over the table.

He laughed, running a hand through his limp hair.

"You're sitting there like this is my fault but really, it's all her."

"I won't fucking warn you again."

Under the table, my fists clenched.

"Just think, if she didn't say anything, if you didn't have

her wandering the house like a free-range hen, then neither of us would be here."

My teeth pressed together so hard I heard them squeak. His mouth was reckless because he thought himself safe in this room.

*Think again, Nixon.*

In a split second, I was over the table, smashing his face down into the metal surface. I was rewarded with the sweet sound of cracking bone and a splatter of red on the otherwise shining surface.

Nixon brought his hands to his busted nose just as the door opened and I fell back into my seat opposite him.

"What the hell happened?" the guard boomed.

I shrugged. "Bastard smashed his face into the table."

I kicked him beneath it.

"Didn't you?"

Nixon glared at me, nodding his agreement before bringing his hands back from his face. "Well don't just stand there," he shouted at the guard. "Get me a fucking tissue."

"Want a lolly, too?" The guard snorted. "You have five minutes."

He turned on his heel, leaving Nixon to wipe the blood from his face with his orange jumper sleeve and spit on the cement floor.

"Satisfied?" he asked me, lifting a brow.

"Not even remotely."

He sniffed, wincing. "You never should've brought her in."

"I know you're not telling me how I should run my business."

"I could do it a hell of a lot better than you, that's for

damn sure," he lobbied back, eyes rolling as he tipped his head back, trying to staunch the flow of blood.

"That's a hell of a statement from where you're sitting."

He looked down at his scrubs, then back at me with a face that said that I had a point.

"I can't believe you let some pussy cloud your mind."

"I can't believe you're giving one the credit for your downfall when you orchestrated it so beautifully all by yourself," I clipped shortly. I didn't want to hear another word about her. Not from him. Or anyone else.

Emily hadn't done anything but report what was already happening.

"You took her because—"

"Is this why you called me here?" I asked. "To talk about..."

Jesus fuck I couldn't even say her name.

"*Emily,*" I ground out.

As soon as I lingered too long on thoughts about her, my mind froze, stuck in a loop. A reel of her face, her voice, her body, playing over and over again like a hypnotic mantra.

"Heard you sent her back."

I resisted the urge to ask him who he'd heard that from, knowing he wouldn't rat out his rat. But he wanted me to know he still had one. He knew it would make my fucking skin itch to know there might still be a filthy traitor in my ranks.

"You're stalking her again, aren't you?"

He smirked, seeing something in the twitch of my expression that he thought gave me away. "I knew it. You can't get enough of that bitch."

"I'm going to relish the sight of the light leaving your eyes."

His jaw flexed. The guy in front of me continued to cleave a clean line down the version of him I thought I knew and the one sitting before me.

I never knew Nixon. Not really.

Did anyone really know anyone else?

I knew there wasn't a soul walking this earth who could ever understand the depth of my mind. The things that forged me. What I dreamt about when the world went quiet and the incessant buzz of life evaporated between my fingers.

I wasn't naive enough to think I sat on my throne uncontested, but I hadn't seen this coming. Not from Nixon.

It would never happen again.

Violent shame gripped me from the inside, twisting my gut. The fact this had been brewing in my ranks all this time and I hadn't noticed...

And worse, my faith in Nixon never shook, even when I suspected the client breach at Delirium was an inside job. I never imagined it could be him.

I dismissed Emily when she brought it up; someone with no reason to lie to me. Maybe a foot soldier was responsible, someone lower ranked, but not him. Not my right hand man.

Not Nixon.

"Was it worth it? Your blind grab for my position?"

"Oh, fucking, please," he said, his fists balling on the table. He leaned forward, the whites of his eyes flashing. "You act like you're the only one who could do it, like you earned it or something. You were fucking lucky, big deal. Thane liked you. It had nothing to do with your leadership skills. The last straw," he said, pausing, leaning even closer as contempt flushed through his dull complexion.

"The last straw was that slut you were fucking. You'd do anything she wanted. You'd stage all-out war with the Salvadorans down south if she told you to. Someone needed to take care of business, and it wasn't you. It's *not* you. Not anymore."

At this point, I was salting the wound, knowing it was painful but doing it anyway. In some sick way, I needed this. It was catharsis, seeing him this way, knowing I was going to end his life.

I was going to look my closest friend in the face as he took his last breath. I wanted to make damn sure that there was no room for regret. That whatever tiny sliver of mercy I even thought of showing him would be ill-deserved.

I'd accomplished that, though not much else in coming here. Not even his further comment about Emily, spoken only to test my limits, could get to me now. Not with all respect for him lost.

"You made a mistake," I said simply, my chair scraping over the rough floor as I stood.

There was something profoundly destabilizing about finding out that you built so much on the shaky foundation of lies.

"Say hi to Emily for me," he said, one last jab for the road.

In a knee jerk reaction, I whirled, my chest tight with fury as I stared him down. "No need," I hissed. "She'll see your face again. I'll make damn sure *she's* the one who pushes your sorry corpse into the flames."

# 24

## EMILY

I tapped the steering wheel restlessly on my way through the city to Tessa's place. I clenched my jaw, passing the exit I'd taken the last time I drove down this highway. The one that would lead to Carlos' house. Well, not Carlos' anymore. As far as I knew Salem was still living there. She'd called while I was away. So had Carlos' parents. And the police.

But they hadn't come by or called again since my return to the mortuary and I knew in my bones it was to do with Ruarc. He paid someone off, got my name removed from every possible list where it was written in connection to Carlos' disappearance.

I'd been racking my brain trying to come up with a way to let his family know that he was gone and wouldn't be coming back. They deserved to know that at least. To grieve his loss properly. I'd find a way. One that wouldn't implicate me or Dad or even Ruarc.

I took Tessa's exit and shook off the lingering feelings of

anxiety and guilt. After work today, I'd just needed an escape. To get away somewhere, *anywhere* but home.

I'd spent too many nights staring out into the dark beyond my windows, praying for any sign that he might be out there, looking back at me.

Fucking ridiculous.

As I neared her place I tried to draw up some excitement, sitting straighter, turning up the radio, but nothing seemed to help.

It was true no matter what I was doing. It was like being suspended in formaldehyde like a wet specimen. No longer alive, despite outward appearances. I could speak, eat, walk around; superficially, I was all there. In reality, it was like walking through water, eating without taste, hearing as though through cotton.

Like... I was the ghost all along.

Tears slid down my face, surprising me. I sniffed, hurriedly dabbing them with my sleeve and clearing my throat.

Outside Tessa's apartment building, I parked. A minute went by, and then five minutes, and then almost ten. My eyes glazed over, hazing my sight. I pictured it; turning around, speeding back down the highway toward home only to pass by it, go straight down toward the dead-end where the long curving driveway led to him.

Would he make good on his promise to kill me if I returned?

Did I care?

Getting sucked slowly back to reality, where I was sitting in my car and he was nowhere in sight was like jumping into a pool of ice water.

The only time I could get away from my wandering

thoughts was when I was asleep. Otherwise, he didn't leave me alone. Before I could start crying again, I got out of the car and called Tessa as I entered her building, asking her to buzz me up.

She was waiting at the door when I arrived.

"Who shat in your cereal this morning?" she asked, pausing with her hand on her hip, and the other on the door. My stomach dropped. God, was it that obvious? I tried to put on a smile, tensing like a spooked animal.

"Sorry, came straight from work," I lied. I'd forced a bowl of leftover macaroni and cheese down my throat and showered *and* blow-dried my hair before coming here, but she didn't need to know that.

"Empty-handed, too?" she lifted a brow.

I laughed, the sound real instead of forced. The normalcy of her giving me shit for not bringing a bottle of wine making me feel the most at home since I left the mansion in the trees.

"Shit, I forgot," I said. "I'll run out and grab something."

"No, no, don't worry about it. I have everything we need. Just giving you a hard time. I always bring a bottle to yours, you know," she said, ushering me in.

We hung out in the living room, having the place to ourselves tonight.

Her roommate was a really nice girl named Grace who spent more time at her boyfriend's place than at home. There was pizza and wine waiting on the coffee table in front of the lumpy couch in their living room.

I wasn't hungry. My stomach rarely asked me to feed it these days and everything I put in my mouth tasted like sawdust. I tried to force down a slice though, telling myself that if I couldn't fall back into my normal life, I'd have to take it back by force.

"So where have you been lately? Any good trips?" I asked through a mouthful of pizza. Tessa giggled, bringing her wine glass to her lips. She was home but she still had her makeup from the day on. She had ditched the leather jacket she wore like a second skin though and was in a faded, oversized t-shirt and athletic shorts.

"I should be asking you that."

Tessa didn't know anything that happened. As far as she was aware, I had taken a little vacation myself. My father came up with the shaky cover story that I was actually in Florida staying with some distant relatives who needed some help with a move.

I had no relatives anywhere that I knew about. Both my father's parents and my mother's parents were dead and outside of that, the one sister my mother had lives in South Korea. I only heard from her once every few years on Christmas.

"It was nothing special," I said nonchalantly. "I'm really sorry I missed the signing event, though. Hope you were all right without me."

She frowned. "We managed. "Where did you go, again?"

I paused for a beat.

"Florida."

Her lips pursed.

"Didn't manage to get a tan while you were there?" she asked lightly.

"Well spotted."

I was such an idiot. Why didn't I come up with something to tell Tess in advance? I mean, of course she was liable to ask why I virtually fell off the face of the earth. Dad's excuse that there was spotty cell service only held up so well. That coupled with the few text messages he *had* sent her wouldn't have done much to convince her of our cover story.

Tessa was smarter than that. She knew there was something going on, but she also wasn't the sort to pry into other people's shit on account of having so much of her own with her family.

I didn't want to lie to her but the truth wasn't an option, either.

Not that she'd believe it anyway.

"So?" she pressed gently. "Are you going to tell me where you really were or is it like a state secret or something?"

I emptied my lungs, allowing myself to imagine the freedom of no longer carrying this all by myself. Of telling another person. Telling my best friend.

Except I couldn't. Well, I couldn't tell her *all* of it. There were certain parts, certain *lines*, she wouldn't be able to cross and come back from. She'd want to kill Ruarc, to call the police... to do the right thing. But... I didn't think I wanted those things, too, and she wouldn't understand that. No one would.

"I don't know how to start."

"If it's too much, you definitely don't have to say anything. I mean, like, if you're not ready to talk about it or if you just think I should shut up and mind my own business, I totally get it."

She reached over, giving my knee a squeeze. "I can just tell it's eating at you and you know I'm here if you need me, right? You can tell me anything."

A sad smile pulled at my lips. Maybe not *anything,* but at least something.

"I know." I drew in a steadying breath, pulling apart everything that'd happened and separating it into piles in my mind. The safe-to-tell pile and the absolutely-fucking-not pile.

"You have to let me finish talking before you say anything," I warned preemptively and Tessa's eyes bugged out of her head, adjusting herself in her seat, getting ready for me to spill the tea. She had absolutely no idea the *bomb* I was about to drop on her.

Tessa mimed sealing her lips and throwing away the key.

I took another deep breath, this one shuddering from my lips slowly.

Maybe the way I could finally let this go was by first letting it out.

"Do you remember when I told you I had a weird feeling whenever I was in my cabin? Like I was being watched?"

I paused for her to nod yes.

"Well, I was."

My voice shook.

I paused, clearing my throat, and looking down. My tears flowed so easily these days, they were pouring down my face in no time.

"Hey, hey, it's okay," Tessa said, scrambling to hand me some napkins. I blotted them on my face, smelling vaguely of pizza crust.

"Is that why you had to leave? Did something happen to you? Or were you just afraid of this mystery stalker?"

I tried to say something, but my tears had other plans, choking my throat and suspending all other body functions so I could weep. I blubbered pathetically over the man who kicked me out of his life. Over everything gained, and *lost*.

"No. No." I tried to compose myself, taking a pitiful sip of my wine. "I wasn't afraid of him. Not really." I felt the truth of that statement rattle in my bones. Because knowing he was out there hadn't frightened me. Not really. It excited me. It made me feel alive.

"Him?"

I nodded, unable to say his name aloud and knowing I probably shouldn't anyway.

"He took me, Tess. My dad got himself into trouble with some dangerous people and this guy, he took me."

Her face paled. "You were kidnapped?"

She stared at me, incredulous, skeptical. I would be, too. My father hadn't reported me missing. There were no manhunts. Nothing on the news. I was just *gone* and my dad covered for my absence. And now I was back, here on the couch across from my best friend drinking wine like it never happened.

It was like something out of a movie.

"Sort of," I replied, chewing the inside of my cheek. "The man, he kept me to leverage my Dad, and then, eventually, he let me go."

"Oh my god," she scooched forward, drawing me in for a hug that almost had me breaking in her arms. She rubbed my back and I could feel her heart pounding against my chest, fast while mine felt like it chugged through mud.

"What was your dad into?" she asked gently.

I barked a short laugh.

Where the hell did I start?

The explanation rested firmly in the absolutely-fucking-not pile, so I shook my head. "It doesn't matter now. It's over."

She pushed my unruly hair back from my face. "Did this man hurt you?"

I clenched my jaw. The blush that spread up my neck and over my cheeks was hot, forcing me to avert my eyes.

"Oh god, babe," Tessa said, imagining the worst.

"It wasn't like that," I said, my voice watery. "Well, I guess it was. But it also wasn't. I thought he was a monster, but I was wrong. He's..." I choked. "I... oh fuck, Tess, I don't know what's wrong with me."

Tessa's brows cinched, her gaze jerking between my teary eyes, trying to understand. But how could she? How could anyone?

"Oh fuck," Tessa said on an exhale. "You fell for your fucking stalker?"

I sobbed hard, my stomach twisting with guilt and shame.

She drew me back in, holding me tight, hushing me with long strokes against my hair.

"Just say it," I sobbed into her hair. "Just tell me I'm fucking crazy."

"The whole bloody story sounds crazy, babe."

I sniffed, prying myself away from her to drown my pitiful sorrow in more wine.

"There's something wrong with me."

She shook her head, taking my empty wine glass from me to fill it back up to the fucking rim. "No. Not crazy. *Human*. And as insane as the story sounds, I know you wouldn't lie to me, but damn, girl, that shit sounds like something my boss could've written, you know?"

I laughed, but it sounded hollow even to my own ears. I

searched for judgment in Tessa's eyes but found none and felt strangely unburdened. Some of the weight lifted from my chest. Telling her about him made it feel more real. Joined together the part of my life that felt like a dream with my stark reality.

"So," Tessa said, eyeing me deviously over her wine glass.

"So?"

"Tell me about him."

And I did. I told her more than I planned to. The push and pull. The dirty, rotten, bad, and the good that was so good it made me shudder at the memories alone.

Only the most intimate moments I kept to myself, holding them close to my chest, keeping them just for me.

I wound up spending the night, with too much wine in my system to stand up straight let alone drive.

In the morning, Tessa pumped me full of ibuprofen and coffee and lent me some clean sweats before sending me on my way. The last thing she said to me as I left her apartment rang in my ears all the way home.

"I know you said it couldn't work out between you and your mystery guy, but stories like yours deserve a better ending."

## 25

### EMILY

With Tessa's words rooted in my head, I went most of the day distracted, just going through the motions. Grocery shopping in a trance that almost saw me bowling over a toddler. Running two stop signs on the way home and nearly rear-ending someone at a red light.

Back at the cabin, I settled in on the couch and put on a series I'd watched several times already, letting its familiar dialogue drone out everything else for a few hours to eat up most of the day.

I almost hoped for a last minute drop off from hospital overflow, just to have something to do. To keep my hands and idle mind busy. But a call from Dad never came and he insisted I take at least one day off each week.

Around eight my brain felt numb enough to drag myself through a warm shower and get ready for bed.

I tipped my face back under the stream of water, lathering shampoo through my hair, sighing.

My lips parted, letting in a stream of soapy water as I

stopped. The sound of the water hitting the floor drowned out everything else but I *felt* it.

Rinsing my face, I peeked out of the shower booth through the open door to my bedroom.

The sound of the TV series playing robotically to no audience droned in from the living room.

I shivered, sensing the familiar interruption in the atmosphere around me. The presence and persistent glare of something that could see me but I couldn't see. It was back.

He was back.

I rinsed off quickly, rushing out of the shower, every inch of my skin alive and tingling.

Wrapped in just my towel, I hurried through the cabin, searching each window for his face until I got to the front door. I threw it open.

Crickets sang in the grass, a cool breeze swayed the trees in the woods. The temperatures dropped recently and the wind raised goosebumps on my skin, but I didn't see him.

"Ruarc?" I called out, his name a ball in my throat. A plea.

Leaving the door open behind me, I padded across the chilled wood of the porch and down the stairs, each one creaking beneath my weight.

Air stuttered into my lungs, scrutinizing every shadow. Every potential hiding place.

All the progress I thought I made in getting over him was undone at the mere suggestion that he might be close.

I shivered in the wind, closing my eyes, trying to hone in on that feeling. The one that told me he was near, but no matter how deeply I dug for it, I couldn't find it anymore.

Was he gone?

Was he ever really here?

Was I so obsessed with him that I was conjuring the feeling?

I walked back inside feeling bereft, my footsteps heavy. I couldn't fucking do this again. It was barely nine but there was nothing I wanted more than oblivion. The quicker I fell asleep, the quicker it would be morning and I could go to work.

In bed, I pulled the covers up to my chin, curling into a ball against the sheets. My body tingled with unresolved energy, unspent tension. Getting that hit of adrenaline just before bed was not going to make sleep easy tonight. Opening my eyes, I stared into the dark until shapes appeared. Shapes that I could pretend might be my monster in the dark.

I didn't know if there was a way back to who I used to be before him. Ruarc came into my life like a hurricane, destroying everything that made me who I was, forcing me to rebuild. Still, he'd been as intangible as a ghost. Maybe that's all he would ever be.

A ghost. There one minute and gone the next.

# 26

## RUARC

I vaulted onto the porch, landing lightly on the balls of my feet to pad around the edge of the cabin and press my body tight against the rough wooden exterior.

The front door opened and she stepped outside.

I'd been so careful these last few days. Overly cautious about when and where I watched her, but each time it was as if she could sense my presence, her haunting green eyes drawn to my exact location.

Except in sleep.

In sleep, I could stand by the foot of her bed, watch her chest heave and her lips part. I could imagine those lips around my cock as I stroked myself, pumping into my fist. She didn't wake up when I rubbed the tip over her lips, depositing little spurts of my seed into her mouth. Claiming her as mine even if I wouldn't have her.

I *couldn't* have her.

Not in the way I wanted.

Owning a person wasn't the same as having one

devoted to you. Possessions could break. They could be bought and traded, borrowed and bent. They could be lost.

I couldn't lose what I didn't have.

"Ruarc?" she called into the night, my name in her mouth like a siren's song. I closed my eyes, cursing silently as my stomach twisted and my cock thickened in my pants.

My breath burned in my lungs as she walked across the porch and down to the grass.

This was a bad idea.

Every passing day, I thought *this* would be the day that I forgot her.

The last time I came here.

It would be the day that I didn't care anymore. Where she wouldn't be the first thing I thought about in the morning. That thoughts of her wouldn't linger in my mind when everything was still.

Her hollow steps retreated and I chanced a sidelong glance around the edge of the cabin to watch her walk back inside, her head hung low. The door shut behind her, but she didn't lock it. She never locked it anymore.

I clenched my teeth so hard it hurt, willing myself not to read into that.

This was the woman I took from her home and held against her will. Whatever I felt and whatever she felt were not the same things. There was a gulf between us and there wasn't enough sex in the world to fill it in and make it solid ground.

Drawing the image into my mind sent a rush of blood to my cock.

I moved away from the wall, inhaling sharply, the clean pine air filling my lungs.

*Go home,* I told myself.

*Leave.*

I had shit to attend to. Delirium still stood on shaky ground and there were still a few more strings to pull to have Nixon released so that I could give him the ending he'd earned.

*Leave, you bastard.*

My hands raked violently through my hair, unable to force my feet to move.

Like my wiring was shoddy. Nothing connecting as it should.

My mind would tell my feet to move and they wouldn't.

I would try to keep my mouth shut but words would pour out anyway.

My thoughts got loud like a roar of rain hitting a tin roof in a thunderstorm.

*I just want to see her.*

That would be enough. Five minutes and I could leave.

I cringed at how pathetic I sounded but it didn't change my mind. I waited until her lights were off, and then I waited a little longer, just in case.

When I was near certain she'd be asleep, I crept across the porch, ducking low to peer into the windows for any sign of life.

Emily's cabin was extremely easy to get into for anybody who wanted access. A fact that bothered me to no fucking end even if I'd taken advantage of it more than once.

Even if she hadn't left the door unlocked, it was an old key-handle type. The ones anyone with half a brain and a hairpin could pick. The windows slid open easily enough as well since she never locked those anymore, either.

I pushed my way inside, lifting the door slightly to

avoid the worst of the creaking hinges and the way the warped bottom sometimes dragged noisily across the floor. I froze, my muscle tightening at the sudden creak of the hinges.

The cabin's interior was warm, sheltered from the wind outside. I sucked in a deep breath, the hair on the back of my neck standing up. Her scent had a growl sticking in my chest, my eyes rolling back. *Fuck*. If I could, I'd fucking drown myself in it.

Almost in a trance, my feet carried me across the creaky floor to her bedroom, memory helping me avoid all the noisiest spots. My pulse pounded so strongly, I felt it in my fingertips.

I wanted to *see* her. That was it.

*Five minutes,* I reminded myself. *No more. And then never again.*

The darkness of her room swallowed me up, and it took my eyes a minute to adjust as I stood at the foot of her bed.

The suffused moonlight filtering in from the gauzy curtains was just enough for me to make out the lines of her body under the covers, slowly rising and falling with her breath.

She was so fucking beautiful. Even in sleep, when the lines of her face softened, I couldn't imagine another person ever being as perfect as her.

A slow smile spread across my face before I could banish it away.

My hands shook. The visceral need to get closer, to touch, to *taste,* commanding every nerve ending.

Several long, silent moments passed and even with my mind signaling that time was up, my feet wouldn't move. They might as well have been glued to the floor. I was a bystander, watching from somewhere above, removed, apart. Unable to do anything to stop myself.

My little lamb moved suddenly, shifting under her covers and sighing softly.

Seeing her wasn't enough. It was never going to be.

Her soul called to me, beckoning me into the light.

Emily ruined me just as surely as I ruined her.

Why the hell did I ever think I could let her go?

Home felt empty without her.

I craved her voice, to feel her body in the bed with me.

Emily didn't buckle and fold under me, she fit into all my grooves and empty parts. She fought it hard, this *thing* between us, but ultimately, she accepted me, even broken and covered in blood.

She gave in willingly. Trading a piece of her soul to the devil in exchange for *life*. For feeling. To make that heart beat like it never beat before.

Being among the dead so long and so often, I had to wonder whether she'd ever felt alive before our eyes connected in the basement of the mortuary. It would be so easy to fall into a mind-numbing routine of work, sleep, eat, and repeat out here in the trees.

Was that it?

Did she only crave my darkness because it felt better than nothing?

I clenched my jaw, watching her legs slide over one another beneath the covers as she rolled onto her back and rubbed her cheek against her pillow, making little cooing sounds that made me rock hard.

My vision narrowed to a single-minded purpose, focused on her face in the dark.

It was more than that, I told myself as I dropped to my

knees, feeling along the edge of the bed to pull the covers from her.

...I'd prove it.

The comforter whispered over her mostly bare skin as I slowly drew them down, tugging them from her body and off the bed to drop them in a pile next to me.

I marveled at her lithe body, dressed in nothing with simple black panties and an oversized shirt.

My throat constricted. *My* shirt. The one she'd been wearing in the office when I'd bent her over my desk and had my way with her, needing one last taste of her before I could send her away.

Carefully, I reached for her hips, pulling her panties down. She stirred, but didn't wake, trying to draw her legs closer to herself for warmth.

*Uh uh, little lamb.*

Holding her legs apart, I slipped onto the bed between them.

I shuddered as I bent my head between her thighs, my tongue flicking out to taste her.

I groaned as her sweetness coated my tongue and a soft sleepy moan fell from her lips.

Pressing my tongue flat against her clit, her back arched, pressing her pussy into my mouth.

Her taste... her scent...

I was going insane. She was driving me to madness and was boarding the bus willingly, urging her to hit the fucking gas.

*I'll have her tonight. One last time.*

A lie. And not even a good one.

The goalposts kept moving and I let them. It would never be enough.

Sucking her clit into my mouth, I let my teeth skim over the supple flesh while pressing my fingers inside her.

She jerked in her sleep, wriggling under me, her fingers twisting in the sheets as she came up from dreamland. Slowly at first, with little whimpering moans and then all at once with a yelp as I began to fuck her with my fingers.

She pushed at my head, but I hooked an arm around her thigh, locking her to me as I kept up my assault with my fingers and tongue.

"R-Ruarc?" she stammered, her hands no longer shoving at my head. Instead, her fingers pressed into my hair, gently at first, in wonder as if she thought perhaps she was dreaming, but as I sunk another finger into her sweet cunt and flicked my tongue wickedly against her clit, those fingers twisted. She gripped handfuls of my hair, moaning loudly into the dark.

She fell back on the bed, her back arching. Her moans sliced through me like a knife. My cock swelled.

I felt her clench and pulse around my fingers as she began to move, thrusting her hips, fucking my mouth, bucking like she might combust if she didn't find release. Her moans grew louder, into shouts, and I licked her through it, violently stroking that sweet spot inside with hooked fingers.

"*Ruarc*," she screamed, coming around my fingers with a watery sob.

Her body convulsed and trembled and when it was finished, she sighed.

I pulled back, but her fingers in my hair tightened, holding me close. "Don't," she begged. "Don't go."

Her voice was sleepy and full of lust and I could not fucking deny her. Even if I wanted to.

I climbed over her body, kissing a line up her thigh, biting the supple flesh just above her knee. I pushed up her shirt, kissing and teasing until I had her breast in my mouth, making her cry out again.

Her arms and legs wrapped around my body like she thought I was going to disappear. I groaned against her tit in my mouth and she shivered as I released her, moving to take her lips.

She whined against my mouth, her body clenching as I kissed her hard, an almost painful ripple tearing through my abdomen, drawing a moan from my lips. I pushed in with my tongue and she opened for me, her broken cries swallowed up with every stroke of my tongue.

"Please," she begged when I pulled back for air. "*Please*."

I groaned, reaching between us and freeing my cock from my pants. I was hard enough to crack.

Her fingernails bit into my lower back, pulling me into her as I thrust my hips, burying myself so deeply in her tight cunt that I saw stars.

She screamed, throwing her head back.

Her tightness took me, stretching and yielding for my length and I knew I'd never find another cunt that took me this good. Not in a hundred years. Not in a thousand women.

My Emily.

My perfect little lamb.

*Mine.*

Going slow wasn't an option. I fucked her like it was life and death.

Because knowing I'd still need to walk out that door when this was over made me feel like I would die and if I did I wanted this to be the last memory that chased me to my grave.

Her mattress bent and flexed with every brutal thrust, bouncing her on my cock, bringing me close to the edge already.

*Not yet.*

I wrapped a fist around her pretty throat, knowing what it did to her. She whimpered, her eyes rolling back in ecstasy as she lay there and took that dick like a fucking pro.

I allowed her a little gulp of air and she gasped, her walls clenching around me. "I'm not on birth control anymore," she said in a rush before I could go back to doing the devil's work around her neck.

"*Fuck,*" I hissed, my body responding in a way that shocked me to my fucking core. The primal need to plant my seed, to breed her, to claim her in a way that couldn't be undone had me seeing stars.

I squeezed her neck, silencing her as I savaged her pussy and pressed my mouth to hers.

She whimpered, trying to wriggle free as she came on my cock. Her ecstasy spurring my own. I let her take a full breath and watched in awe as twin tears streaked from her eyes at the raw pleasure wracking her body.

"*Damn,*" I groaned, blind with lust.

Her eyes met mine in the dark and I gritted my teeth. Her lips parted, recognizing how close I was to my own end and wanting to watch me get there.

I groaned.

"Ruarc, pull out," she muttered, her hands pressing on the bones of my hips, making me fight against her to continue my bruising pace between her thighs.

"*Ruarc*," she insisted as I hit my apex, throwing my head back in a silent howl.

"Ruarc!"

I barely made it, jerking out of her slick folds to come onto her abdomen and thighs. The loss of her warmth like a slap in the face as my body wrung itself dry on her skin.

I should have buried my seed in her. Buried it so deep that she couldn't claw it out no matter how hard she tried. I should've hung her upside down, ensuring every fucking drop made it to that place deep inside that would bind her to me in a way that couldn't be undone.

Why?

Why hadn't I taken it? Taken her?

I pushed back, off her body, shifting from the bed as the high leveled out and I realized what I'd almost done. What I'd almost allowed to happen.

My nose wrinkled, upper lip twitching in disgust as I adjusted my pants, searching the floor for a lost shoe.

What was I thinking?

I wasn't.

Another side effect. What was next?

"Where are you going?" she demanded, rolling from the bed to clean herself with a towel from the floor.

"Home."

"What? No."

She bolted forward like a fawn on unsteady legs, grabbing my arm as I turned to leave.

I cut her a glare. "Emily—"

"*No*. You can't just come here and do... whatever that was and then just walk out like it never happened."

My jaw tightened. "What do you want?"

"I'm not your whore, Ruarc."

My brows lowered, seeing the fire in her eyes. The one I'd seen that first night in the mortuary, burning bright.

She still didn't get it.

She was the furthest thing from being my whore.

She was the only woman I ever fucked more than once. The only one whose name I not only remembered but woke with on my lips in the dead hours of the night.

It was because she wasn't my whore that I needed to keep her at a distance. I had to push her away before she could decide to withdraw from me herself. If she did, I wasn't sure how I'd react. There were so many nights I imagined my mother returning. Some nights, she would come sweeping in and I'd hug her tight. Other nights, I'd put a bullet between her eyes.

Emily couldn't leave me. Not if she never had me to begin with.

It was the only way to keep her safe.

"I know," I admitted, my voice barely cutting through the space between us. I was fucking scared, did she want to hear that? I wanted her so much; I was afraid I wouldn't know what to do when she walked away. "I won't come back. You have my word."

She cocked her head at me, her eyes narrowing to angry slits. "Is that what you think I want?"

"You should."

Her jaw flexed. "I left the door open because I knew you were still out there, even when I couldn't feel you."

"You wanted me to come."

"Yes, you idiot."

So reckless, my little lamb. Rude, violent, tender, she never held back, even when the glimmer of fear was so bright in her eyes.

"I need you to hear this, Ruarc."

"*Mmm?*"

I blinked, flinching as she settled a warm palm against my chest.

"The little boy in here who's been building walls his whole life..."

My stomach twisted.

"I need him to understand that I'm not going to leave him. He can fight and he can roar and he can go on building his walls, but I'll just keep climbing them. He can't keep me out."

*Fire.* It burned in my chest. In my eyes. In my throat. I forced it down. Out. *Away.*

"Stay with me," she said. It wasn't a question. Numbly, I let her lead me back to the bed, sitting heavily on the squeaking mattress.

Emily took off my shoes, setting them neatly next to the bed before retrieving the covers from the floor. She removed both my blades, the one from my belt and the other from my ankle, patting me down for any other weapons before crawling into bed next to me.

I'd fallen asleep beside her before, but this was different.

Emily curled into my side and a lump formed in my throat as I pressed my lips to her dark hair, inhaling her.

The cracks in *us*, the ones I put there, broke wider. Letting voices of dissent pass through, reminding me that everything I loved turned to ash on my tongue. And that I'd killed the part of myself capable of that emotion a long time ago.

I couldn't have her.

There was a world she belonged to before I pulled her

into mine. One that didn't do the shit I did to her. She had people who loved her. A future that didn't involve violence and blood and pain.

I wasn't alone because people left. I was alone because anything that came too close died. Starved for sunlight in my hollow darkness.

*I won't be the death of her.*

*I won't let her be the ruin of me.*

Sleep came in short, uncomfortable bursts until the darkness in the windows began to brighten.

Sliding out of her bed and getting dressed, I let myself out, the tight ball in my chest unfurling as clean air entered my lungs, untainted by her scent. Allowing me clarity of thought.

Would she think it all a dream when she woke?

Something pulled uncomfortably in my chest.

Eventually she would see, all nightmares ended with bright mornings, and they faded just as quickly.

# 27

---

## RUARC

The hard leather steering wheel creaked under my grip as I stared out the windshield, taking in Snow's Mortuary as dawn crept over the horizon.

My gaze tracked right, the small footpath scoring the earth around the side of the building. The one that led back to the cabin I'd only just left. As if she was about to run out and stop me. Beg me to come back. I scoffed at my own pathetic longing, jamming the ignition button before I could sink any lower.

Thoughts roiled in my head. Nothing, *nobody* ever made me so slow and uncertain. Emily Snow was not the sort of person I should be coveting. I needed to be acquiring more assets right now, not liabilities.

I squeezed my eyes shut, but even then I couldn't escape her. Vivid images flashed over the backs of my eyelids, a projected silent film of every forbidden touch. I saw her eyes, wide and open. Pleading. Ready to surrender to me, to give me everything.

I opened my eyes and threw the car into reverse, roaring into the silent cabin as I hit the gas. Fucking enraged.

Was my little lamb any better than an illicit drug? My body ached for her as if in withdrawal.

Drugs were everywhere when I was growing up. In my mom's nightstand, in her purse, in her veins. In the pockets of most of the other teenagers in our neighborhood.

I vowed never to touch them and I *never* had. I couldn't have something else control me like that.

But Emily wasn't just flowing through my veins, she'd seeped into every cell and fiber of my body. She'd broken down my defenses and permeated every thought, tainting it with her unique essence.

Her grip on me was tighter than any drug I could've shot into my veins, and just as lethal.

Driving away from the mortuary, it didn't stop. If anything, the sensation worsened. I felt the call, the pull of her drawing me back.

Sweat beaded at my temples.

Air pushed hard out of my lungs.

I never should've come back here.

I focused on the brightly lit road ahead, pushing the Aston to its limits, letting the whine of the engine and the force of its speed drown out my incessant thought patterns. Always looping back to *her*.

Nixon would have some choice words seeing me right now. The worse fucking part was that he'd be right.

Flashing lights in my rearview broke the spiraling chain looping thought. I glanced up into the rearview, spotting a car right on my tail.

Either they'd appeared out of nowhere, or I wasn't paying enough attention. I was betting on the latter.

It was a rarity, having company on this road, especially at this hour.

There was virtually nothing between the mortuary and my estate aside from a few dirt side roads leading to all but abandoned mansions owned by the wealthy and powerful who had no time to use them.

I accelerated, and the other car did the same, gaining on me until he was right on my ass. I hit the gas again but not before he clipped the back of my Aston.

Mother*fucker.*

Adrenaline flooded my veins as I fishtailed, regaining control.

This early in the morning?

I wasn't in the fucking mood.

The car fell into line behind me again, accelerating.

*Bastard.*

I put my seatbelt on, having to work twice as hard to keep control of the vehicle at high speed with one hand. It clicked into place and I pulled the belt tight over my chest, bracing with two hands on the wheel as I hit the brake.

The car's slick engineering brought it to an absolute halt in seconds, the tires screeching against the pavement for an instant before the inevitable crash.

My body lurched forward and I was ready with my blade as the airbag deployed, stabbing it dead before it could crush my nose.

The ear splitting ring of breaking glass and twisting metal assaulted my ears as the car collided with mine.

The Aston whipped across the road, coming to a tire-whining stop just off the side of the road.

"Fucking jackass," I muttered, my chest aching from where the seatbelt bit into me. I unfastened, leaning over to take the Glock from the glove compartment before pushing out of the ruined car.

The rear was caved in beyond recognition and I sniffed, tasting blood in the back of my throat as I set my sights on the mangled late model Honda with its hazard lights flashing in the middle of the road.

My upper lip curled.

Whoever it was picked the wrong damn day.

The driver hunched over the wheel, immobile. I wrestled the door open, cutting my palms on the jagged metal. It groaned before giving, coming entirely off its hinges. I tossed it to the pavement and wrenched the man from his seat onto the broken glass covered pavement.

He moaned, coughing as he rolled from his back to his side. I staggered back a step, recognizing his face.

Blood ran down into his eyes from a gnarly gash in his forehead and it looked like his right leg was broken. Yep, the white pressing through his denim jeans couldn't be anything else but bone.

I grabbed the back of his head, forcing his head up into the light to be sure.

I never bothered with names but I never forgot a face. This little fucker worked for me.

"Give me one good reason why I shouldn't put a bullet between your eyes," I snarled, releasing him. He groaned, dropping his head. And then he swung. It was a weak attempt at a punch, but with as much blood as it looked like he'd lost, I'd give him applause for trying, even if he missed.

The sound of a bullet blasted through the air, momentarily stopping everything around it, the air, my breath, my body, before I grasped for his arm, pinning it to the ground.

He cried out.

I slammed his arm to the ground again, knocking the weapon free and kicking it across the road and into the ditch.

"Who sent you?" I demanded.

He glared up at me through one squinted eye, the other still battling the river of blood running down his face, and losing.

He ground his teeth together, determined not to talk.

"Talk, you little shit." I sneered, kicking his injured leg.

He screamed, reaching for it, the sound at odds with the golden glow of sunrise and the birdsong in the trees.

This had Nixon written all over it.

"The only way you have even the smallest chance of surviving the next five minutes is by opening that useless fucking mouth and telling me exactly what I want to hear.

I bent to a crouch, tugging my gun from my waistband to press it into the notch under his jaw.

He went from screaming to utter silence in the blink of an eye, his breaths hissing out between his lips. "What exactly was it you were trying to do?"

"I-I was at the mortuary," he stuttered. "I followed you."

"On Nixon's orders," I said, not a question, but the dead man nodded into the barrel of my gun anyway, confirming it. "When did you speak to him?"

Nix was still in lock up, but that didn't mean the traitor couldn't make calls. I thought I'd weeded out all the potential conspirators from my ranks, but this fucker still managed to slip through.

How many others were still out there?

My blood cooled, coming to terms with everything I'd allowed to happen because I wasn't paying attention.

"Y-yesterday. He wanted me to follow you. Said you liked going to the m-m-mortuary. He wanted me to—"

"Enough."

I felt something small tug in my chest for the boy. He was barely into his twenties. Barely a man. Easy to manipulate.

"Sir," he tried. "I–"

"Stop talking."

His blue eyes quivered. I recently learned a hard lesson about trust. If I couldn't trust Nixon, everybody was out. If this boy existed, there had to be others.

"Who else is there? Who else did Nix have working with him?"

"N—nobody else," he blurted and heat poured down my back.

"I don't like having to repeat myself," I warned.

"*Nobody*! Nobody. I swear. It's just me. He told me it was just me. He was going to make me his right-hand man when he..." His words died in his throat feeling the gun press into his skin.

I breathed in deeply, forcing it out hard.

"Well, *right-hand man*, I hope it was worth it."

I moved the gun, tapping it against his breastplate through his blood-soaked shirt.

He was gone quick, fluid flooding his lungs, taking his dying breaths through choked moans. I watched the light leave his eyes, until the dull sheen of a lost soul clouded his irises.

I left his corpse on the road as I went back to my car, but before I could settle back into the seat, the rear left axle snapped and the tire rolled away down the road.

I chuckled darkly, taking a calming breath as I turned my face to the sky.

What kind of sick, twisted, luck was it that after dragging myself away from her, this piece of shit would see me returning to the mortuary, corpse and cash in hand.

Muttering a string of curses, I dug around near the pedals, finding my phone. The broken screen sliced into the tip of my pinkie finger and I growled as I jammed the screen, blood marring the dial pad.

"Boss?"

"I need a cleanup crew three miles out to the east on the main road. Two vehicles to clear. And bring me my Lincoln. Tarp the back for me, would you?"

"You got it, boss."

I hung up, tossing my phone back into the car as I leaned against the frame to wait.

A minute later, another car came down the road, *not* from the direction I expected. My throat tightened, seeing the boxy dark shape, picturing Emily behind the wheel. But the vehicle slowed and the driver's side window rolled down to reveal a bearded gawker with a lit cigarette between his fingers.

"Shit, man, you all right?"

I stalked over to his car and he recoiled back in his seat but didn't speed off. I drew my gun and lazily rested it against the base of the window frame, drawing a gasp from his mouth.

"You saw nothing," I said, plucking the cigarette from his fingers to put between my lips. I took a long drag, shuddering at the release. Much as a good fag after a good fuck. A good little hit of nicotine after a kill was just enough to take the edge off. I blew the smoke in his face, flicking the cigarette over his lap, making him pat out the still-hot ashes.

"I saw nothing," he repeated, his face paling, eyes jerking between me and the road, begging for me to release him.

I reached in, patting him on the shoulder. "Good man. Off you go."

Watching his taillights vanish over the hill to the west, I couldn't help thinking Emily would appreciate my show of mercy. The old Ruarc would have added the gawker's corpse to the pile for burning, just to be safe.

But there would be enough bloodshed in the days to come. If nothing else, this little incident proved it was time to finally put an end to it. I'd been holding back. Drawing it out.

No more.

It was time for Nixon to meet his maker.

# 28

___

## RUARC

Wind blew through the open bones of the abandoned construction site.

The project had long since halted. It was to be a mixed-use complex and only got as far as the foundations and the building's skeleton up to two parking levels. After several stops and starts due to some petitioning the destruction of a wetland ecosystem, the construction hadn't been active for almost two months.

On the outskirts of town with an unused lot on one side and nothing on the other, I was sure we wouldn't be disturbed.

Rain tapped against the windshield as I tapped my fingers against the steering wheel.

Nixon would arrive at any minute.

If it'd been anyone else, I'd have opted to finish it at the house. Perhaps in the woods out back, or in the courtyard gardens at the heart of the mansion.

But the thought of allowing Nixon back on the property disgusted me.

I tried to pull it back, but I was too late. Thinking about the mansion and the other people who were allowed intimate access to me and my space, Emily came bursting into focus.

A breath shuttered from my lips

Tonight, her face in my mind was not going to be motivation.

It would be the distraction Nixon warned me about.

I glanced at the time displayed on the dash. Well past midnight.

He wasn't yet late. I was just early, and fucking impatient to get this over with.

When I killed Nixon tonight, there would be no one else.

No one who could betray me in a way that would twist in my gut like a knife.

The raindrops on the outside of the car seemed to come down harder, magnifying the sound inside.

I'd pictured his end in so many different ways. Maybe I would show mercy, maybe I would be quick, maybe I would make him suffer, but only one of us was leaving here alive.

Headlights filled the rearview.

Crunching over dirt and gravel at a glacial pace, one of my men chauffeured Nixon to his gravesite, parking opposite me in the rain.

It'd been a bitch to organize, and cost me more in bribes than I cared to share, but I'd seen to Nixon's release. And then I'd seen to his pick up and the deliverance of a message. One I knew he would not refuse. Not if he still wanted a shot to take what rightfully belonged to me.

I lifted the nondescript black duffel from the seat next to me and pushed out into the cool rain. I heard the doors of the other vehicle open, but didn't bother to look as I stalked to the half built, sheltering under the ceiling of the first level.

I shook off the rain from my hair and dropped the heavy duffel to the cement floor with a thud.

"This is the place you picked? Really?" Nixon asked, approaching with an easy swagger, my man on his heels placed himself by the exit, hands clasped at his front. He wouldn't intervene, no matter what. His role was purely an observant one. In the off chance I didn't leave here alive, he would corroborate Nix's triumph to the others, helping to facilitate his ascension to the throne.

Not something I intended to allow.

In jeans and a plain collared black shirt, Nixon appeared a little too at ease, his damp hair falling forward into his eyes.

Besides the shadow of a beard growing in and some weight loss, he didn't look like a man who'd spent the last month in a prison cell.

"Apologies," I snapped sarcastically. "I should've allowed you your choice of grave."

He smirked, sinking his hands into his pockets and looking around the unfinished building like it was a potential investment rather than a coffin.

Nix wasn't stupid, he had to know the likelihood of his success here was undeniably slim. I may not have had occasion to get my hands dirty since taking over, but that didn't mean I didn't know a hundred different ways to kill a man. And it definitely didn't fucking mean I would hesitate.

"Someplace with trees might've been preferable. Though, what I really want to do is go home and sleep on a real bed," he said with a hollow laugh.

I flinched, the casual sound of his voice disarming me. Despite everything, I still saw *him*. The Nixon beneath the greedy bastard who tried to orchestrate my downfall. I shook my head, reminding myself they were one and the same.

Inhaling sharply, I bent to unzip the duffel at my feet and drew my blade.

I kicked the duffel towards Nixon, the remaining collection of blades clattering together before several spilled out over the dirt covered concrete.

He looked over his options with no expression on his face.

As soon as I realized I needed to be the one to do it, I knew it had to be done in this way. Nixon had challenged my reign, if he'd had a fucking spine in his back he'd have challenged me to my goddamn face we'd have settled it like men.

Like *this*.

Guns were fast. Efficient. They were also impersonal.

If I was going to end Nixon, it had to match the gravity of what he did to me. Deep, raw, with his blood on my hands.

"Don't just stand there. I don't have all night." I seethed, flipping the blade around in my palm, adjusting my grip on the handle.

He bristled slightly, showing a hint of apprehension for the first time since he showed up.

"So this is what it comes to," he said on a breath.

I scoffed, digging the balls of my feet into the ground as five and a half inches of steel glistened in the moonlight.

"This is what it comes to," I confirmed, running my

tongue over my teeth, a surge of power awakening in my core, flushing heat out to my extremities.

He bent and pulled out the twin blade from the duffel. He slipped it from its sheath and held it in his hand testing its weight. Looking up at me, he slowly rose to his full height.

The expression on his face made something twist in my gut.

He smiled, but his eyes hardened with pain.

"What are you waiting for?" I yelled, eager now, nearly bouncing on my feet, my skin prickling with unspent energy.

"You wanted a chance, here it is. *Take it.*"

Nixon bit his lip, looking down at the ground. His stance was uneven, unsure. With any other person, this would have ended already but here I was. Fucking stalling.

I needed him to make the first move. To wave the red flag for the charge.

"*What are you waiting for?*"

My muscles tensed, on high alert, watching him for sudden movements. My teeth gritted with annoyance, frustration scratching up my back like rats.

Fuck him for getting us to this point.

Fuck him for making me do this.

"*Come on!*"

Nixon's lips pulled over his teeth, finally showing me his fangs.

I poised for the attack, ready to parry, and strike.

Instead of advancing, Nix growled, hot air lifting from his mouth as he dropped his blade.

"I'm not going to fight you," he shouted. "So, if you're going to kill me, get it over with."

Frost bloomed in my core, a cold sweat slicked over my chest, making the blade slippery in my palm.

"Fight back, you fucking coward!"

He stood, his hands in fists at his sides, his jaw set.

"*Fine*," I hissed.

He wanted an execution, I'd give it to him.

Gladly.

I charged and he ducked to the ground, drawing an evil grin to my lips.

*Yes.*

*Fight, you fucker.*

Anticipating his next move, I jerked back when he arced back up, fast enough to get out of the way of the blade he'd picked back up from the ground.

He wanted to fight dirty? Fine.

Nix aimed his next attack for my arm, trying to fuck up my grip.

He swung wildly, driven by the instinctive need for survival.

His mistake.

I dodged the attack, parrying to the right to drive my knife downward into his extended shoulder. He threw himself out of the way, stumbling, but not before I could carve a deep gash into the muscle and flesh just below his shoulder.

Blood soaked his dark shirt, running in rivulets down his arm to coat his hand, making his grip on the blade there slippery at best.

He bared his teeth at me, a mutt in a fight meant for wolves.

"Fucking bastard," he hissed, charging me again, his arm raised, chest puffed out, shoulders broad.

I waited, widening my stance, ready for the impact.

His blade glanced off mine, deflected as I bent low, ramming my shoulder into his middle to heave him over my back. He rolled awkwardly from my spine, landing in a coughing heap on the concrete.

"Get up!"

Nix spit into the dirt, pale from the blood loss. I caught my breath, blood pounding in my ears. I wasn't ready for him to lurch up without warning, flying at me like a bat out of fucking hell.

A sting of pain bloomed on my face as he slashed his blade over my cheekbone, opening a long cut that leaked warmth down to my chin.

His eyes went wild with bloodlust as he recovered from the inertia of the attack and pivoted, coming at me again, mouth pulled in a grimace.

"Come on!" he yelled, his voice strained with manic desperation. "Stop fucking holding back."

"Have you always been so eager to die?"

I stepped to the left and him to the right, parroting each other's movements in a slow circle as we both searched for weak points, biding time for the next blow.

Truthfully, I was hemming. Stalling the inevitable. Even after everything, it turned out I wasn't exactly who I thought myself to be.

He should be dead at my feet by now.

"Come on, Ruarc. Don't you need to get back to your little whore?"

Whatever small thread of hope I'd been carrying that Nixon might repent his sins, admit his mistake, own up to his greed, and beg my forgiveness, snapped. Cold settled in my chest. My hand tightened on the knife.

Thunder roared above us, distant but resonant, an echo of the growl rumbling in my chest.

"That bitch was always going to be your downfall. You'll see. She's your greatest weakness. I should've killed her when I had the chance."

A curse roared from my chest and I was on top of him. He crashed to the ground, his knife knocked from his grip as I sunk mine smoothly between two ribs.

His eyes widened, mouth opening in a silent gasp.

*"You're wrong."*

Emily didn't make me weak. She wouldn't be my end. She made me strong. She would be my new beginning. My salvation. The light in my darkness. The thread of purity woven into my ugliness.

My reason for existing.

Hands on the blade, I watched him through the static of my red-tinted rage. He grabbed for me, clumsily groping until he gripped my shoulder. He choked, unable to speak for the blood filling his mouth and sloshing down his cheek.

"And I should've killed you the instant you laid a hand on her."

His hand loosened and his eyes lost focus. As the red pool beneath him grew, his body sagged. I twisted the knife, drawing one last weak croak from his lips before he was gone.

I didn't stand until every ounce of life left his eyes.

My head spun as I pushed to my feet on unsteady legs, looking down at my handiwork.

I hurled the knife across the ground, pushing my hair back from my face with blood soaked hands, breathing in the crisp air as I looked up through the dripping planks of the ceiling to the slivers of moonlights between.

Pain slowly began to register; Nixon got me in the chest and face with his blind strikes.

I did a mental check, assessing the damages, finding more blood than I'd anticipated.

His? Mine? Both, most likely.

I'd killed Nixon in every way that mattered before coming here tonight, but still his lifeless corpse drew pity from my core like poison from a wound.

"Sir?" my man by the wall spoke, reminding me of his presence. "Shall I load the body into the Lincoln?"

I closed my eyes, sighing as the tightness in my lungs relented.

"Yes."

"Shall I handle the disposal, sir?"

I shook my head, rolling his offer around in my mouth before replying.

"No," I said finally, my jaw tight as I realized what an absolute fool I'd been. "I'll handle it myself."

## 29

### EMILY

Sleep danced on the edges of my consciousness, just out of reach.

Sighing heavily, I gave in, opening them with a muted groan to stare into the dark.

The silence was so keen tonight it almost felt heavy. Like a physical weight on my chest, like pressure all around me. It had a presence all its own in the cabin. More than presence, though, I recognized it for what it was behind the mask it wore.

Absence.

Absence of hope, absence of desire, the absence of him.

My lips twisted as the pain came, but I'd grown used to it now; That hollow ache in my chest every time I thought of him.

It didn't knock the breath out of me anymore at least. I hated it those first few weeks, chastising myself for having ever felt anything for him at all.

Now, though...

Now, I welcomed it. The leftover pain of his absence was the only reminder I had that I'd ever really lived.

*Stories like yours deserve a better ending.*

I tried.

Since that night of confession with Tessa I'd gone to his house three times.

He wouldn't see me.

The doors were always locked, and no one came no matter how hard I banged on the solid wooden panes. No matter how loudly I shouted. Even though I knew he was in there. I could sense him, feel his eyes on me from the windows even if I couldn't see him.

On the third night, I tried to force my way into Delirium and when they refused me, I'd thrown a brick through the front window next to the door, right into the foyer. Shocked at my own penchant for violence. At the hurt that propelled it.

His men did open the door then, but only to drag me back to my car and stuff me inside, ordering me to leave.

It hurt and I fucking hated him for it.

Hated him for being as stubborn as a goddamned mule and just as immovable. For making me into a husk of myself. For ruining me inside and out.

I rolled onto my side, staring at the wall until my eyes adjusted.

Another sleepless night. I wouldn't care much if the exhaustion didn't affect my work. You could still damage a dead body if you weren't careful and I'd almost botched the filler on two corpses this past week.

*I bet he slept like a baby.*

My eyes caught on the stack of books on the nightstand. I hadn't cracked a single spine since they showed up on my doorstep. A stack of six, tied together with a satin red ribbon. There was no card but I knew where they came from. Who ordered them.

Why even bring them? Why not throw them out? Burn them? Drop them in the goddamned ocean?

I certainly wouldn't be reading them.

*Yes, little lamb, I'll order your filthy books.*

I shuddered, my stomach clenching tight.

They'd make the hours pass, but I knew they'd also just remind me of him. In the same way certain scents did now. Certain sounds. A certain type of music.

I reached out, shoving the books from the nightstand to the floor before groping under my pillow for my phone. My eyes burned at the brightness of the screen but I endured it until they adjusted.

What was social media good for if not endless hours of distraction?

Eventually, my vision started to blur. It faded out and then snapped back into focus. My eyelids drooped. My hand's grip around my phone loosened until finally, I was sucked under.

As I slept, there was a distant tapping. It was sharp enough to pierce my drowsy reckoning, but I ignored it, stuffing my face into my pillow.

It came again, three hard, succinct bangs.

*Knock. Knock. Knock.*

My eyes opened, registering everything at once.

It was still dark. Late. Middle of the night. And there was knocking.

*Ruarc.*

I sat up, the cloud of sleep dispelled in an instant as I looked around my cabin, kicking my blankets off.

My feet hit the cold floor and I sucked in a breath through my teeth, reaching for my robe.

*He's here.*

My brow furrowed as I threw open my bedroom door and footsteps slowed on their path to the front door.

But... Ruarc wouldn't knock.

He didn't ask for things, he took them, again and again.

Every time he'd been inside my cabin it was without my opening the door to let him in.

"Hello?" I called tentatively, swallowing hard when no reply came.

Licking my dry lips, I pulled the robe tighter around myself, rushing to the kitchen for a knife from the block before going back to the door.

Steeling myself, I adjusted my grip on the chef's knife, flicked on the porch light, and flung the door open.

The porch light brightened one side of his face, leaving the other largely in shadow. My breath caught in my chest, holding there, making my lungs burn. I exhaled slowly.

"I thought you were never going to open up," he said, a small smirk pulling the side of his lips. And then, I saw the blood.

"Oh god."

He took a small step forward, unsteady, swaying on his feet. He held onto the railing around the porch to balance himself.

"What happened?" I asked, setting the knife down on the small key table by the door as I stepped out, my heart in my throat.

"Ruarc?"

He grunted as he turned to me, his eyes bright against

the river of darkened blood marring the other side of his face.

I gasped, searching the lawn behind him and the driveway for danger before grabbing him by the arm to drag him inside.

"Who did this to you?"

He laughed, the movement reopening the long slash in his cheekbone as I directed him to sit on the couch.

With the full lights on, the damage was even worse than what I'd seen. The white shirt he wore was splattered with dried blood. But worst of all were his hands. They were soaked in it. Every wrinkle and crevasse filled with red.

"You should see the other guy," he said lightly.

I put a hand to his forehead, checking for fever but finding his skin cool to the touch. With a grip on his chin, I forced his head back, tilting it so I could examine the wound on his face.

The gash looked uncomfortably new. Whatever happened, it happened tonight. Hours ago if not less.

It was unusually intimate being allowed to see him in this way. I knew what he did and what that meant, but I never saw it in front of my eyes. He kept that part from me. Until now.

"Wait here."

I went to the bathroom to find some Neosporin. My reflection, spooked and wide-eyed, looked back at me from the mirror.

In spite of the fear and uncertainty, I felt keenly *alive*.

I'd missed this. Wanted to grab hold with both hands and refuse to let go.

Ruarc was still there on the couch, sitting obediently where I left him when I came back out. It was a good start.

"What did you do?" I asked, kneeling in front of him.

His dark eyes roamed my face, appreciating me from the new angle with a tight jaw and heat behind his stare.

He didn't say anything, instead reaching for my arm and pulling me from the floor. He guided my thighs over his lap with blood stained fingers before settling them at my waist, holding me there in a straddle over him.

My breath caught at the feel of him, hard beneath me. Solid. *Real.*

When I looked into his eyes, I didn't see the ghost looking back at me. I saw flesh and blood. Not a monster. A man.

*My Ruarc.*

His grip on my waist tightened and my body responded, arching into him as my arms threaded around his neck. Ruarc pressed a rough palm to the middle of my back, clutching me close as our mouths collided.

He kissed me. *Hard.* Stealing all the breath from my lungs as he wrapped his muscled arms around me and squeezed tight. He groaned against my mouth, and a delicious ache spread through my belly, awakening a desire that'd been dormant since our last encounter.

"*Emily,*" he whispered against my mouth, breaking the spell.

I pulled back, our lips breaking apart but our bodies still fastened by the tight grip of his arms.

He tried to press the back of my neck, tried to bring me back to him but I remained at a distance, fighting his insistent touch.

"I am not your whore," I said, leveling the full meaning on him. Needing him to see how much I meant it.

I craved him more than I'd ever craved anything else, but I wouldn't be that for him. I couldn't.

I wanted it all. Or I would have nothing.

His lips pressed into a thin line, but he released my waist, lifting a hand to gently brush the hair back from my face, tucking it behind my ear before running his fingers down the line of my jaw, dragging a shuddering breath from my lips.

"Oh little lamb," he said, a light in his eyes now. "You never were."

"But..."

"I was just too ignorant to see it. To much the fucking coward to reach out and take it."

My face fell. "You're not making sense. What are you saying?"

"I'm saying, Emily Snow, that I love you."

A sob grew in my chest, halted by my complete inability to breathe as tears stung my eyes.

"You hurt me, Ruarc. You just fucking left. You just..." The sob finally came out and I choked it down, sniffing, trying to regain control.

He nodded, pursing his lips.

"I know." He cupped my face between his palms and I swallowed as a tear escaped and he rubbed it away with his thumb. "All I'm asking is that you let me try to make it up to you."

"I don't know if you can."

He licked his lips. "Well I've got our whole lives to try."

"Don't say that unless you mean it."

"I do."

A shuddering sigh shook my lungs as I dropped my head, feeling weightless and anchored all at once.

I wiped my nose on my sleeve and moved to crawl from his lap. "I need to clean and stitch that cut in your cheek before it gets infected."

He pulled me back, inclining his head to the door. "Before we do that, there's something I was hoping you'd help me with."

I followed his gaze to the door.

"Nixon's in the trunk."

I stiffened in his grasp.

"He's here?"

His Adam's apple bobbed as he swallowed, nodding. "His corpse is."

Soft lines were drawn at the corners of his eyes, making his gaze unbelievably vulnerable. Reflexively, I wrapped my arms around him, tight. He seemed like the last person in the world who would need to be held, who needed comfort or reassurance, much less from me, but he didn't stop me, pressing his face into the crook of my neck.

"I'm so sorry."

"I need you to get rid of it," he said, voice muffled. I let go of him, my hands on his shoulders as I looked into his face.

"Me?"

"You."

I felt there was more he wasn't saying and I bit my lip, waiting for him to continue.

"Nixon, and whoever else comes next. I want it to be you, not your father."

I struggled to close my dropped jaw, reading between the lines.

He wasn't just asking me to take over for my old man, this was him asking me if I could do this. *Really* do this. If I could accept that being tied to him meant also being tied to the syndicate. To crime. To *sin*.

My father handled cremations. He always had, but there were times when I needed to assist. Or times when he was too ill to do it himself. I knew how. It wasn't difficult.

It wasn't an open flame or anything, it was a very high-tech incinerator. The bodies were placed in simple wooden coffins and the conveyor system slid them into the flame. When it was finished, we collected the ash. That was it.

But could I feed a body, *a soul*, into the flames knowing that somewhere out there, someone would be missing them?'

I considered Ruarc's request, my gaze meeting his hard patient stare.

A monster who killed other monsters.

I nodded gravely. "Only the guilty," I said, drawing my line in the sand. "I won't be responsible for vanishing innocents. I can't."

He nodded back. "Okay."

"What about my dad?"

His arms were loose around me, settled comfortably on my hips while mine were on his shoulders. Our embrace almost comically laid back for what we were discussing.

"What about him?"

I stared at him, waiting, willing him to elaborate until he finally sighed.

"Your father betrayed my trust, Emily. I can't work with him."

My jaw clenched.

"As a favor to you, I won't harm him. He can go on

performing autopsies and whatever else he does until he kicks the bucket."

This time when I climbed out of his lap, he let me.

"Let's go."

He eyed my outstretched hand before taking it, wincing as he used it to help him stand.

After the rain earlier, the air felt light and refreshing as we exited the cabin, a balm to my frazzled nerves.

"Where is he?"

"In the back of the Lincoln, parked near the road."

I nodded, renewed by a sense of purpose, a morbid thought passing through my mind.

"Drive 'round to the service entrance. We'll use the lift to bring him down. I'll go fire up the old beast."

Ruarc scoffed before walking away into the dark, down the narrower path to the main road, while I veered to the right, traipsing through wet grass in my bare feet.

I was glad it was Nixon; the first corpse I'd feed to the flames.

I remembered the rough way he'd nearly dislocated my arm. The cruel things he'd said. The fact that he'd tried to hurt Ruarc only compounded the interest of my hate for the man.

It would be easy to watch him burn.

*I might even enjoy it.*

I got to the building first, punching the code into the rear door to enter. I paused as I pulled it open, the familiar sensation that I was being watched washing over me.

Instinctively, I turned my head to the right, squinting past the security lights to Dad's house in the distance.

No lights, no activity. Ruarc came straight to me, but

there was a chance my dad was watching. That he might see me.

I laughed at the ridiculousness of it.

*Never enter the mortuary after midnight.*

I didn't think I'd ever break that rule again and yet here I was, willingly tying myself to the midnight hour and to everything that came with it.

Smirking, I wedged the wooden door stop in the base of the door and went down to the basement, flicking on the lights in the cremation chamber.

The controls were simple and even though I hadn't had cause to use the cremator in a while, I managed to get it going within a couple minutes.

I heard the elevator's hum out in the hall and grabbed the clean trolley from the hall to meet him. The doors opened and Ruarc stepped through with a lifeless Nixon over his left shoulder.

His steps were slow, panting as he brushed past me into the hall.

"Put him down on this," I said, pushing the trolley toward him. He heaved the body, dropping Nixon on the slab with a clatter.

I stilled, taking in the full extent of the damage.

He'd clearly lost a lot of blood. His shirt was soaked in it and I saw rips in the shoulder and chest where he'd been punctured with a knife. His eyes were half open and his skin chalk white.

"You used a knife?" I asked.

"It was personal," he replied, like that explained everything.

Spotting the watch around his wrist, I lifted his arm so I could take it off. It wasn't going to burn in the incinerator. I took his rings, too, fighting to pry them from stiffening fingers.

I held the jewelry in my palm, checking his pockets for anything else before I was satisfied. The gold and silver pieces in my palm looked expensive. I held them out to Ruarc.

"Do you want to keep these? The incinerator won't destroy them, I'll just have to pick them out of the ashes afterwards."

His cool, hazel eyes looked at the items for a long moment. I started to retract my hand thinking he didn't want them, but he reached over, plucking the watch from my grasp.

He held it between his hands, rubbing the crusted blood from the surface with the pad of his thumb.

Okay then. I discarded the rings on a tray. We'd have to come up with something else to get rid of those. I wondered what my dad usually did with them.

"Anything else the incinerator won't destroy?" Ruarc asked, clearing his throat.

"Metal fillings, artificial joints, screws, plates. Those things won't burn, but everything else will."

Ruarc's eyes were downcast, flitting between Nixon's body and the watch in his hands.

I'd seen the look before. Granted, not on the face of someone staring down at the man they'd just murdered, but... what did I know?

"Do you want a second alone with him?"

His eyes came up sharply.

"No."

I nodded.

"There will be more," he said ominously before I could begin to wheel Nixon away.

"What do you mean?"

He inclined his head to Nixon's broken body. "Like him. There will be those who try to succeed where he failed before I have time to put it all back together."

My stomach turned, but I pushed my shoulders back, taking a steadying breath.

"I'll do it," I replied. "If someone tries to hurt you and you hurt them first, I'll make sure there's no evidence it ever happened."

The ghost of a smile twitched at the corner of his mouth and for some reason it made me feel defiant. He had no right to look so damn smug.

"*But,* we have to talk money."

His eyes darkened, but that smirk remained.

"I don't need a disposal fee or whatever arrangement you had with my father. I just want to know that if I do this for you–"

"For *us*," he corrected and damnit if I didn't get a mad case of butterflies.

I cleared my throat.

"If I do this for us, I need to know that this place, my family's mortuary, will be safe. It's the only thing I have left of hers. My mother. And I mean, it's a win, win. You make sure it's financially able to remain open, and you can use it for your *needs*."

"Is that all?" he asked, cheeky now. Maybe I should've asked for more.

"That's all."

"Done."

He reached out his hand over Nixon's corpse and I

clasped it in mine, sealing our bargain. When I tried to pull away, his grip tightened, hauling me in close over Nixon to steal a kiss from my mouth.

Euphoric lightness fluttered through me. Ruarc was no hero. He was broken, jagged, and damaged but I didn't need him to be perfect. I didn't need a storybook romance. Not *that* kind of storybook, anyway. Kissing a man in the cold room of my family mortuary while the incinerator heated up to cremate his long-time friend was far from the happily ever after I imagined. But this wasn't the end, it was just the beginning.

"Is the oven preheated?" Ruarc asked, a dark brow lifted as he pulled away.

I cringed, but laughter filled my throat. "Please don't call it that."

# EPILOGUE

## Ruarc

### *Two Months Later*

"Y ou're still here?"

Her voice was like honey, coating me with soft warmth.

Her long, dark hair was draped over her shoulders.

Wearing a white dress, she looked ethereal walking into the darkly furnished room. I lowered the top of my laptop and motioned her toward me. She smiled, approaching my desk.

"I thought you'd be at the party by now," she said.

"It's still early. Besides, what would I do there without you?"

I held my arms open and she came around to slide comfortably onto my lap. I slid my hand up her thigh, teasing a hitched gasp from her lips. Of all her sounds, that was one of my favorites. Second only to the sound of her screaming as she came all over my cock.

"What did you do when you went there without me before?" she asked, her brows going up, anticipating the worst.

Nothing. I watched. Reveled in the debauchery. Rarely did I indulge and I didn't miss it. There wasn't a single other woman who'd left her mark on me the way she had. Hers was the only face I saw when I closed my eyes. The only voice I wanted to hear calling out my name.

It took some getting used to. Having her here but allowing her to come and go as she pleased. Leaving in the morning to work with her father at the mortuary and returning in time for dinner with me.

The normalcy of it made me want to laugh. I never thought I'd become this domesticated.

Well, perhaps not domesticated, but something closer to it than I'd ever thought possible. It helped that she was never alone outside of this house. Anytime she left it was with an escort, much to her annoyance, and the mortuary was a secure building now. With proper surveillance and armed men at the exits while she worked.

I protected what was mine.

I pressed my lips to her neck.

"I don't like what you're suggesting," I said. "Did you think there was a long line of women before you, little lamb?"

She giggled, tightening her arms around me.

"I didn't suggest anything," she argued sweetly.

I pressed another kiss to her neck. Sitting on my lap, the hem of her dress rode up her thighs, only just covering what needed to be covered for her to be decent. Hoisting it up and gathering the white fabric around her waist and bending her over the desk would be the easiest thing in the world. I began to harden just thinking about it.

I wanted to throttle my past self for ever thinking that I'd be able to throw her away once I'd had her. If anything, every joining only made me crave her even more. And in other ways I didn't know to crave before.

Like lazy Sunday evenings spent with my arms around her on the sofa watching thriller movies. Teasing her with lazy strokes of my fingers near her entrance until she was shaking with need by the time the movie was through. It'd become one of my favorite nights of the week.

The rare times she didn't return in time for dinner, I found myself waiting until she did to eat, ordering the cooking staff to keep the food warm until her arrival.

"What are you thinking?" she asked, her eyes crinkling on the edges with her curious smile.

I squeezed her hips, a breathy laugh escaping my lips. "How thoroughly you've ruined me."

Her brows lifted. "*Me* ruin *you?*"

She cocked her head. "I kind of think it's the other way around. I was perfectly normal and happy before I met you."

It was my turn to look doubtful. "Is that so?"

"It is."

"*Hmmm.*" I pushed her hair back. "I see it a bit differently than you, I think."

"Go on."

"You say I stole you away. I say I set you free."

Her throat bobbed.

"You called this place your prison once but that was only because you were too afraid to admit that you've never felt more at home."

She blinked, her gaze dropping to my lap. I lifted her chin, finding the gleam of some foreign emotion in her green eyes.

"You've never felt more *you,* than when you're with me."

She leaned in, pressing a soft kiss to my lips before sighing against them. It was her way of admitting I was right without the need for words. Though I didn't need her to tell me. I knew it from that first night down in the cellar. From the moment she admitted she knew I was watching her. That she liked it.

She pursed her lips, thinking.

"I was thinking that I could go with you tonight," she said in a soft tone, changing the subject back to the club. "Once you're done here."

We hadn't been back to the club together since the night I first had her. It took time to restructure the syndicate and rebuild client trust. There were several weeks where it remained closed to accommodate the shifts. And then several weeks more where we offered bonuses and private rooms at a lower rate, doubling security.

Emily had asked me more than once to take her back to Delirium, and each time I'd declined her. Not wanting to share her with another soul on this earth.

I didn't even want another man to look at her. Didn't trust myself enough not to take his eyes now that she was mine.

I mulled it over.

"Please?"

A hot breath passed my lips and I ran my fingers down her arms. "Is there something wrong with the bedroom?"

"No."

She wasn't going to let this go.

"All right."

"All right?"

I nodded. "But I have rules."

"I don't want to be collared."

My jaw clenched, the urge to bend her to my will despite her wishes flared through me like fire. "*Fine*," I gritted out. "But no one else may touch you. Male or female."

"I don't *want* anyone else to touch me."

Such a good girl.

My lips twitched into a smile. "Very well, then." I lifted her off my lap, giving her backside a hard slap that brought a red stain to her cheeks.

"Go ahead of me. Pick any available private room and I'll come find you. You will wait on the bed, naked, until I arrive. Ass up, face down. Do not touch yourself or pleasure yourself in any way until I arrive. If you do, I will know and you will be punished."

She grinned, her eyes alight with mischief that told me she didn't intend to follow my instructions. The woman loved her punishment.

"Don't threaten me with a good time," she crooned with a wink, slinking to the door like a cat.

"One last thing..."

"You have my permission," she said before I could finish. "...anything you want."

I stared at the door after she retreated, my cock harder than if she'd just sucked it.

Of course, it helped that wherever she went off the property, she wasn't alone.

I let twenty minutes pass before packing up and heading to my room to grab a mask. Instead of going through the entrance on the upper level, I went downstairs first. I wanted to take my time, and survey the atmosphere before I got to Emily. Going down to the heavy, ornate door, I looked into the biometric scanner and let myself into Delirium.

Warmth, darkness with muted red light, ambient music, primal sound, and pulsing, writhing bodies greeted me only steps into the entry.

I meandered through the hall, nodding to my patrons as I passed, taking it all in. Everything that was almost taken from me, but thanks to Emily, I'd managed to save.

Heading upstairs, my anticipation heightened. My senses becoming hypersensitive. My steps quickened, knowing she was waiting for me, damning my mental request for delayed gratification.

I peered into the open doors of the other rooms as I passed, but I had a feeling I knew which one she'd have chosen.

Sure enough, I was met with a closed door near the end of the hall and straightened my jacket before pushing inside without knocking.

A hungry grin spread across my face finding her on the bed, legs spread on her back with her fingers knuckle deep inside her cunt.

"I thought I told you not to start without me," I scolded.

She jumped, clamping her knees together like I just caught her stealing, her flushed face whipping to the door.

"You were taking too long," she said, breathless.

My instructions were clear.

"Such a bad girl. What am I going to do with you?"

She bit her lip, provoking a growl from my chest.

I went for the large armoire off to the side of the room, wrenching the doors open to see if it held what I was looking for.

It did. That and more.

I pulled the bar from the shelf and one other thing, keeping it hidden as I approached the bed.

Emily scrambled backward, catching sight of the item, her eyes darting between it and the bar tight in my grip.

"Ruarc, what is that?"

I tossed the massive plug onto the bed and grabbed her by the ankle, dragging her closer before she could escape. Her eyes widened as she struggled, but I only pulled her harder. "You'll only make it worse for yourself, little lamb."

She stilled, her chest rising and falling rapidly.

I gave her a look before releasing her ankle. "Clothes off," I ordered.

She'd already removed her white dress from earlier, but now she did as she was told, tugging off her bra, her tits on full display.

"Lie back."

Emily swallowed, lying flat against the luxurious duvet. "Legs."

She lifted them and I angled the bar, clamping her ankle in the manacle at one end before moving to do the same with the other, the bar keeping her legs spread about a foot apart. When I was finished she marveled at the device, testing it with her legs, trying to close them, bend her knees.

I grinned, reaching for the leg spreader rod to pry it out

to its full extension, forcing her legs wider. She gasped, her hands instinctively going to her wet cunt, to protect it in the way she no longer could with her legs.

"*Uh, uh,*" I chastised her. "That's mine tonight."

Without warning, I lifted the bar high, kneeling over her on the bed, folding her legs over her chest.

"Hold on," I ordered her and she reluctantly moved her hands from between her legs to grip the bar above her head.

"Good girl."

I reached for the plug and she squeaked, her cheeks flushing. "Ruarc!"

I grabbed hold of the rod, holding her down before she could try to flee. "Did you disobey me, little lamb?"

The wave of her breaths rolling over her chest made me thirsty to taste her, the engorgement of my cock so strong it thudded with its own pulse.

*Not yet.*

Emily nodded. Shook her head. "I won't do it again."

I smiled. "Yes, you will."

She bit her lip again and I thrust the plug into her wet pussy, making her spasm at the sudden intrusion, a sharp moan rising to join the club music pounding all around us.

I slunk low, trailing my tongue over her clit while I worked the plug in her pussy, getting it nice and wet before it made its second entry.

Emily bucked against my face, throwing her head back, her hands on the rod between her legs white-knuckled.

I withdrew the plug, keeping pressure with my tongue as I moved it lower, pressing the tip against her other entrance. A fearful breath shuddered from her lips and her grip on the rod weakened, her legs fighting her to be let down.

"Relax, baby," I crooned, pushing the plug in an inch and waiting, helping her keep her legs up with a hand between hers on the bar.

I flicked her clit with my tongue, pushing it in another inch.

"*Fuck*," she hissed, her arms shaking. "I can't. Ruarc, I can't."

"You will take every fucking inch, Emily, do you hear me?"

She whimpered as I pressed the massive plug deeper into her channel.

"Ruarc, *please*."

"Have you learned your lesson, Emily?"

Before she could answer, I pushed the plug the rest of the way into her, making her shudder and flex her hips, a cry on her lips.

Her eyes watered as she lifted her head to look at me through lust-filled eyes.

I cocked my head, still waiting for my answer.

Running my fingers up and down her slit, I drew a moan from her mouth before slapping my fingers against her. The slap had her gritting her teeth, throwing her head back as she writhed on the bed.

"Emily?"

*Slap.*

"Yes!"

*Slap.*

"*Yes!*"

I rubbed her clit, bringing her the rest of the way to her first climax as she screamed my name. She gushed on my hand, squirting all over the bed between my legs as hers tried and failed to close for the rod keeping them apart.

My hardon pulsed with white fire and the need to bury my cock in her intensified to the point of fucking blackout.

Did she just... squirt?

"*Oh my god, Emily,*" I said in a breathy groan, ready to worship at the chapel of her perfect pussy for the rest of my goddamned life.

I couldn't get my pants off fast enough, getting them low enough with wild messy kicks, crawling over her, thrusting deep.

Emily whimpered at my savage entry, baring her teeth as I settled into her deepest place thanks to the angle of her hips and the bar between her legs.

"God, Ruarc, you're so deep."

"Does it hurt, little lamb?"

"Yes."

"*Good.*"

Slowly, I eased back, building up her anticipation before thrusting deep once more. I watched as she took me into her, every inch, buried to the hilt.

I eased back again, reaching between her arms to curl my hand around her neck, pulling her up. "Look, baby, see how good you take that cock."

She struggled to see, breathing erratically as I fucked her good and hard, until her legs shook and her face reddened. Until I couldn't watch her beautiful cunt taking my cock anymore, not unless I wanted to come before my little lamb and that was *not* an option.

"Ch-choke me," she stuttered, getting close and I left her to hold the rod while I wrapped her neck in my fist, keeping a punishing pace between her thighs.

She nodded, telling me to go harder, tighter.

*More.*

She always wanted more.

"Fuck, Emily," I moaned, fucking her recklessly, brutally, beautifully, lost to my own desire as my body tightened for the release.

"*Come for me,*" I hissed and her eyes narrowed as her body exploded into an orgasm so powerful it pulled me down with it, her walls milking every drop of my release as I poured into her, her name a broken plea on my lips.

She gasped for air as I released her throat and sagged against her, her legs falling over both of us.

Her heart pounded through the cage of her ribs against my ear, echoing my own.

"I love you," she whispered, her arms going around me, fingers brushing the back of my neck, pushing into my hair.

The three little words I'd been waiting to hear since I'd spoken them to her in the cabin raced over me, through me, consuming me in a way that I knew I'd never return from.

Emily was *mine*.

But now I belonged to her, too.

### THE END

Read the next book in this standalone series, *Sinful Temptation.*

Thank you for reading *Twisted Devotion*. I had so much fun writing this book and truly hope you enjoyed reading it! If you did, please leave a review 🖤

*Sign-up for the Petal & Thorn Newsletter and never miss a release from Poppy St. John!*

**ROMANCE WITHOUT RESTRAINT**

Poppy writes steamy contemporary romance with a focus on all things forbidden, dark, and taboo. She likes her main men morally gray and has always had a thing for bad boys who will do anything to win the hearts of the women they love. All her stories end with a hard-won HEA ♡

Join the Petal & Thorn newsletter:

https://www.subscribepage.com/petalandthorn

Made in the USA
Monee, IL
12 January 2025

76691449R00214